After stripping out of the dirty hiking clothes, Alexis started filling the tub and then went to find her waterproof vibrator. Dark clouds had gathered on her walk home, and she could hear the beginnings of another storm. It'd be raining soon. She lit a few candles in the bathroom and turned on a Norah Jones CD, then settled into the tub slowly. The one good thing about Westside Apartments was that there was no extra charge for hot water. The bathtub was steaming, and the smell of the lavender-scented candles filled the air.

Alexis soaped herself and then rinsed off. She leaned her back against the edge of the tub and spread her legs. Her fingers played with her clit, lazy and slow. She was thinking about Sandy, of course, and imagined what she'd like to do to her if they'd come home for the same bath. Finally she reached for her vibrator and slipped it under the water. The tip rested just below her clit, where she liked the vibration most. Her eyes closed and she felt her body getting warm.

Visit

Bella Books

at

BellaBooks.com

or call our toll-free number

1-800-729-4992

Sign on the LINE

Jaime Clevenger

Bella
BOOKS
2006

Bella Books, Inc.
P.O. Box 10543
Tallahassee, FL 32302

Printed in the United States of America on acid-free paper
First Edition

Editor: Cindy Cresap
Cover designer: L. Callaghan

ISBN 1-59493-052-X

To all my friends, thanks for the dyke drama, and yes, I changed your name. To all my exes, thanks for teaching me the tricks, and yes, I made you better in bed. To Corina, thanks for the kisses, and I wouldn't change anything. To Cindy, thanks for letting me keep my favorite naughty part in the story. To Emily, thanks for giving me the Portland scoop. To Tiffany, thanks for all the publicity. To Liz, thanks for the threesome jokes. To Jackie, thanks for sharing secrets. To my readers, thank you and enjoy!

About the Author

Jaime Clevenger lives in northern California with her partner and three lazy pussies. Jaime spends her days riding her horse, teaching karate and writing. By night, she works as an emergency veterinarian. She has also written *The Unknown Mile*, *Call Shotgun* and *All Bets Off*. She hopes very much that you enjoy this book. If you would like to contact Jaime, please visit www.jaimeclevenger-books.com.

Chapter 1

A high-pitched alarm broke the relative silence of dawn in Alexis Getty's bedroom. The room was never really quiet. One drapeless bay window faced a busy intersection, and though the squeal of tires and scratching brake pads could be heard any time of day, the noise worsened with the morning commute. When it rained the cars rumbled past like crashing waves. And in Portland rain came as regular as junk mail. Unfortunately, the wet street scene wasn't as picturesque as the ocean-like sound suggested. But the rent was cheap.

The alarm's incessant beeping continued, and Alexis fought the urge to hit the snooze button. Maybe it was Saturday morning and she could roll over and drift back to sleep. She couldn't recall if yesterday was Thursday or Friday. Forcing her fuzzy mind to think, she remembered meeting Paula at the bar after work. They were only going to play one game of pool, so Alexis hadn't bothered to change out of her delivery uniform. Inevitably, the night ended many hours later. Now the black pants and blue polo shirt lay in a crumpled mess near the door, and the toes of her Doc Marten boots stuck out from the bottom of the pile. Her bra and boy-style boxers were a few steps from the bed.

A horn blared and she decided it must be Friday. Drivers were always impatient at the end of the week. Why rush to join the commuters? Her head was pounding from one too many dollar shots, and the alarm was suddenly intolerable. Reaching toward the nightstand, her hand brushed over a cardboard sleeve from a coffee cup. Alexis reread the number penciled on the cardboard and the name Tina. Details from last night came back quickly. She'd first met Tina, a tall brunette with long red nails, at a hair salon on 23rd Street Thursday morning. Alexis was delivering a package for one of the hair stylists and had nearly collided with Tina on her way into the salon. Judging from Tina's primped femme look, Alexis had tagged her as straight, yet her lingering stare made her wonder. Alexis watched Tina leave the salon and then pumped her stylist for information. According to the stylist, Tina was married to some blow who was having an affair. She was filthy rich—as in owned a mansion on Lake Oswego, came to the salon every week for "a style" and used no color enhancers. Tina's lush brunette hue was all natural. "In other words," the stylist had told her, "she's out of your league."

Alexis didn't care what league the stylist had placed her in. Tina wasn't her type. She had no time for straight married women. But then Tina had shown up at the cafe that afternoon, and Alexis was struck by her intense gaze and furtive smile. Once she realized that Tina was indeed checking her out, Alexis decided to introduce herself. In a five-minute conversation outside the cafe, she discovered a few more details. Tina drove a new jet-black Porsche, her blow's name was Joe, and she liked women with strap-ons. Tina had scribbled her number on the cardboard and pressed it into Alexis's hands before disappearing into the crowd crossing the boulevard.

"Lex! Turn off that damn thing!" Drew Riverton pounded the wall. "You know I need my beauty sleep."

"Don't I know it," Alexis mumbled.

"Aren't you late for work?" Drew asked. He lived in the adjacent apartment, and their bedrooms shared a common wall that was uncommonly thin. Although it had only been a few weeks since Alexis had moved into the Westside Portland Apartments, she already knew too many bedroom secrets about Drew. He had a habit of entertaining multiple lovers, all men. The first week there was a different man each night, all with names ending in "y." There was a Johnny, a Danny, a Sammy, a Perry and a Ricky. Fortunately, he got tired of the "y" name endings and the next week had moved on to a troupe of men from a traveling circus. Alexis also kept a busy evening schedule with multiple lovers, though not as many as Drew. So far, her partners all seemed to enjoy the challenge of outdoing the loudness of the neighbors. Alexis and Drew had formed a fast, if not unlikely, friendship, in part because of the thinness of their common wall.

Alexis rolled over and reached for the alarm. It was a quarter to six. Too late to stop for coffee on her way into work. Drew stopped pounding the wall as soon as the buzzing ceased. Alexis dressed in a clean uniform and went to the miniature washbasin in the bathroom to splash warm water on her face. The bathroom was not the selling point of the apartment. There was only one light, swinging on a chain above a pre-WWI washbasin, and its dim glow barely lit the nearest wall. The apartment manager jokingly referred to this as mood lighting and called the bathroom uniquely antique. The toilet had no lid, and instead of a shower there was a cracked claw-footed tub.

Alexis ran her fingers through her hair and glanced at the four-inch mirror she'd positioned on the shelf above the washbasin. She'd gone through several hairstyles and colors over the past few years, including everything from a buzz cut to a bob to braids, and several shades of brown, black and blonde. Currently, she had a shaggy bed-head 'do in platinum with obvious brown roots. She added a pair of cobalt studs and silver hex bolt loops to her ears and her favorite silver ring on her right hand. Surprisingly, her dark blue eyes had no telltale puffy lids or hint of redness. After a warm splash of water, her skin felt smooth as usual. Alexis was usually careful to hide any apparent signs of a late night out. Standing on her tiptoes, she glanced down to fix the collar of her shirt and smooth out a few wrinkles. After a month in the apartment, she still wasn't used to the little mirror. She'd tried everything from kneeling to craning her neck in awkward positions to get a better angle. Often, she ignored the mirror altogether.

"Hey, Lex, you're running late," Kate said, handing her a cup. The other delivery drivers had already hit the break room and left, littering the place with newspapers and half-empty coffee cups. "Not that it's anything new with you. Coffee's black and bitter. I figured you'd want cream and sugar, but we're all out."

"I guess I should be happy as long as we're not out of caffeine." Alexis grimly took the cup.

"Around here, yes. You know it was your friend that stole all of the little sugar and cream packets."

"Mossinni?"

"Apparently she slipped in the break room right after Ace fired her."

"To steal cream and sugar?" Lex couldn't imagine why Moss would take all of the coffee condiments. She guessed one of the other delivery drivers had fabricated the story and taken the items home. Most of the guys who worked at APO were not above-average on the honesty scale.

Kate wiped down the table where someone's half-drunk coffee had left a wet ring. "Gotta love this place, eh? By the way, Ace wanted to see you when you got in. He's up in the DC office."

DC was short for Distribution Center. Ace was the bigwig of the Portland APO Distribution Center. APO stood for Air Post On-time, though it often wasn't carried by air or delivered on time. Alexis sipped her coffee. "You're right. Bitter as shit. Wish I had stopped at the cafe for real java."

"Go on, Lex. Ace will be pissed if you keep him waiting. He's already upset that you missed the morning meeting."

Kate pushed Alexis toward the staircase leading up to the DC office. Ace's office was the only place with heat. The rest of the warehouse was kept on a thermostat that made sure the temperature stayed as cold inside the building as outside. To keep from freezing, the graveyard warehouse crew wore parkas and scarves. At least once a month one of the package handlers was caught with vodka in his locker.

"Hello, Ace." Alexis greeted him with a tight smile. "Kate said you needed to talk to me."

Ace nodded. He was seated at his mahogany desk with his feet stretched out, watching the line of trucks slowly pulling out of the warehouse. The morning delivery lines were starting to take off, late as usual. He sipped something from a thermos and then eyed Alexis. His wife had probably made coffee for him, and she enviously guessed there was a full spoonful of sugar and cream in his thermos.

"You heard that I let Moss go yesterday?" Ace let the women in Personnel take care of hiring, but he made sure all firings went through him.

Of course Alexis knew Moss had been fired. Gossip flew through the warehouse faster than the delivery crates. What was he getting at? "Yep. You mentioned she got herself a DUI last week." Alexis thought Ace enjoyed firing people more than any other part of his job. She'd seen his eyes light up when the shit hit the fan about Mossinni's DUI. Alexis was sad to see Mossinni leave. But she'd earned her own ticket out. Still, it didn't make sense to steal the sugar and cream packets. No one liked getting fired, but it didn't do any good to take out frustrations on the one sanctified vice of your comrades still stuck in the trenches. And now that Moss was gone, Alexis was the only lesbian at the warehouse.

"Well, she also stole some things."

"I know. My coffee's black and tastes about as sweet as motor oil."

He nodded. "She also ripped the labels off a half dozen packages." Ace pushed his chair away from the desk and stood up. He went over to the storage closet and pulled out a box. "I guess it's better than pulling out a semiautomatic and going postal on us," he continued, staring at the box.

Alexis had to stop herself from smiling. The idea of Mossinni wielding a semiautomatic willy-nilly through the warehouse was comical. Moss had once described herself as one of a small minority of short, overweight, curly-haired, God-fearing, Italian lesbians west of the Appalachian Mountains. She was a big talker and strong as an ox, but everyone knew she was too sweet to even squish a spider on the warehouse floor. Alexis watched as the next to last delivery truck pulled out of the building. Her own truck was already filled and waiting. The deliveries would be late if Ace held her up here any longer. "So why'd you call me in?"

Ace handed her the package he'd been staring at. "Here's one of the items that Mossinni pulled the label off of. I was having Gale try to track down all the deliveries that weren't made yesterday, hoping we could figure out where the six packages without labels were supposed to be sent. We figured out that this one was en route to Westside Portland Apartments. Gale said you just moved there."

Gale was Ace's secretary and the biggest gossip in the DC, so Alexis wasn't surprised that she knew where she lived. "What's the apartment number?"

"Yeah, we don't have that info." Ace sneered. "If we had that, then I wouldn't be asking you for this favor."

She hated his condescending tone. "Favor?"

"Westside isn't that big of a complex. I'm sure you can just ask around and see who was expecting something. If you can't figure it out, let me know and I'll have Gale contact the New York DC where the package originated. But you know I'd rather not do that. We've been able to trace the other five packages to the correct delivery addresses, and I know I can trust you'll get this one delivered without any problem."

"There are too many apartments at Westside for me to knock on every door asking if anyone wants this box. Come on, Ace, just talk to New York and get the apartment number."

He shook his head and glanced at his watch. "Your deliveries are going to be late, Lex. Better get a move on."

Alexis stowed the unlabeled box in her locker and then went to the dispatcher to get her delivery schedule. Since she'd started running deliveries at APO a year ago, Alexis had always covered the same route on the southeast end of downtown. During that time, she'd moved four times and managed six serious breakups in six casual relationships. In fact, her last attempt at a serious relationship had ended over three years ago. She'd fallen in love with Virginia, the assistant professor from her Intro to Feminism class, moved into her apartment and spent one blissful year planning ways to help save the world. Then the morning after Alexis graduated, she found a one-line note from Virg taped to their refrigerator: "Larry and I have decided to give our engagement a second try—hope you can understand." Alexis was single and broken-hearted for six months, then she cut her hair and started dating anyone who said yes when she asked. She usually ended the relationship after a few months or as soon as the topic of cohabitation came up.

Ron, the dispatcher, handed her a delivery schedule and then tapped his wristwatch. "Tick tock, tick tock. Lex, your first delivery is ten minutes delayed. You had better find a way of picking up the lost time, or I'll be on your ass with this afternoon's pickups."

Alexis faked a smile and turned on her heels. She had no desire to give Ron an excuse for her tardiness. Ron reminded her of an overfed junkyard dog. He always wore the same sweat-stained blue shirt, and the buttons at the apex of his beer belly threatened to pop under the tension. His scowling expression rarely changed—even while he was chewing tobacco—and he rarely bothered with breath mints, or showers for that matter. After confirming the packages in the truck with her delivery list, Alexis pulled out of the warehouse.

The first delivery turned out to be to Anderson Software on 35th. She breathed a sigh of relief when she saw this. Bonnie at the service desk of Anderson had a crush on her, and she never minded what time the deliveries arrived so long as Alexis had a moment to flirt with her. It was Mossinni who had first advised Alexis to play up to every one of her regular customers, male or female. More often than not, she found that the subtle or not-so-subtle philandering paid off in the long run.

"Well, well, it's Lex come to see me again." Bonnie smiled and pushed her chair back from the desk. She stretched out her legs and then crossed her knees, showing off a pair of fishnet stockings. With a toss of her head, her dark red curls fell over her shoulders. "What'd you bring me this time, love?"

"Diamond rings, in Netware boxes, of course." Alexis wheeled the dolly out of the entryway. "Nice stockings."

"You should see the garter belt," Bonnie replied, biting on the end of her pen. "And my leather collection."

"Maybe another time. Business first." Alexis didn't avert her eyes as Bonnie uncrossed her legs and spread her knees apart, dangling the pen at the edge of her black skirt. "Such a tease," Alexis said, finally turning her focus from Bonnie's clearly visible firm thigh muscles to nod at the boxes. "Where can I put these?"

"All work and no play, huh? Oh well, I'm sure I'll survive." Bonnie pointed down the hall. She stood up as Alexis rolled her dolly past the desk and then she brushed her hand on Alexis's hips when she stopped.

Unloading the four boxes, Alexis tried to ignore Bonnie's gaze and smiled uneasily as Bonnie's hand touched her butt. Finally, she passed Bonnie a clipboard with the delivery order. "Can I get your signature?"

"Where?" Bonnie asked, rubbing the pen between her index finger and thumb suggestively.

Pointing to the X-mark on the bottom line, Alexis watched Bonnie lick the tip of the pen before signing for the items. Alexis took the clipboard from her. "Any packages you need to send?"

Bonnie shook her head. She clicked her pen then spun it between her fingers and kept her eyes locked on Alexis. "I'll be at Decker's with some of my friends tonight. I've seen you there before, haven't I?"

"Maybe."

"I think you should come tonight. Maybe you can practice your pickup lines."

"How do you know I need to practice?" Alexis grinned. She was enjoying all of the innuendos. Only a week ago she'd sworn off dating people from work, but Bonnie was obviously not interested in anything serious. And apart from Tina—the rich, married brunette from last night—Alexis didn't have any other plans for the weekend. She doubted Bonnie would be anything more than a one night encounter and decided it wouldn't really count as a date anyway. Besides, it was hard to turn down such a blatant offer from an attractive woman with curves in all the right places, full lips and a tongue stud. "I'll see what I can do," Alexis said finally.

Apparently satisfied with this, Bonnie let Alexis push the dolly through the service room. Conscious of Bonnie's gaze on her back, Alexis glanced over her shoulder just as she reached the elevator.

"Tonight," Bonnie said, raising her hand to her lips as if she were about to blow a kiss and then slipping her index finger between her lips instead. She pulled the wet finger out of her mouth slowly and then winked.

Alexis shook her head and stepped into the elevator, feeling cocky. Although she never trusted the sweet, smiling type, Bonnie had a good nature, even if she was a little overbearing. As the door closed, she eyed her list for the next delivery. "One down, twenty more stops before lunch."

The last morning delivery was only five minutes late, and Alexis ended up back at the DC warehouse exactly at noon. She handed her keys to Ron and headed across the street to Blue's Cafe. The head chef, Sandy, made the best salads with freshly fried seasoned croutons. The soups were top-rate. Soup and salad was Blue's Friday lunch special, and Alexis hadn't missed it for the past three months, mostly because she looked forward to seeing her favorite chef at the end of the week. She loved to get a seat at the front counter so she could watch the kitchen where Sandy was always flying about during the lunch rush.

All of the wait staff at Blue's knew the regulars and fully expected that they would seat themselves. When Alexis entered the cafe, she took her usual place at the far end of the front counter. Sandy, who had glanced up as soon as Alexis sat down, gave her a friendly smile and nod. The two cooks on Fridays, Juan and Sandy, rarely ventured beyond the kitchen during the lunch rush, but on occasion Sandy had been known to slip out for a break to chat with Alexis. She always wore a white apron, tied twice around her thin waist, over a pair of tight Levi's. Her auburn hair was pulled back in a ponytail, and her bra straps poked out from the edges of her blue tank top. Alexis's mother had warned her never to trust a kitchen with a thin cook, but Blue's had proved Mom's wisdom didn't always hold.

"Good to see you, honey. How's your week going?" Sandy asked, almost yelling over the clatter of the dishes and the hiss of the grill.

"Better now. Missed you."

"Yeah, I bet you did! Ha!" Sandy stepped out of the kitchen and dried her hands on her apron as she headed toward Alexis's seat. "I've heard the rumors about you all over this town. I'd bet you've had ten pretty young things distracting you this month alone!" Sandy leaned over the counter and kissed Alexis's cheek. She straightened up and grinned down at Alexis. "You only remember me on Fridays."

Ten? Well, it was a good guess. Since she'd made it a common practice to ask out nearly every interesting woman she met, she had quite a full schedule. Unfortunately she usually had little desire to continue past one date with half the women she asked

10

out. "I'd love to remember you this weekend. What are you doing Saturday night?"

"Working."

"Sunday?"

Sandy brushed her finger under Alexis's chin. "You come here every week for the past three months and only now ask me out on a date?"

"I didn't think I had a chance with you."

"And I didn't figure you'd be a shy one!" She laughed. "Sunday it is. Give me a call here on Saturday night to set things up."

Alexis nodded. "By the way, how's the soup today?"

"Could use some more spice," Sandy said over her shoulder as she headed back to the kitchen. "But I baked some cornbread this morning and it smells wonderful. It has a sweet, nutty flavor that complements the minestrone well. I think you might enjoy it."

"You know I always love whatever you make."

"Don't tell me that, Lex. I'll get lazy if I know you're easy." Sandy disappeared into the kitchen.

Chapter 2

On the bus ride home from work, Alexis occupied herself with planning her weekend schedule. She'd meet Bonnie at the club tonight and hoped Tina would agree to dinner on Saturday night, leaving Sunday open for Sandy. At some point, she wanted to drop in at the farmer's market to pick up some fresh produce and then she had to stop by Mossinni's place to find out how she was taking the layoff. Maybe Moss still had the package label for the box she needed to deliver. It'd be a lot easier asking Moss for the label than knocking on everyone's door in Westside Apartments. Her thoughts with the weekend plans so occupied her mind that she didn't notice the woman sitting opposite her until they both stood to get off at the same stop. Their knees bumped as the driver did a double tap on the brakes as he announced the bus stop intersection.

"Sorry. I've got bad balance," the woman said. "Guess I should have taken Tai Chi instead of art classes." She smiled.

Alexis felt her skin blush as soon as she recognized the woman. Darcy Callahan had moved into Westside Apartments a week ago, and Alexis still hadn't managed a complete sentence of conversation with her. Something about her tall, dark, brooding look, the chic, short haircut and her quick wit made Alexis immediately clam up each time Darcy started a conversation. Darcy had moved into the third apartment on their floor, directly opposite Drew's place. Alexis had been smitten with Darcy the first time they'd met in the apartment building's mailroom, and she had to stop herself from watching the sway of her hips each time she'd passed her in the halls that week. They had similar schedules and often met on the stairwell or the mailroom coming or going from work.

Unfortunately, Alexis knew few personal details about her. For instance, was she straight? She dressed in conservative business suits, which seemed tailored perfectly to complement her lanky build but offered no mark of sexual preference, and she wore no ring or any other jewelry aside from two silver hoop earrings. According to Drew, the resident apartment snoop, she'd had no male or female visitors at her apartment since she'd moved in. Alexis prided herself on an ability to ferret out the women-loving-women from any crowd, yet here she was stumbling.

Darcy climbed out of the bus first. She took the stairs up to the apartment building's entrance slowly, and Alexis thought of asking if she'd had a long day, but didn't. She could flirt with anyone unless, it seemed, she really wanted more than a flirt. Then she couldn't even handle small talk. They parted in the mailroom, with Darcy finding her mailbox empty and quickly waving her goodbye to Alexis.

As soon as she'd disappeared down the hall, Alexis banged her fist against the metal mailbox. She wished that she'd at least managed to be polite to Darcy. Balancing a pile of junk mail on the unlabeled box, she headed up the stairs to the third floor. The sound of canned laughter drifted out from Ruth's apartment, the fourth and last apartment on the third floor. Ruth was in her eighties and hard of hearing. She spent her mornings arguing with the

Channel 3 News anchormen and the weatherman, her lunchtime watching soaps, late afternoons arguing with talk show guests, and her evenings conversing with the game show hosts. Ruth's lights were turned off by nine o'clock every night.

Alexis knocked on Ruth's door. She waited a minute, not hearing any sounds beyond the TV chatter, and knocked again, this time louder.

"Hold your horses, I'm on my way!" Ruth hollered. "Don't get your panties in a knot."

A few minutes later, the door finally opened and Ruth smiled. "Oh, it's you, honey. I wasn't expecting any visitors, and my, I'm a mess." She giggled, brushing at the wrinkles on her pink blouse and then pushing her curled hair into place behind her ears.

Although she rarely left her home, Ruth was better dressed than most people Alexis met out on the street. Alexis held up her grocery list. "Do you need anything at the store? I'm going over to the mini-mart and thought I could pick you up something to save you a trip this weekend."

"Isn't that sweet? You like delivering things, don't you?" Ruth always made some comment about liking the postal service and package carriers. Nothing brightened her day more than picking up the mail. "Well, a carton of milk would be nice. I was planning on a trip to the store myself, but I hate carrying home the milk. You wouldn't mind? And I like my milk whole. None of that skinny, fat free, pale stuff."

"Sure." Alexis started to leave and then remembered the package. "Oh, Ruth, one other thing. You aren't expecting a package from anyone, are you?"

"Oh, I'd like to say yes." Ruth shook her head. "It's been a long time since anyone sent me a package. One of my lovers in the seventies used to send me a little something once a week at least." She smiled coyly. "Now about all I hope for is a note from Ed McMahon and the Publishers Clearing House. They've both promised me a hundred thousand dollars, but I believe the money won't come in a little box like the one you have there." She nodded at the box under Alexis's arm. "I'd like a handsome young man with a bow tie and a large check! But if you open up that box and find a love letter inside with my name, I won't mind accepting it. Or the lover that goes along with it." She laughed without any tinge of cynicism.

"If there's a love letter inside, you'll be the first to know." Alexis hoped to find out who the box belonged to without opening it, but maybe the contents would give her a good clue. "I'll drop by with your milk later."

Alexis went to her apartment and found a note on the door. She unlocked the door and read: "Drop by my place after work. I want you to meet my new best friend. He's a real charmer. (heart) Drew."

Drew hadn't mentioned any guests. She entered her apartment and dropped the box, along with the junk mail, on the kitchen table. So far, she'd only set up two rooms in the house—the kitchen and the bedroom. After living with roommates for the past few years, she'd never had any need for living room furniture. She didn't own a sofa, a TV or even a coffee table. The living room was really only a big empty space with one wall decorated with black-and-white prints that she'd made in a college photography course. Instead of furnishing the living room, she was saving up to buy a potter's wheel. Ever since she'd left home, she'd thought of having her own wheel. Growing up in Arizona had made Alexis realize the worth of dirt. There was plenty of it, like the rain in Portland. Sometimes she'd dream of Sedona dirt, red as fire, mixing with the torrents of Portland, and the mud became life in her hands. Her mother was a potter in Sedona and had taught her how to work the mud. It had been three years since she'd last seen her mother in the Sedona studio. They'd made a set of pasta bowls together.

Alexis stripped out of her uniform and changed into a pair of jeans and a button-down black shirt. Finding the cup sleeve with Tina's number, she called her and left a message saying she'd be hoping to meet her at Decker's on Saturday night. Since she was meeting Bonnie at Decker's tonight, she figured it'd be easier to keep the location the same for both nights. Little things like that helped when you were dating multiple women. God help you if you stood someone up in this town. Her own answering machine had a message from Moss, but she decided to call her back later. She finished off some leftover Pad Thai noodles and downed half a Coke before heading over to Drew's place.

Drew greeted her with a towel around his waist and a toothbrush in his mouth. He had obviously just stepped out of the shower, and water was dripping off his skinny legs onto the doormat. His brown mop of hair was doing a perfect Elvis-style wave. He smiled and waved her inside, then held up one finger and headed down the hallway to the bathroom, his hips swaying and the towel threatening to slip off his backside.

Alexis sat down on the black leather sofa in the living room and flipped through the *Portland Mercury*. She eyed the half-full beer on the coffee table. It was one of Portland's microbreweries and Drew's favorite, but she didn't like the smell of it. "So where's this new best friend?" Alexis asked. As soon as she spoke up, she heard a whining sound coming from the bedroom and then a scratch on the closed door.

Drew poked his head out of the bathroom. "I've got him locked up in my bedroom. Go on in and meet the boy, if you dare."

The whining gained intensity and soon a half-fledged bark came from behind the door. "Drew, you didn't get a dog. Tell me you're just babysitting him."

"Go on and meet him. He's a love. And I promise he won't bark."

Of course the dog barked again, as if in answer to this promise. Alexis shook her head and followed Drew's urgings to go and meet the beast. She opened the door, and a beagle puppy came rushing out to greet her. He licked her hands and wiggled his butt, then ran in a circle around her feet, refusing to hold still. "Shit, he's like a windup toy on meth. You know the apartment manager is going to kill you."

"Isn't he beautiful?" Drew asked. He passed Alexis and patted the puppy's head. "I saw him and just had to have him. I'd rather be kicked out of this dump than not keep this cutie. I think I'm going to call him Apollo."

"Has he started to pee on your carpet yet?"

"Why are you being so pessimistic?"

Alexis laughed as the dog tried to lift his leg against a potted ficus tree. Drew immediately scooped him up and plopped him down on a white-papered pee mat in the bathroom. "I can see he's not quite as smart as he is handsome. Just like most of the males in your life."

"Well, I can't argue with you there." When the puppy had finished, Drew gave him a chew toy and praised him for his peeing. "We have a little work to do, but it can't be worse than dealing with some of the other men I've brought home."

"Potty-training?"

He laughed. "Oh, I could tell you some stories."

"Please don't." Alexis sat down on the carpet and whistled to get the puppy's attention. He came bounding out from the bathroom, eager to greet her again just as if they had never met.

"So do you want to be a foster mom?"

"Hell, no."

"But he's so cute," Drew cooed. "How could you turn him out?"

"That's what they say about little kids." The puppy tried climbing up onto her lap, but he couldn't seem to coordinate all four legs. She scooped him up and rubbed his belly. His charm was nearly irresistible. Nearly. "And why are you trying to pawn him off already?"

"I'm not." He headed into the bedroom, then started cursing about his lack of clothing. Alexis had seen his closet and guessed he had twice as many shirts or pairs of pants as any man she'd ever met. His shoe supply rivaled most women's collections. After a moment he came out dressed in a pair of black slacks and a tight gray sweater. He sat down on the couch to pull on his socks. The puppy thought this was a game and did his best to help pull off the socks as quickly as Drew placed them. "The problem is I'm not home every evening. I've got a busy schedule, you know. And though I absolutely adore this little rugrat, I won't be able to say no to every hot date with the excuse that I've got a puppy with bladder control issues waiting for me."

"You could bring him along for the ride."

"He's only eight weeks old. I'm not going to stick a carsick puppy on a date." Drew screeched as the puppy took hold of his toe, teeth piercing through the thin sock. He pried the puppy off his foot and shook him gently. "You're lucky you're so handsome. Otherwise, you'd really be in trouble for that little love nip. Come on, Lex, how could you turn this guy down? It would just be every once in a while. I promise I won't abuse your offer."

"What offer?"

"Please?"

"Are you begging now?"

"I can grovel, too," Drew offered.

"Don't. I'm sure you have enough experience doing that to get dates." She winked at him, and he shoved her shoulder playfully. "Okay, I'll take him. But only every once in a while. I'm not agreeing to be anyone's foster mom. You know how much I hate commitment."

"Deal." Drew set the puppy on the ground and took a sip of his beer. "So what are your plans for the evening?"

"Grocery store, then I'm heading over to Decker's to meet a woman who's been flirting with me ever since I started delivering packages to her job site."

"God, I'd love to have your job. Is she a hottie?"

"I think so." She wasn't going to tell Drew about the fishnet stockings or the references that Bonnie had made to her leather items. Suddenly she remembered the package she had left to be delivered. "Hey, Drew, you aren't expecting anything, are you? I've got a package to deliver to someone here at Westside, but no name or apartment number."

"I don't know. What's inside? I'll tell you if I want it."

"I haven't opened it. It's kind of heavy though."

"Doesn't sound like lingerie or a jockstrap." Drew furrowed his brow as he thought. "Well, it's probably not mine. But if you open it and find a pile of gold coins or a silk jockstrap, then you know where to find me."

Alexis shook her head. "So what about your plans tonight? Staying home with this guy?"

"One of the trapeze guys is coming over for a nightcap after the circus. But I don't expect him 'til after eleven. He's got some nice pecs, let me tell you."

"I hope you're talking about his chest muscles. So how long is the circus in town?"

"One more week. I'm still trying to get the wrestler to flirt with me. He's not really my type, but I like the challenge." Drew laughed. "Hey, speaking of challenges, have you talked to our snobby model next door, Miss Darcy Callahan, yet?"

"No. I tried tonight. We rode home on the bus together." She didn't think that Darcy was as snobbish as Drew declared. He called everyone who was quiet and attractive a snobby model. And although Darcy certainly had the height to be a model, she wasn't skin and bones.

"Oh! I didn't tell you what I found out!" Drew set down his beer and clapped his hands, mocking his own excitement. "I enticed the apartment manager to part with some gossip about our Miss Darcy. Turns out she's a professor in anthropology at the community college. And according to her apartment application, single."

"Damn. I knew there was a reason I froze up every time she says anything."

"Bad memories of college professors?"

Alexis hadn't told Drew about Virginia and didn't intend to. As much as she had grown to love Drew, she didn't like the fact that he had a big mouth. He didn't need to know her little heartbreak story. "Something like that, yeah."

"Well, I can understand that. For years after I graduated college

19

I had nightmares about missing exams and crazy professors hunting me down for late papers." He shook his head dismally. "Anyway, I knew you had a crush on her, and I just had to snoop. Though really, Lex, you've dated women that were much better looking, and you know the quiet types aren't always as much fun in the sack."

"Just because she seems quiet now doesn't mean anything. I've heard some of the guys you've called quiet screaming your name at two in the morning."

He blushed. "Yes, well, I sometimes have a way of helping men break out of their shell."

Shaking the puppy hairs off her shirt, Lex stood to go. "I've gotta get to the grocery store before it starts raining. I promised Ruth a carton of milk. Hey, do you want to go to the farmer's market with me in the morning?"

Drew nodded. "But not too early. I don't know how long the trapeze boys like—"

Holding up her hand, Alexis headed for the door. "Don't go any further with that. I don't want to know."

By the time she returned from the grocery store, there was a message from Tina. She agreed to meet her tomorrow night outside Decker's at midnight. For some reason, Tina didn't want to go inside the club. Alexis dialed Mossinni's number, hoping to ask her about the package. She'd bumped into three other Westside residents, and none of them were expecting a package. Moss didn't pick up the phone. Alexis left a message inviting her out to Decker's. Though after losing her job, Moss was probably not in the mood to party.

Decker's was always busy on Friday nights. The bouncer didn't ask to see Alexis's ID. He passed her inside with a nod to the new cashier to make sure she wasn't charged. The regulars were treated well. Alexis found Paula and Jen already at the bar and with drinks in hand. She'd known Paula since college, and they'd dated for a few months. Fortunately, it hadn't worked out. Now they were much better friends. Jen was new to Portland and new to Paula's life. The two women had been dating for the past month and still showed the annoying symptoms of fresh lust. They kissed each other at least a dozen times every hour, and it was difficult to talk to either of them without placing a hand between their close-pressed bodies to lasso their attention.

"Hey, girls," Alexis said.

Paula pulled herself out of Jen's arm hold to give Alexis a hug. "Hey, Lex. How's it going, babe?"

"It's Friday. No complaints here."

"You got your weekend lineup yet?" Paula asked. She turned to Jen and continued, "See, Lex spends all week flirting with women while the rest of us with real jobs stare at our computer screens. Then, by the time the weekend rolls around, she's already got a half dozen women waiting for her call."

"Okay, that's an exaggeration. I'm lucky if I have two dates set up by Friday, and as for a real job, I work just as hard as anyone else."

"And you get to wear such a sexy little uniform, too," Paula continued.

Alexis could tell she was fishing for an argument and wondered what was wrong. Maybe she had grown tired of Jen's fierce attachment to her and was wishing for a more fancy-free weekend. "I'd rather not wear the APO badge across my left boob, but other than that, I don't mind the uniform. And you're right. It doesn't hurt my chances of flirting with the gals."

Jen pulled Paula back to her side and whispered something to her. Alexis scanned the bar, searching for Bonnie. She wondered if Bonnie liked to dance. There was a wall separating the bar and the pool tables from the dance floor.

Paula interrupted her thoughts, pointing over to the pool table. "One of the tables just opened. Do you want to join us for a three-way game?"

"No. I'll let you kids have your fun alone. You're both better at

21

pool than I am, and I'd just slow down the foreplay," Alexis admitted. She never had much luck in getting any ball except the cue to sink in a hole. "Anyway, I'm supposed to meet a date here."

Blushing after the comment about foreplay, Jen tugged Paula's arm toward the pool table. Paula glanced at Alexis and then trudged after her. She acted reluctant to be alone with Jen, and Alexis wondered if they had quarreled.

Alexis searched the club for Bonnie without any luck, and finally found a place at the bar and began chatting with Erin, one of her favorite bartenders. When the second game of pool ended, Jen headed to the restroom and Paula joined Alexis at the bar. With Jen out of earshot, Alexis asked, "Something the matter between you two?"

"Yeah . . . we still haven't . . . you know."

"What are you talking about?" Alexis asked. Paula adjusted her seat on the stool and ordered a gin and tonic.

"Sex."

"I know what you meant, but I can't believe it."

Paula sighed. "At first, she said she wanted to go slow. And I thought, no problem. It's her first time with a woman. We can go slow. Lex, it's been over a month and she's still saying, 'Let's take it slow.' We've spent nearly every night together over the past three weeks and done nothing more than kiss. I'm going crazy. Either she doesn't really like me, or she's changed her mind about wanting to be with a woman."

Alexis had to stop herself from laughing. She knew Paula had a strong appetite for sex, and waiting for a woman was torture for her. "A month isn't that long. I can think of someone who I waited an entire quarter for. Three whole months to get that girl in the sack."

Paula pushed away from the bar and leaned back on her stool. "Oh no, that was different. I was only eighteen."

"Completely different, right?" Alexis challenged sarcastically.

"It was. You were a year older than me and had already been with half the sorority girls. Hell, you had a hippie for a mom. My parents were straight out of the Family Channel. They never talked about sex. I just needed some time to come out."

"And Jen doesn't?"

Paula sighed. She turned to look at the restroom door just as it opened. Jen smiled over at them. "I swear she's driving me to drink," Paula said under her breath.

Alexis slid off her barstool. "Patience is a virtue. At least that's what you once told me. I never really believed you though."

As soon as Jen reached them, Alexis spotted Mossinni walking into the club. She apologized for leaving Paula and Jen alone again and headed over to greet her ex-co-worker. "Moss! Good to see ya, girl."

"You too." Moss reached up to hug her. "And where's your woman tonight?"

"What do you mean? I'm always single."

"Single? Well, I don't think I've ever seen you single for an entire night at Decker's. There's always some pretty young thing trying to catch your eye and squeezing your firm biceps by the end of the night. How often do you go home single?"

Alexis shrugged. Moss was exaggerating of course. "At least a couple times a month."

"And tonight? I'm sure you have someone picked out by now. Are you playing hard to get?"

"No." Alexis glanced at the door. "I am supposed to be meeting someone here. We'll see if she shows." She didn't like the sarcastic way Moss had of calling her out on things. Moss was always looking for a way to attack someone, even with friends. "So how have you been?"

"You mean after the DUI charges?" Moss shrugged. "I've had better days. Then again, I've had worse."

"You've been all the talk at APO. By the way, did you take the cream and sugar packets from the break room?"

"What gave you that idea?" Moss laughed.

Alexis knew from Moss's sly grin that the rumor was true. "Why the hell did you do that?"

"I was trying to get back at Kate. She's the one who told Ace about my DUI. Ace wouldn't have even known about it otherwise."

"You shouldn't have been driving drunk."

Moss shook her head. "Don't I know it. Damn, it was a stupid thing to do. Listen, if I could do it over again, I'd have called in sick a thousand times over rather than show up to work toasted."

"And why'd you take the labels off your leftovers?" Any packages that weren't delivered, for whatever reason, were less than affectionately termed leftovers. Drivers usually accumulated leftovers because no one was home at the delivery address.

"I don't know. I was mad, I guess." Moss shrugged. "I'm thirsty. Wanna go to the bar?"

Alexis followed her over to the bar, though she wasn't interested in a drink or in continuing her conversation with Moss. Unfortunately, she needed information. Jen and Paula were dancing in the other room. She still didn't see Bonnie and wondered if she was going to get stood up.

"Ace was pissed about the ripped off labels?"

Alexis nodded. "I got stuck with one of them. They traced five of the packages to the correct addresses. But one of them was to an apartment complex, specifically, my apartment complex, and there is no record of an apartment number. Now Ace has given me the job of figuring out who the damn thing belongs to. You don't remember, do you?"

"Are you kidding? Remember, I wasn't entirely sober. Just open it up."

"Seems sacrilegious."

"Fortunately for me, I've never been religious." Moss laughed. She ordered a Diet Coke and watched the bartender fill a glass with ice.

"Sworn off alcohol?"

"For a while," Moss admitted. "It was starting to become a

habit." She patted her belly. "Someone asked me how many weeks pregnant I was, and I knew right then that I was drinking too much beer. Well, it was either that or the DUI that made things hit home."

"Too bad you got that DUI now with the holidays coming. We need extra drivers as it is. Maybe you can find a job working retail." It was the beginning of November, and APO's busiest shipping time paralleled the retail industry.

"As long as no one asks to check my last job references." Moss shrugged. "Ah, it doesn't really matter. I just need to find a rich girl." She chuckled cynically and took a sip of her Coke. "You know, I'm meeting someone tonight as well."

"Really? Well don't keep any secrets. Who is it?"

"Don't know exactly. I answered a personal ad this morning. Got an e-mail this afternoon telling me to be here at midnight." She glanced at the bar clock. It was nearly midnight. "We'll see if she keeps her promise."

Alexis was wondering the same thing about Bonnie. Her pride would be wounded if Bonnie stood her up, and she was going to be disappointed if she never found out what sort of leather toys Bonnie liked. She had had enough eye candy at the bar to awaken more than a few erotic nerves in her body.

"Hey, Lex, don't look now, but the hottie who just came in is checking us out. She's in line to have her ID checked."

Alexis spotted Bonnie at the door. "Well, looks like I'm not getting stood up after all."

"She's your date tonight? She doesn't look legal. I wonder if she can watch R-rated movies alone."

Alexis didn't reply to this comment. Moss had a quick jealous streak. "You gonna be okay if I leave you alone here?"

"No. Bring her over and introduce me. I hate sitting at a bar alone."

Alexis didn't want Moss to be the third wheel tonight and hoped the online friend she had mentioned would actually show. Fortunately, Alexis passed Paula and Jen on her way to the door.

They had just stepped off the dance floor, and Alexis directed them over to the bar to keep Moss company. Paula and Moss were old friends and Alexis knew she could entertain her.

Bonnie was just about to pay the cashier when Alexis stepped up. The cashier nodded at Alexis. "Hey, Lex, this pretty gal a friend of yours?"

"Yep, she's with me." Bonnie was looking especially attractive tonight. She wore the same short black skirt that she'd had on earlier that day with the fishnet stockings. But she'd changed out of the conservative gray sweater to a red tank top. She was carrying a leather jacket, and Alexis immediately thought about Bonnie's comments that morning about her sex toys. Bonnie also had a leather armband with spikes. As soon as Alexis noticed the spikes, she hoped that S&M wasn't Bonnie's specialty. Leather was nice, but pain wasn't.

The cashier turned back to Bonnie. "Well, hon, Lex already took care of your cover, so put your money away. Go on and have a good time."

Bonnie smiled at Alexis. "You know how to work people, don't you? I'd bet that you never pay a cover in any club in Portland."

Alexis smiled. "It's good to have friends."

"So is that your posse?" Bonnie pointed to the bar where Paula, Jen and Moss were all sitting.

"My posse?" Alexis only considered Paula to be her friend, but she didn't want to go into details of her relationship with Moss or Jen now. "For tonight."

"I dated the one on the left. I think her name was Jen."

"You dated Jen?" Alexis stopped herself from blurting out the next thought. So much for her story about being a lesbian virgin.

"Yep. We broke up about three months ago." Bonnie shook her head. "I didn't think I'd see her around here. Small world."

"Sometimes it's too small."

Bonnie nodded. "To make a long story short, we didn't end on very good terms. I haven't talked to her since I kicked her out of my house. I caught her with this other woman, spread eagle and buck naked, in our bed."

Wow, TMI, Alexis thought, trying to shake this mental image of Jen. "So let's go somewhere else. I'll tell my friends that you're dragging me off for mad sex."

Bonnie blushed. "Oh really? Is that a challenge?"

"Or a plea bargain."

"Whatever. You know, I'm a good girl who never has sex on first dates. Maybe we can find another club for dancing tonight. I feel like some Latin music."

Alexis nodded. So much for the leather toys. Well, Salsa dancing was a good alternative to hot sex. "I know just the place."

The Latin club a few blocks down from Decker's was a straight club, but the crowd was friendly. Bonnie admired the dancers on the floor as soon as they had ordered their drinks. "Do you want to dance?"

Alexis nodded. Virginia had taught her the basics, but it had been a while. They headed through a crowded section of the dance floor and wormed their way to the center of the mass of dancers. Fortunately, with a crowded dance floor it was easy to follow along, and no one really noticed mediocre skill levels. After the first set of songs, Bonnie leaned close to Alexis and said, "Hope I didn't scare you with that story about Jen. I don't usually kick people out in the middle of the night."

"No, I was already scared with your comments this morning." She had to shout this twice before Bonnie heard her. Then Bonnie looked at her with a puzzled expression.

"I can't remember exactly what I said. I do remember grabbing your butt." She smiled coyly. "It was hard to resist. I've been trying to get up the courage to ask you out for about a year. Ever since you took over for the last APO delivery guy. I think I just needed to wear my fishnets for an extra boost. I saw you looking at my legs and knew."

"Knew?"

"Knew where your eyes wanted to look."

Alexis was glad that Bonnie couldn't see her blush this time. The room was hot, and feeling Bonnie's skin under her hands was enough to make her boxers wet. Bonnie's red tank top accentuated her curves well, and she didn't flinch when Alexis passed her hand over her breasts as they spun on the dance floor. Her hand brushed there on accident, mostly, and though she apologized, Bonnie gave murmurs of approval. The other dancers, sweaty men and scantily clothed women, were too wrapped up in their own moves to notice what the two women in the center of the floor were doing. Alexis shifted closer, dancing hip to hip with Bonnie. Every time she thought about kissing her, something made her pause. Finally, there was a break in the music and Bonnie caught her eye. They stared at each other, both feeling the heat of the other's intended gaze. Alexis brushed her hand over Bonnie's cheek and then kissed her. She felt Bonnie respond immediately, pulling her into a tongue dance. And they only separated when one of the other dancers stumbled back, pushing against them.

After an hour of dancing, Alexis noticed that Bonnie was slowing down. She pulled her to the edge of the dance floor. "You look tired. Do you want to take a break?"

"I've had a long day," Bonnie admitted. "Will you walk me home? We're only five or six blocks from my place."

"Of course." Alexis found their coats and they headed out of the club. The streets were wet and Alexis took a deep breath. She loved the fresh smell after a rain. She glanced at her watch. It was nearly two. She wondered if Paula was sleeping with Jen tonight. Paula had told Alexis that if nothing happened this weekend, she was going to have "That Talk." Alexis thought about the story Bonnie had told her about her breakup with Jen. She guessed there was more to this story than what Bonnie had mentioned.

"So I have to tell you something," Bonnie said. She gazed across the street, then straight ahead and finally down at the sidewalk. Everywhere but at Alexis.

Did she have some STD? Did she live with five dogs and a monkey? Was she engaged to a guy? Alexis had heard just about everything, she thought grimly. There was no need to be melodramatic and draw it out. After nearly a minute of silence, Alexis finally asked, "Okay, what is it?"

"You know how I told you that I don't have sex on first dates?"

Alexis nodded.

"Well, I wasn't lying."

Good, no monkeys.

"Usually I don't do anything more than kiss."

"Usually?" An argument that Alexis had with Drew came into her head.

He'd insisted that gay men were better dates than most women because, "Overall, they had no problem getting into the fun part, even on the first date." She'd insisted that this was a misconception of males and that most women were more than ready to "get down with the fun part," if they had the right partner.

"Yes. But I was thinking that I've never really liked my rule."

Alexis couldn't help smiling. She'd have to tell Drew about this later. Liking the direction that this was heading, she decided to push one step further. "Does this mean I get to see the garter belt that goes with those fishnets?"

"Maybe. It's under consideration."

They reached Bonnie's place, a townhouse with a big staircase and a view of the river. Unfortunately, her two housemates, two women who looked about Bonnie's age, were both in the living room watching a movie. Bonnie didn't bother making introductions. She pointed upstairs and Alexis followed her up to a loft. A futon covered most of the floor space, with one corner reserved for a dresser and a narrow walkway around all sides.

"Sorry about my housemates. I didn't think anyone would be awake this late." Bonnie pulled off her shoes. "I'd offer you a seat, but there's only the bed."

Alexis kicked off her shoes and set her jacket on an empty space of floor by the door. She sat down on one corner of the mattress, surveying the room. She could tell that Bonnie was nervous and tried to avoid looking at her. Spotting the stereo and a pile of CDs, Alexis went over and picked out an album. She'd made out to every type of music and was always willing to try a new band. This time, though, she went for a guaranteed get-you-in-the-mood Sarah McLachlan CD. As soon as the music started, she turned to face Bonnie. "This okay?"

Bonnie nodded. She blushed as soon as Alexis touched her cheek, then apologized. "Damn, I feel like a beginner. Lex, I swear I've done this before. It's just that . . ."

"Just not usually on your first date." Alexis took a step back. "You know, we can just hang out. We don't have to do anything."

"No." She reached out to grab Alexis's belt and unhooked the buckle, then pulled it slowly out of the belt loops. As soon as she had the belt in her hands, she smiled. "I've had a crush on you for so long. I don't know how many times I've undressed you. In my head."

"Well, don't let me stop you now." Alexis kissed her again then ran her fingers through her hair and along her neck. Her tongue pressed inside briefly with another kiss, teasing. She took Bonnie's hand and kissed her palm. "Go ahead. I love being undressed by beautiful women."

Bonnie fingered the first button on Alexis's shirt deliberately, as if she were still considering Alexis's offer. She laughed nervously. "I can't believe you're here. On my bed. Do you think we should take things a little slower?"

"Are you really asking me that?" Alexis had no desire to slow things down. She wondered what had happened to Bonnie's aggressive sexual drive. An awkward lover was often a turn on, but only if Alexis could lead the play.

In the next moment, Bonnie had unbuttoned Alexis's shirt and the material gapped, exposing her bra. Bonnie pulled the shirt off her shoulders and slipped her cool hands under Alexis's tank top. She caressed each breast while tugging the tank top off. Bonnie left

Alexis's bra on and focused next on her jeans. Her fingers moved methodically, like she'd practiced this, and she didn't say a thing. When she spotted Alexis's boxers, dark blue with a yellow happy face at the front opening, she finally smiled. Alexis could feel Bonnie gradually relax with each piece of clothing that came off. Finally, she stood naked in the middle of the room, with Bonnie smiling at her, getting a full view. A cool draft sent a shiver up her back, and she reached for Bonnie, wanting to take off her clothes quickly so they could get under the covers.

Bonnie pushed Alexis's hand away as she tried to slip under the red tank top to feel her breasts. "I want to touch you, but you can't touch me yet."

Alexis tried to argue, but Bonnie was firm. She had to ignore the demands of her body. Bonnie strummed Alexis's nipples while she explained that only she could do the touching for now. First ground rule. Her fingers massaged Alexis's breast, and she started to suck on the nipples. As she did, Alexis tried again to slip her hands under the tank top. This time she got a firmer rebuke from Bonnie.

"Why do you want to stay dressed?"

Bonnie bit her lip and took her hands off Alexis. Maybe she was losing some of her nerve. There was a moment of hesitancy on her face. "I've always imagined it this way. I mean, in my head. I was at work when I fucked you, but this is just as good. Just tonight, okay?"

Alexis sighed. "Of course I'd like to have you naked, but I'm not going to push it for now." Everyone had fantasies, and she didn't mind playing a part in this one. Still, it might be uncomfortable to deliver packages to Anderson Software come Monday morning. Maybe they wouldn't get any deliveries for a while.

Bonnie nodded. She went to her dresser and pulled out a pair of leather handcuffs. She arched her eyebrows as she looked back at Alexis. "These might be a little snug, but . . ." Slipping them on Alexis's wrists and tightening the straps, she continued, "I don't want you to break your promise and touch me yet." She fit the link between the cuffs to a metal ring drilled into the wall above the futon pillows.

"Was this in your work fantasy?" Alexis asked, smiling. She'd been tied up before, but was a little uneasy letting Bonnie do this when she was still fully dressed. Despite her uneasiness, she could feel moisture welling up between her legs and was desperate to have a little pressure on her clit.

"Well, no, but I thought it was a good idea to add it in." She finished tying the knot and pushed a hand on Alexis's chest, directing her down to the bed. Bonnie straddled Alexis's hips and then sat down, her jeans brushing against Alexis's trimmed hair. "Now I have a few things I want to try on you."

"Should I be scared?" The muscles between her legs were already contracting and releasing, ready for whatever Bonnie had in mind.

Bonnie flashed her eyes and smiled, tight-lipped. "I know your reputation. I doubt if you're scared of anything."

Alexis could feel herself getting wet. She watched Bonnie pull a pen out of a backpack near the futon. Bonnie uncapped the pen and touched the tip to her tongue. She drew a thin line across Alexis's belly just above her hairline and then paused. "Are you wondering if this is permanent ink?"

"I'm praying it's not." Alexis pulled against her handcuffs, trying to slip free from the leather binding. The last thing she wanted was to have Bonnie's name signed below her waistline. As she pulled against the leather, the knots tightened, chafing her wrists.

"You can't get away. I've got you caught, finally." Bonnie pressed one hand on Alexis's belly and moved her knees up to pin down Alexis's hips. She made an X-mark at the start of the line and then wrote "fuck me now" in swirling cursive. She smiled as she admired her handwriting. "You know, I've always wanted to sign that on the delivery forms."

She capped the pen when she'd finished and then started to

trace the cap over Alexis's nipples and down between her legs. She shifted lower on Alexis's thighs and pressed the cap on the swollen clit. "I want to put this inside you."

Alexis waited for her to move the pen, but instead she kept it pressed against her clit, occasionally drawing a slow circle around the pen with her fingertips. Her muscles were shivering now, begging to feel the pen, anything, inside. She spread her legs further. Still, Bonnie waited to push it inside. With the pen on her clit giving constant pressure, Bonnie bent her head and started to suck on Alexis's nipples, massaging with one hand while the other stayed between her legs. Alexis arched her hips up, hoping the pen would slip inside or Bonnie would give in and move a few fingers to fill her need. Her body was straining for an orgasm, and all she needed was something, anything to press her G-spot. She pulled against her tether, and the knot on the ring tightened with her tugging.

Bonnie started to move lower on her body, leaving her nipples wet and erect. She paused as soon as she was between Alexis's legs and drove the pen and her two fingers inside just as her tongue touched the swollen clit. She squeezed her legs together as Bonnie moved her hand in a slow circle, pushing deeper. Her muscles tightened as she was caught in the rush of an orgasm.

Chapter 3

By the time the handcuffs were off Alexis's wrists, she was already planning her way home. The orgasm had been exactly what she needed, but she wasn't comfortable sleeping with Bonnie. She'd only half listened as Bonnie suggested places they could go for breakfast and slipped into her pajamas. Unfortunately, it was too far to walk home, too late to catch a bus, and cabs would be sparse at three a.m. She didn't trust Bonnie not to try something while she slept. And knowing her own habit of sound sleeping, she was worried that she might awake to find messages written all over her body, or her hands cuffed again and strange objects strategically positioned between her legs.

Somehow Bonnie convinced her to stay. She awoke to sunshine pouring in through a skylight. The loft was colored with the warm, golden tone of a bright day after a storm. Bonnie was still asleep, curled on her side with her head resting on Alexis's arm. Trying not to wake her, Alexis shifted a pillow under Bonnie's head and moved her arm, then crawled off the futon. Bonnie slept on while she dressed. She found a notepad and a pen, smiling when she realized it was the same one that had been inside her, and wrote Bonnie a quick note. It wasn't exactly a "Dear Jane" note, more of a "Let's just be friends."

She caught a bus heading west and made it home just before ten a.m. As she passed Drew's apartment, she heard something scratching at the door. In response, she knocked on the door and the scratching immediately stopped. Ordinarily she wouldn't have knocked this early, but she guessed the sound was probably from the puppy trying to tell somebody he needed to go out and do his business. A moment later, Drew opened the door and the puppy ran out into the hall, squatted on the carpet runner and proceeded to poop.

"Oh, I thought he might be telling me something." Drew shook his head. "You wouldn't believe how fast his little system works. He eats and not more than ten minutes later you better be running out the door." Drew went to the kitchen, leaving the door open, and returned with a plastic bag. He made a disgusted face as he cleaned up the puppy's mess. Thinking that this was a game, the puppy wriggled happily on the floor and pushed his nose at Drew's hand. He latched onto Drew's pant leg after being shooed away for the third time.

"Still think he's the most beautiful creature ever?"

Drew shook his head. "Well, I don't think Apollo fits him. I was thinking of calling him 'No, bad dog.' He seems to respond to that."

"That name's overused."

Drew picked up the puppy and headed back to his front door. "Come on in, Lex. You look like you had a rough night."

"Ah, not bad."

"Well, a little oj will fix your mood."

She followed him inside, thinking that what she could really use was a shower. Drew poured two glasses of orange juice and set a bowl of water down for the puppy. "You still up for the farmer's market?"

Alexis nodded. This was the last weekend of the market until spring, and she was hoping to find some good end of the season apples. "You bringing the puppy?"

"Of course. You know dogs are magnets. I'll be meeting gay boys like crazy."

"I thought dogs were *chick magnets*," Alexis countered. "Are you sure this pup will rope in men?"

"Oh, like bees to honey."

"We'll see, I guess." She finished the orange juice and rinsed her glass in the sink. There was only one fork and one plate on the drying rack. "Were you alone last night?"

Drew sighed heavily. "The circus pulled out of town a day early. They're heading to Reno next and have a gig tonight. Anyway, I got a call from the trapeze lead sometime around eight this morning apologizing for standing me up. I was pissed and hung up on him. You know, it's one thing to stand someone up and another to wake them up the next morning just to admit that you're a dick."

"Sorry. That sucks. If it makes any difference, I didn't have a great night either." She lifted her shirt and showed him the marks that Bonnie had left.

"Oh, Lex, don't go back to that one. She didn't even capitalize the F." Drew started laughing and had to set down his juice to keep from spilling.

"Whatever." She wasn't that upset about the writing. But she didn't like that Bonnie had kept her clothes on, and maybe the handcuffs had rubbed her wrong. She liked to be the one in control unless her lover was a stronger lead. "I'm going to go clean up. Hopefully the ink will come off. Otherwise, I'm going to have a quiet weekend here with you and the puppy. Will you be ready in a half hour?"

He nodded. "Make sure you scrub hard."

"Thanks," she replied sarcastically. The puppy followed her to the door and then whined as she pushed him out of the way to leave.

◈

Apollo was indeed a hit at the farmer's market. Before they had reached the fruit and vegetable vendors, Drew had two guys' phone numbers and a dog walking date for Sunday afternoon with an athletic, short Austrian named Johann, who probably had a lifetime gym membership and was as well ripped as his dog, Brute. Drew was excited about this catch and kept mentioning the size of Johann's neck muscles. Although by his enthusiasm, Alexis suspected he was thinking of Johann's other body parts too. They toured the aisles, rubbing the squash and poking the apples. Drew stopped at a bakery table to pick out a loaf of bread and ended up in a discussion about organic winter wheat varieties. Apollo was straining at his leash to move on, but Alexis could see that Drew liked the baker too well to just buy the bread and move on. She took the leash from him and pointed down the aisle at a table overflowing with apple barrels. "Take your time. I'll meet you over there."

Apollo had to sniff each table, and it was a slow walk to the apple barrels. Alexis didn't mind the puppy's speed. It left her plenty of time to watch the woman who was in charge of the apples. She stood under a sign that read Kingston Apples, and she looked about Alexis's age, or a little older, had a friendly smile and tanned skin, unusual in Portland this time of year. The woman seemed about Alexis's height and had a similar athletic build. Her dark brown hair was trimmed to just below her ears and pulled back from her face with a black headband. Alexis liked the woman's rustic, no makeup type beauty and eyed her left hand, hoping she wouldn't have a ring. An older couple had her attention for the moment, and she was filling a bag with Pippin apples and talking about pies. The old man finally paid the woman, and his wife took the bag from her.

Alexis was sorting through a barrel of Fujis, picking out a few that looked appetizing, and trying to keep the puppy from wandering too far under the table. She noticed the apple seller watching her and smiled briefly, then went back to sorting through the barrel.

"Have you tried a Pink Lady?"

"What?" Alexis asked, glancing up at the woman. She had a knife in her palm and was slicing an apple. The skin was dark pink with hints of green and a dimpled surface. Alexis took a bite of the apple that the woman offered. Surprised, she found the flesh was crisp, despite the bumps on the outside, and the tangy sweet flavor was better than any Fuji or Granny Smith. "This is delicious."

"I picked them just yesterday. They were the last ones on the tree, and they've sucked up all the last bits of sweet sun." She paused. "You have a cute puppy."

"Oh, he's not mine. I'm just walking him so a friend of mine can flirt with the baker."

The woman laughed and then leaned over the table to whisper, "You might want to let your friend know that the baker's gay."

"Don't worry, so is my friend," Alexis replied. She pointed Drew out and then smiled as the woman nodded with approval. An apple picker. I'm in love with an apple picker, Alexis thought, taking another bite of her slice. "Can I have ten of these?"

"My pleasure." She started filling a bag with enough care that Alexis could tell she was getting above-average fare. The woman handed her the bag and took her money.

Alexis thanked her and started to leave, then turned back to the table. "It's such a beautiful day. Too bad you're working. We don't get many days like this in November. Are you stuck here long?"

"No, I'm just staffing the table until my mother gets back from her break. My family owns the apple orchard that these all came from, and I come up every fall to help out with the harvest."

"Where do you live the rest of the year?"

"Santa Barbara."

"Oh, I'm sorry," Alexis replied. Then seeing that the apple picker couldn't tell that she was joking, she quickly added, "I'm just jealous. I lived in Santa Barbara for a year and I miss all the sunshine. They get days like this all the time down there."

"I miss the rain. In fact, I've decided to stay here a month longer than planned so I could get a good dose of rain, and my family, before heading back to Southern California and the endless summer." She extended her hand. "I'm Elana, by the way."

"Alexis." She shook her hand. "You know, my friend and I are going to have lunch here in the park. He'll probably convince the baker to join us, and I'd love if you did too, if you're not busy here."

Elana nodded. "If I can get away . . ."

Just then an older woman appeared wearing an apron with an embroidered quote: "An apple a day keeps the doctor away!"

After brief introductions, Elana told her mom that she was taking an early lunch break. The old woman nodded, pleased that she was getting out of the market tent to enjoy the sunshine, and then told Elana to ask the baker along. There were two people running the bakery table and only one was really necessary, Elana's mother insisted.

Alexis and Elana headed over to the bakery table, with Alexis carrying Apollo. He'd grown tired of the leash and refused to walk. As soon as they were out of her mother's earshot, Elana said, "So my mother's been trying to set me up with the baker for the past five years. She doesn't seem to understand that there's no hope for a match."

The baker waved to Elana as they approached. Drew took the puppy, thanking Alexis, and with a wink, congratulating her on the new acquaintance. Ben, the baker, couldn't take a break from the table. Apparently his assistant wasn't feeling well and was heading home early, leaving Ben to man the table alone for the rest of the afternoon. Drew said he wanted to take Apollo home anyway and asked the group if they would like to meet later. Elana proposed Blue's Cafe for dinner that evening. She mentioned that the restaurant had been reviewed in the Dining section of the newspaper, and she was looking for an opportunity to try out a new place before it went out of vogue. Alexis tried to suggest another restaurant, but Ben and Drew quickly agreed to Elana's plan.

Drew left the market with Apollo tucked under one arm and a loaf of bread under the other. Ben's eyes followed him as far as the entrance gate. Elana and Alexis headed out of the tent as well, choosing a spot in the sunshine with a view of the river.

"I'm excited about our double date with the guys, if you can call it that," Elana said as they sat down on the park bench.

"Yeah, Ben seems as animated as Drew is. Tonight could be entertaining with those guys flirting around." Alexis smiled, though she wasn't happy with the dinner arrangements. She liked double dates, but wished they were going to a different restaurant. If Sandy saw her, she'd be in a tight spot. She hoped the dinner crowd would be bigger than the usual lunch crowd, leaving Sandy too busy in the kitchen to notice she was there. "So what do you do in Santa Barbara?"

"You mean, my real life away from apple harvesting?" Elana laughed. "I'm a photographer. Landscapes are my passion, but I do weddings and any paying gig really. I travel around quite a bit."

"Weddings?" Alexis couldn't imagine Elana as a wedding photographer. She would have more easily passed for a wildlife biologist or a nature trail leader.

"Gotta pay the bills somehow." She shrugged. "I've spent too many hours trying to catch that one shot that says *wedding day bliss.* You know it's bad when the bride asks why you're pointing your camera on the sunset when that angle obviously doesn't include anyone from her wedding party."

"Women with princess fantasies can be a force to be feared."

"Don't I know it. And what about you? Job, hobbies, wife and kids?" She paused and then added quietly, "Or do you spend all your time flirting with women? You seem to be pretty good at it."

Alexis had been called out about her flirting often enough not to blush anymore. "I work for a package delivery service." And you'd be surprised how much of my day is spent flirting, she thought. "As far as hobbies, I'm a potter with no wheel, but a lot of muddy ideas. And you know, I like walks on the beach, cozy fireplace conversations and jazz music."

Elana smiled on cue. She interrupted Alexis to point at an old couple walking slowly down one of the park paths. "Weren't they the ones who bought my apples?"

Alexis squinted at them. "I think you're right. Yep, there's the bag you sold them in that old guy's hands."

"I want to be like that one day." Elana quickly added, "I mean, not married and old, but you know, spending the day with someone you know that well. Taking a walk, planning dinner and having a reason to make a pie. Unfortunately, independence seems more valuable now."

They watched the couple stop at the gates at the end of the park path, as if trying to decide which direction they'd come from or where they'd left their car. Finally, they decided on left and turned to head that way. Alexis touched Elana's hand, tracing a scar that ran along the edge of her thumb. She wanted to ask about the scar and realized at that moment how interested she was in Elana. Too bad she lived in Santa Barbara. "You don't seem like the type who'd be single for long. I'm surprised you're not happily settled with some girl and already making pies together."

"Well . . . I broke off a relationship about a month ago. We'd been going together for four years. My mother was hoping we'd marry." Elana paused just as Alexis let go of her hand. She shifted her position on the bench, pulling her knees up to her chest and dangling her toes off the edge. "When he finally asked, I said no." She sighed. "And that was the end of four years."

Alexis was momentarily stunned. She'd assumed that Elana was a lesbian and couldn't believe that she was straight or bi. "Why'd you say no?"

"The real question is why I would wait four years to say it." Elana stood up suddenly and held her hand out to Alexis. "I want to stretch my legs. Mind if we walk down to the river?"

Elana kept Alexis's hand while they walked, heading down the same path that the old couple had taken, but veering to the right to head to the river. Her palms were callused like a kid who had spent all day swinging from the monkey bars, though Alexis guessed the sores were from climbing ladder rungs or carrying baskets of apples.

"I'm sorry I mentioned my ex."

"No worries. I think I brought it up." Alexis didn't want to think of Elana's ex. Of course it was hard to avoid. Her head was filled with questions. Had Elana only dated men? She seemed experienced at flirting and none too shy. Did she just flirt with women? Alexis always tried to avoid falling for someone who was just out of a long-term relationship, or someone who lived in another town. She was also uneasy about women who primarily went with men, thanks to Virginia. But with Elana, she wasn't ready to give up too soon. After all, the man was out of the scene. Elana was single now, and apparently interested in her. What was more, it didn't sound like she had a pressing reason to return to Santa Barbara. They walked the rest of the way to the river in silence.

"And why aren't you settled down with some girl?" Elana asked as they picked their way along the riverbank. "Wait, let me guess. You don't like commitment."

"I commit to women all the time." She smiled. "Usually for the whole night."

"That's what I thought. I like people who are honest." Elana crossed her arms and raised her eyebrow as though she were considering if she should trust Alexis. "And what happens if you meet someone who you want to spend more than one night with? Would you ever be happy with just one person?"

"I'd like to hope so." Alexis shrugged. "Sometimes I kind of feel like I'm in a department store trying to figure out which jeans fit me best. It gets old trying on so many different pairs. But how else do you find the perfect jeans that make you feel comfortable and sexy at the same time?"

"Good question. Nothing's perfect. But some jeans come close." Elana stared out over the water. "After five years being complacent, it's hard to start shopping again. You start thinking maybe your hips are too wide for jeans anyway."

Alexis stepped in front of Elana. She set her hands on Elana's hips. "Can I kiss you?" Elana didn't reply. She leaned forward and met Alexis's lips. The kiss was tentative at first and she started to move away after a soft peck, but when Alexis met her lips a second time, it was Elana who pushed forward. Alexis moved her hands off Elana's hips, and brushed against her lower back as she pulled back. After they'd parted, Elana's eyes stayed closed for a moment, as if she'd been waiting for their kiss and didn't want to let it end too soon. When she noticed Alexis watching her, she blushed and turned away. Alexis caught her hand. "I'm sorry. Maybe that was too soon. I know we've only just met."

"Don't apologize, I'm just . . . getting used to this again." Elana touched Alexis's shoulder, then traced the line of her neck up to her chin. She continued, "I had a girlfriend in college, but we were both too scared to do much more than flirt." She laughed, almost sadly. "I need more practice." Still holding Alexis's chin, she took a step forward and they kissed again, this time Elana driving their moment. When she let Alexis go the second time, her cheeks didn't blush. She slipped her hand around Alexis's waist and they walked back up to the park. They separated just before they reached the market tent. "You'll be at Blue's Cafe tonight?"

"At seven," Alexis agreed.

"I'll enjoy waiting to see you." Elana paused and then asked in a puzzled tone, "Where are your apples?"

"My apples?" Alexis looked at her empty hands. "Shit, I left them at Ben's table."

"Stay here. I don't want to explain this one to my mother." Elana disappeared into the tent and a few minutes later returned with a full bag of Pink Lady apples. "Ben had saved the bag, hoping he could give them to you tonight. He said you looked a little distracted and wasn't surprised that you'd forgotten about apples."

"Yeah, I guess I was a bit distracted." Alexis took the bag, wondering how tonight would go with the foursome. Drew and Ben might be fun, but she'd rather be alone now with Elana. "Thank you again for the apples."

Drew hated public transportation. He had a shiny new Beemer and loved to drive, so Alexis wasn't surprised at the look of disgust he gave her when she suggested taking the Number 9 bus at half past six.

"Only you, Lex, would entertain the notion of showing up for a date with your bus pass in hand," Drew replied.

"Maybe you could lighten up a little. People who ride buses are saving the air for your ungrateful lungs," she teased.

"I'm not arguing with a save the whales lesbian who thinks of doomsday every time someone mentions the word *nuclear*. Come on, if we drive together it'll be half the pollution."

Alexis finally agreed, knowing that Drew was hopelessly addicted to driving. She also noted that some dark gray clouds had taken the place of the earlier blue skies, threatening a rainstorm at any moment. A bus ride in the rain was less than inviting. Alexis went downstairs first, planning to meet Drew there. She had decided to leave a note about the unlabeled package on the message board near the mailboxes, hoping that the rightful owner would call her to claim it. So far, she had knocked on half the doors in the apartment building and found no one who was expecting the box, but everyone was willing to take it off her hands if she found any money or jewelry inside. She didn't want to open it yet. Just as she finished posting the note, Darcy came into the mailroom.

"Hi there, mind if I sneak by to get my mail?"

"Oh, sure," Alexis mumbled, stepping aside to let Darcy into the mailroom. Startled at the unexpected meeting, Alexis stared awkwardly at the message board. Her tacit excuse for lingering was to read a posting about a lost cat. She tried to memorize the cat's description, "Fat Orange Male with White Paws wearing a Leopard print collar. Answers to Tweetie." Since her thoughts were really focused on Darcy, who had just opened her mailbox, she had to read the description several times before it made sense. Who would name a fat male cat *Tweetie*? She snuck a glance over at Darcy, appreciating the three-quarter length black stretch pants that exposed well-shaped calves and outlined the lean muscles of her legs. Darcy's half unzipped blue sweatshirt and white sports bra peeking out from underneath had Alexis obviously staring. There was a triangle of moisture between the curves of her breasts, and her running shoes had left a trail of wet prints on the carpet. Too bad she's just finished a run, Alexis thought, I would have loved to join her for a workout.

Darcy closed her mailbox after sorting out the junk ads. She tossed the junk pile in the recycling bin and caught Alexis's eye.

"What a waste of trees."

"Yeah, totally." Totally? Why had she said that? She couldn't manage even a hello and now was reverting to her high school vocabulary. She tried to laugh and it came out as a half-hearted grunt.

Darcy continued, "Looks like you're all dressed up for a night out?"

"Just dinner. Just friends," Alexis answered in a quiet tone that was so unlike her normal voice that it was almost comical. But at least she was holding up her end of a conversation. The more she stared at Darcy the more she was reminded of Virginia. Darcy seemed to bring out all of the insecurities she'd felt dating Virginia. Maybe it was a professor thing.

"Well, enjoy. By the way, it was drizzling out there for a few minutes. You might want to take an umbrella."

"Oh. Probably."

Darcy nodded and an uncomfortable silence followed. Finally Darcy stepped past Alexis and left the mailroom.

"God, I'm pathetic!" Alexis kicked the lower row of mailboxes. She wished she could have a simple conversation with Darcy without feeling like a preteen hormone-raging dyke. She wondered at Darcy's history, reminding herself that whether she even dated women was still up for debate. This question didn't stop Alexis from fantasizing about making out with her in the mailroom. Would Darcy prefer being on top or on bottom? And would she like using toys? Just fingering? How much lube?

"Who's pathetic?" Drew bounced down the steps into the mailroom. He slipped his arm around Alexis and whispered, "I just passed *our* Miss Darcy in the hall. Did you two finally talk? What did you say? Anything brilliant?"

"No," Alexis admitted. "I can barely manage monosyllabic responses. God, I hate crushes."

"How about just goosing her the next time you two meet? It would save a lot of time, and then you'd know exactly how she felt."

"No, then I'd know exactly how a woman's slap felt."

"Nothing like a little foreplay," Drew said, turning his usual high-pitched voice to a seductive tone.

"Come on, let's get out of here. If I don't get some lovin' tonight I'm worried I will end up knocking on someone's door."

"Maybe that would be a good thing. Unless of course, you're scared that she'll turn you out," Drew challenged.

"Don't even think about daring me, cause the answer is already no." Alexis pulled Drew toward the door, ignoring his taunts about her crush.

Fortunately Blue's was very crowded that evening. There was no sign of Elana yet, but Ben had met them at the door. He smiled warmly at Drew and shook Alexis's hand. They stood outside with the two boys chatting and Alexis watching the sidewalks for any sign of Elana. She was excited to see her tonight and happy to have Darcy off her mind. After ten minutes, the light evening sprinkle turned to full-fledged rain, and Ben decided they should go in and get a table. He insisted Elana wouldn't want them to wait outside for her.

The hostess immediately recognized Alexis and slipped them into a table just opening up by the window. After a half hour, Elana still hadn't shown up, and the other three had already finished their before dinner drinks. Alexis made two trips outside to check for her, and Ben called Elana's cell number, but there was no answer. Finally they decided to order dinner without her. Alexis asked for the chef's nightly special when a familiar waitress named Brigit arrived at their table. She listened to Ben and Drew place their orders, trying not to think about being a third wheel and fighting the realization that she was getting stood up for the first time. It didn't really matter, she argued, but Elana had poor timing. Seeing Darcy had brought up memories of her breakup with Virginia, and she wanted something to get her mind off that dead-end subject.

Drew launched into a conversation about his puppy's chewing antics, and Ben laughed at all the right times. For a moment, Alexis felt a pang of jealousy toward Drew and was annoyed at the sickeningly sweet way that the two men interacted. In addition to baking bread, Ben ran a computer tech company out of his home and had a college degree in engineering. Adding to this list, he had a handsome smile, good strong jaw lines and a sense of humor. He was by far the best catch of the men Drew had entertained in the past few weeks. Although Alexis was happy for Drew, she couldn't help wishing her own good catch hadn't stood her up.

Shortly after Brigit brought out their dinner orders, Sandy appeared at their table. She was decked out in fancy chef's attire, trading the Levi's and white apron that she wore for the lunch crowd for a spotless white buttoned up smock and black slacks. Her hair was pulled back with a tie, and she had a big chef's hat perched on her head. Instantly, Alexis was happy that Elana hadn't shown up.

"How's everything?" Sandy asked after a warm smile at Alexis and a quick introduction to Drew and Ben.

"Absolutely stunning. I love the linguini with the mushrooms," Drew replied, forking the item in question. "But I think I like the green beans with the red peppers even better. Who'd have thought to add caramelized walnuts? Truly mouth-watering combination."

Sandy blushed with his praise, seconded by Ben and Alexis. She lamented not being able to sit down and enjoy the meal with them and then, addressing Alexis, asked for a second chance in a more private setting. Sandy handed Alexis a slip of paper and left the group quickly, heading back to the kitchen with brief greetings at a few other tables.

As soon as Sandy disappeared behind the Employees Only door, Drew gave an overexaggerated congratulations to Alexis and then begged to hear the note read aloud. Ben laughed, eagerly agreeing that the note must be shared. Reluctant for an audience, Alexis unfolded the note and read aloud, "There's something about you. Just can't get you off my mind. Love that you came here tonight instead of just calling. I want to get out of town tomorrow. Would you be interested in joining me? Call me on my cell." Alexis paused and folded the note in half, fingering the crease that Sandy had made. The note smelled like chocolate, and she wondered if Sandy had been working on the dessert menu when she wrote the note.

"You have her cell number? Wait a minute, are you dating her too? Why didn't you say anything?" Drew asked. He acted like a kid whose best friend was telling secrets to someone else.

"No, I work just down the street from this place, so I come here often for lunch. We're just friends, you know, but we've talked about going out sometime. She wrote her number at the end of the note."

"With a little heart drawing next to her name?" Drew teased.

Ben shook his head. "Even without a cartoon heart, she's interested in more than a friendship with you. And as far as I'm concerned, Alexis, you have my blessing. She's an awesome chef."

Apparently still upset that Alexis hadn't told him about Sandy, Drew grudgingly agreed and then added, "You're damn lucky that you got stood up by Elana."

"Everything happens for a reason, as my mom always says." Alexis tucked the note in her pocket and picked up her fork. "And I wouldn't mind having Sandy cook for me in 'a more private setting,' if you know what I mean."

Drew glanced over at Ben. "I think she was including us in that 'private setting' as well. After all, we don't want to miss out on another showing of her culinary expertise."

Ben agreed. "And if it wasn't for us, then you wouldn't have come here tonight at all."

"Actually, I think we came here because of Elana." Alexis shook her head. She was tired of the day-long roller coaster feeling of her emotions.

Drew lifted his wineglass. "Then cheers to Elana for standing us up."

After finishing dinner, Alexis admitted she wanted to leave the cute new couple alone and catch a bus home. She had plans to go out dancing that evening and was tired of being a third wheel. Neither Ben nor Drew argued, so she left them with cash for her portion of the meal and gave Ben a warning to watch that he maintained Drew's good-boy reputation.

The bus was late, and by the time it arrived, Alexis was soaked. She shook the rain off her hair and coat and spent the ride home shivering. Her phone was ringing as soon as she stepped into her apartment. She peeled off her wet jacket and stomped her boots on the welcome mat before running for the phone. Tina answered the line.

"I just wanted to make sure we were still on for tonight."

Alexis was suddenly tired and gazed at her bedroom door longingly. She really wasn't in the mood for a fling with a straight woman, and Tina was almost certainly straight. The whine in her voice gave her away. But maybe a fling was exactly what she needed to get Elana, Darcy and Virginia off her mind. Despite the note in her pocket from Sandy, Alexis was still licking her wounds from getting stood up. "Yeah, of course we're still on. I'll see you at Decker's."

Tina hung up the line after a too breathy "until then." Alexis headed for the bathroom, passing the APO box on her way through the kitchen, and briefly considered, for at least the eightieth time, just opening the damn box. It reminded her of a Christmas present her aunt had sent her when she was a kid. Her mother had placed the box, received too early, behind the tree to hide it from Alexis's peeping eyes. Somehow, it was forgotten on Christmas Day. They had found the box when the tree was taken down in mid-January. Inside, she'd found an ugly red and green scarf. Her mother suggested that they wrap it up and leave it in the closet until the next Christmas, guessing that they'd both probably forget about it and it would be a surprise then. Strangely, it worked. The scarf box was reopened for five Christmases in a row, each time generating peals of laughter as the ugly scarf resurfaced. Her mother finally donated it, and Alexis pitied the kid who finally ended up with the thing.

Dressed in her favorite pair of loose fitting jeans, a black belt and a tight green tank top that showed off the hard-earned muscles in her shoulders and arms, Alexis pushed her short hair into place with a little gel and clasped a silver chain choker on her neck. She'd thought about getting an armband tattoo, but hadn't gotten up the nerve to do it yet. Knowing how often she changed her mind about everything from her haircut to breakfast cereal and girlfriends, she wasn't ready to commit to any permanent body art. And she hated needles.

Her jacket was still wet on the outside from the earlier downpour and she fished through the moist pockets to find her keys. As she locked her door, Alexis glanced over at Darcy's apartment, wondering what Darcy would say if she invited her to go dancing. She paused at Darcy's door, then lifted her fist up as though she really might knock. But a moment later her nerves gained the upper hand, and she turned to walk toward the stairs. She'd practiced the lines she wanted to say to Darcy, imagining knocking on Darcy's door nearly every time she passed it. Why couldn't she muster the same easy charm she relied on when talking to other women? Again, it was easy to blame Virginia.

Decker's was hopping with a boisterous crowd, and the bouncer had a line of women waiting to get in. Alexis joined the queue pressed against the brick building to escape the rain. The woman ahead of her, a hefty motorcycle dyke with an androgynous look and a very femme partner hugging her middle, lit a cigarette and took a deep drag. She passed the cigarette to her partner, and red lipstick lined the filter after she took her drag. Alexis was dying for a smoke, but resisted the urge to beg a cigarette. She'd kicked the habit last year after a modest stint of only four years and wasn't about to start again. Still, she loved the smell of rain mingled with fresh smoke.

She reached the head of the line after a few minutes of torture watching the cigarette pass between Ms. Motorcycle Dyke and Ms. Lipstick Femme. Janet, the bouncer, nodded at her as she pulled out her ID. "Hey, Lex, you're back again? What's that make, four times this week?"

"No. Three." Alexis shook her head, waiting for the couple in front of her to pay the cover charge so she could pass Janet. "And you know I only come to see you."

"Yeah, right." Janet laughed. In a lower voice, she continued, "And watch what you say, for Pete's sake. You know rumors travel fast at this place."

Alexis had gone out with Janet a few times and would have kept up the romance simply because of the good sex, but Janet's partner of five years didn't like that idea. Just as she was about to enter the club, Alexis heard someone call her name. She glanced at the sidewalk, recognizing no one, and then glanced at the street.

Tina hailed to her from her black Porsche double-parked across from the club. "Over here, Lex."

Alexis apologized and stepped out of the doorway, trying to ignore Janet's whistle. She crossed the street, and Tina pointed her to the passenger side. Fortunately the rain had settled down to a light drizzle, and since she was already wet, she didn't mind a few more drops. The window was down and she leaned into the car, smelling a sweet dose of Tina's perfume that mixed with the scent of the rain.

"Get in," Tina said. She was wearing a black button-down shirt, open at the neck, and gray slacks.

Expensive cut, Alexis thought, eyeing the line of the fabric and the outline of Tina's pale skin. "You don't want to go into the club? We could get a drink and dance, flirt around a little . . ."

"The only reason to flirt is to decide who you want to fuck that night." Tina shook her head. "And I already know who I want to take home."

Alexis liked Tina's no-nonsense reply. Maybe Tina wasn't a whining, kept woman after all. She opened the door and slid into the leather seat. "I'm a little wet. Sorry." She brushed her hand along the console between the seats, trying to dry off the water drops.

"You don't have to apologize about being wet." Tina started the engine and revved the gas, glancing at Alexis. "I find that very sexy."

"Oh, really?" She was going to enjoy this night, she thought. Forget about Darcy or Elana. Tina had her attention now. They sped down the street with "Fuck Me Like an Animal" playing on the stereo, and Alexis decided that if anything, this was going to be a night to remember. She loved topping women with attitude. "What else do you find sexy? If I can be so bold to ask."

Tina reached across the console and rested her hand on Alexis's knee. She slid her way up the thigh, and just before her fingers had reached Alexis's crotch, she let go to change gears. "I like skipping foreplay."

"You're married?" Alexis asked, pointing to the gold band on Tina's left hand. They were on the freeway now, following the signs to Lake Oswego, and the Porsche was happily flying past the SUVs and luxury sedans.

"Yes, unhappily. He's out of town with his mistress."

Alexis considered this for a moment. She'd guessed that Tina was straight, and what did it matter if she was married as well? All she wanted tonight was a good fuck.

"Do you have a problem with that?" Tina asked.

"No. As long as you take off that ring."

Tina immediately pulled the ring off her finger and dropped it in the cup holder. "Any other requests?"

"Not yet."

The Porsche was well suited to the obnoxiously clean five-car garage. Tina parked and clicked the button to close the automatic door. The other car in the garage was a vintage convertible Mustang, and Tina mentioned that her hubby's Lexus was at the airport awaiting his return from Palm Springs. Tina led Alexis into the house and quickly turned off the alarm that had started to beep. Her heels clicked on the marble entryway and she gripped Alexis's hand, pulling her past the dining room and the library, through the kitchen and down a few steps to an enormous living room. Alexis watched Tina's hips swaying with each step, her tight pants advertising a firm butt and well-shaped thighs. Alexis moved toward Tina, brushing her hand down the small of her back and over the rise of her butt.

Tina murmured her approval but stepped away. "In a minute. I want to get a drink. What will you have?" A full bar was set up on one end of the living room and Tina found a bottle of gin and two glasses. "Gin and Seven?"

Alexis nodded. She slipped off her wet jacket and went over to the bay windows opposite the bar. The sky had cleared enough to allow moonlight through the clouds and the dark waters shimmered like silver. A dock led out over the water's edge and an old lantern dropped a circle of light at the end. Waves lapped up to the dock under its glow.

Tina handed Alexis a towel and her drink. She took a seat on the sofa facing the bay windows. "You should see the lake at sunrise. It's beautiful then."

Alexis dried off and then sipped the gin. She knew Tina was waiting, but she was reluctant to turn from the window. The water seemed to hold her captive. "I could get lost in that view for a long time."

"I was thinking the same thing."

Alexis glanced over at Tina, who was unabashedly staring at her. She set her drink on the coffee table and reached out to take Tina's hand. Brushing her lips over Tina's fingers, she straddled her legs and said, "You sure you want to skip foreplay?"

Tina nodded. "I've been wet since you got in my car."

Alexis traced her hand down the center of Tina's blouse, fingering each button. She loosened the bottom button and worked her way up until Tina's breasts were exposed. She wasn't wearing a bra, and Alexis couldn't help but smile as Tina arched her back, helping to press her full breasts into Alexis's waiting hands. Alexis pushed Tina back against the sofa pillows and sat down on her lap, straddling with a leg on each side of her. She massaged Tina's shoulders and then moved to her breasts, sucking on each nipple until it firmed between her lips. Tina murmured encouragement as Alexis's hands moved lower. As she unzipped Tina's gray slacks and ran her fingers under the black silk underwear, Tina started to work on removing Alexis's belt. Tina's hands stalled when Alexis's hand moved from the pubic hair to between her legs and her middle finger dipped deep to feel Tina's moist folds. She shivered reflexively with the touch and grabbed Alexis's hand.

"I want you naked. And I want to get some toys before we go any further."

Alexis was eager to see what toys Tina might have, but reluctant to leave her position on her lap. She loved how wet Tina was already and wanted to see her come under her. "What if I want to fuck you just like this, and the second time around we use the toys?"

Leaving Tina to consider this, Alexis shifted positions on her so she could hold Tina against the pillows with one hand and use her other hand to massage the warm folds under the silk underwear. She could feel Tina's clit already swollen and squeezed it gently as soon as Tina opened her mouth to speak. "I, oh . . . just fuck me."

"That's what I wanted to hear." Alexis pulled Tina's pants off, leaving the silk underwear in place. Tina obviously kept to a gym routine, given the tightness of her muscles, but she had a soft belly and good curves, features Alexis loved to feel under her. She straddled Tina again and rubbed her jeans over the silk underwear. Tina's hands gripped her shoulders while Alexis dipped her hand under the silk again. She fingered the swollen clit and continued to grind her crotch, sensing that Tina was too close to a climax to waste time. Fingernails dug into her shoulders as Tina's muscles tightened, and cum washed over Alexis's fingers in a short burst. It was too quick and easy. Tina relaxed back on the sofa and Alexis pulled her fingers out.

"How long do I get you tonight?" Tina asked.

Alexis grinned. "Sounds like I'm working on the clock. What's my pay scale?"

"A hundred per hour? Cash, of course."

Alexis laughed at the offer. She'd never been paid for sex. "I'd rather this be a two-way sort of affair. No money exchanged."

"Good. That's what I wanted to hear." She pointed at the entertainment unit adjacent to the wall of bay windows. There was one tall cabinet with a space in the middle for the TV and two smaller cabinets for the stereo and video equipment. "My toys are in the bottom drawer. Why don't you pick something out?"

Alexis got off Tina and went over to the cabinet. She pulled open the drawer under the TV and stared at an array of dildos, body paint, lube and leather straps. A thick brown dildo, ribbed for extra pleasure, tempted her. "Would this work for you? Or maybe it's a little big."

"You picked my favorite. And that one fits the harness. Judging from how quick you got me to come, I'm guessing you won't be too shy to try a strap-on."

Alexis found the harness and held it up to her hips. It smelled like new leather. "It's clean?"

"Brand new. I don't like to use things twice, and my hubby doesn't ask for a detailed account of the expense report." She laughed. "We have a don't ask, don't tell policy."

Although Tina was very wet, Alexis decided to grab the bottle of lube. "Slippery When Wet" was essential for strap-on play. She closed the drawer, setting the harness and dildo on top of the TV. "Now all we need is some make out music."

Tina stood up and went over to the stereo. She slipped a CD in and turned to face Alexis with her hands on her hips. "And now you can take off your clothes. I've been waiting to watch you undress in front of me. I love to be entertained."

"Striptease?"

"No, just slow and deliberate. I don't want it overdone." After draping a purple suede blanket over the sofa, presumably to save the expensive upholstery, Tina took her seat again. "You can start anytime."

Alexis smiled. She wasn't nervous about Tina's demands. She'd been with plenty of women who liked to order her every step of the way. And at least this time, even if she didn't get off, she'd still have a nice reward at the end of the night. The music tempo picked up, and Alexis recognized the beat of a familiar club mix. She slipped her belt off and tossed it on the sofa, then started unbuttoning her Levi's. Once the jeans and boxers were off, she took off her tank top and unclasped her bra, feeling Tina's eyes on her every movement.

"Come here."

Alexis went over to the sofa, naked now and feeling a cool draft on her backside. Tina caressed her breasts, plucking each nipple once as if testing it. Alexis had sensitive nipples, and as soon as Tina touched them, she could feel her legs getting weak. Tina's hands moved lower, parting Alexis's folds and cooing as she felt the wetness. "So, I'm not the only one who's enjoying this."

"No."

"Good." Tina pointed at the cabinet. "Let's see what you look like in leather."

Alexis placed the harness on and fitted the dildo in place. The base of the dildo pressed against her clit with an enticing pressure. She loved the weight of it between her legs and couldn't wait to push it inside Tina. Tina had slipped off her underwear and started fingering her clit while Alexis dripped lube over the dildo. She filled her palm with more lube, not caring that some of it landed on the carpet, and then rubbed the length of the dildo, her hips rocking forward to thrust the phallus into her hands. Tina watched, licking her lips.

"You know what you're doing, don't you."

"I've had some experience." Alexis let go of the dildo and approached Tina. "Stand up," she ordered.

Tina hesitated for a moment and then stood, running her hands along the leather straps on Alexis's hips. Alexis pulled the blanket off the sofa and spread it on the floor, covering the light carpet in a swath of purple. "I need more room to work," she explained. Taking Tina's hands, she placed them behind her own neck and then parted Tina's legs with a thrust of the dildo. Her hand was still wet with extra lube, warmed by the heat of her skin. She smeared this between Tina's legs, mingling her own slippery sweet musk with the wet lube. Tina parted her legs, pressing her pelvis forward to offer Alexis entry.

"Not yet," Alexis murmured in Tina's ear. She brushed her lips along Tina's neck and then bent her head to take a nipple between her lips. As it slipped out she bit it, drawing a quick gasp from Tina.

"I want you inside me," Tina breathed.

Alexis shook her head. "You're going to wait for it. I want to fuck you at my pace. Last time was too quick." She rubbed the tip of the dildo over Tina's pubic hair, pressing against her swollen clit with just enough pressure to bring Tina off her heels. Alexis paused in mid thrust and stepped away from Tina. "Get on your back."

Tina dropped to her knees, rubbing the dildo between her breasts, and then sat back on the suede. "God, you're sexy. I'd love to see my husband come home right now. He'd be pissed if a woman as hot as you were fucking me right under his own roof."

"Don't talk," Alexis said, "and lie all the way back." She nudged Tina's legs apart with her foot and then went down on her knees keeping one hand on the slick dildo, erect and firm, waiting to penetrate. With one hand, she parted the folds of skin, and with a quick thrust, the tip of the dildo was buried inside her.

Tina moaned and arched her pelvis up to take in more of the dildo. Alexis pulled back, riding the rim of Tina's pubic bone with the pressure of the dildo. She could see that Tina wanted a little more force, and she would give it to her, but not yet. Tina was going to be dripping in cum before Alexis was satisfied. Alexis pulled out and changed position, placing a knee on each side of Tina's hips. She ran her hands through Tina's hair, nearly black in the dim moonlight, and then traced over her cheeks and down her neck. When she reached her breasts, she stopped to grab a good handful, loving the fullness of her.

Tina arched her back. "I want you in me. Put it inside. I'm ready." Her voice was close to begging.

Alexis shifted lower, her butt on Tina's hips so she could feel Tina's pubic hairs rough on her inner thighs. "You're almost ready." She dropped one hand behind her back to finger Tina's clit. It was engorged to nearly twice the size as before, and Tina murmured with approval as Alexis strummed just above it, just under it, and on both sides. Finally she moved between Tina's legs and the dildo, still wet, pushed inside just as Tina raised her hips. Alexis pressed deeper, harder, and saw Tina's jaws clench. She was enjoying the hard ride.

"Give me more. I want more," Tina whispered between groans.

Alexis thrust her hips faster, driving in and out, deeper and harder. Each thrust pushed on her own clit, and she could feel her own wetness dripping down her inner thighs. She continued grinding on Tina, pressing so deep that their hairs mingled. It seemed that Tina couldn't get enough. She arched her back, tightened her legs and gasped as though she were about to climax, and then begged Alexis to keep riding her as she relaxed again. Alexis was dripping in sweat, and her own body was begging to climax. With her hands on Tina's breasts, massaging and pinching the nipples, she felt Tina grab for her arms, her fingernails scratching her skin as she shuddered and cried out. Alexis gave one final thrust and Tina climaxed again. She fell back on the suede, her groin muscles still tight, holding the dildo in place between her legs. The purple suede had darkened with the wetness of their cum and the sweat of their bodies. Alexis finally pulled out and Tina rolled to her side, pulling her knees up to her chest. After a moment, she relaxed and stretched out, eyeing Alexis.

"You really know what you're doing," she said, as if to confirm her earlier suspicions. "And I like the smirk on your face."

"I had a good time." Alexis paused. She moved onto her knees and drew a line down the front of Tina's chest.

"But?"

"I'm not finished yet." Alexis stood up, adjusting the strap-on so the dildo would press again on her clit.

"I don't think I can come again."

Alexis wasn't interested in getting Tina off again. "But you can do something for me."

"What's that?"

"Get on your knees," Alexis said. She'd never asked anyone to do this before, but she'd fantasized about it plenty of times. Tina got on her knees and gazed up at her, waiting. Alexis reached out for her, placing one hand behind Tina's head and stepping closer so that the dildo was inches from her lips. "I want you to suck on it."

Tina arched her eyebrows, but Alexis didn't wait for her to disagree. With her free hand, she touched Tina's mouth, encouraging her to open her lips. Tina tasted the dildo with her tongue, slowly circling the tip as Alexis moaned with pleasure. Then with a quick thrust, Alexis pushed the dildo into Tina's mouth. The dildo wasn't long, but it was fat. Tina took the length of it in her mouth, and her lips were next to Alexis's pubic hair. Alexis fell into the same thrusting pattern that she'd used to fuck Tina, now watching the woman suck on the dildo as if it were an extension of her own body. She kept her hand behind Tina's head, pressing her face into her with every thrust of her hips, until finally she felt the burning urgency of an orgasm mounting. She thrust faster and faster, the dildo driving hard against her clit and Tina's hands holding onto the leather harness. Finally, her muscles tightened and a tingling wave washed over her. She pulled the dildo out of Tina's mouth and sank down on the sofa, still trembling.

Tina stood up after a moment and left the room. From somewhere down the hall, the sound of water came, and Alexis guessed she was taking a shower. Alexis helped herself to a glass of water and washed the lube off her hands. She found a phone book and dialed the number to request a cab, then went back to the living room and started to dress. By the time she had her jeans zipped, Tina reappeared.

A towel was tied around her waist, but she was naked otherwise. She brushed her hand over Alexis's chest and then traced over her lips. "Leaving me so soon?"

"I called a cab."

Tina sighed. "So you're all business, huh?" She shook her head. "I was thinking how nice it'd be to wake up and get fucked by you again at sunrise." Tina kissed Alexis's cheek. "Another time, I guess."

Tina walked Alexis to the door and offered her an umbrella. Fortunately, there was a lull in the weather and the night sky was clear for the moment. Since the cab was due any minute, Alexis declined the umbrella and buttoned her jacket, bracing for the cool air outside. They said their good-byes with a nod of the head and the uneasiness of every one-night stand.

Alexis didn't have to wait long. By the time she reached the end of the driveway, she spotted a yellow sedan turning down the road toward her.

The driver, an old man with an unkempt gray beard, pulled up to the curb and rolled down the window. "Where to?"

"Downtown Portland. West side."

He nodded and unlocked the back door. Alexis went for the handle and paused. Headlights were approaching. She watched as a shiny black Lexus pulled into the driveway of Tina's house. A middle-aged man wearing a dark suit climbed out of the car and pulled a suitcase from the trunk. He glanced over at Alexis and then up at the house, where the lights shown from several windows. Alexis grinned at him sheepishly, knowing he must be Tina's husband. I just fucked your wife, she thought, strangely pleased at herself. Was he home a day early or had Tina wanted to be caught in the act?

The cab driver called to her, "You ready to go or not?"

"I'm ready." Alexis got in the backseat and watched as Tina's husband closed the garage door. She wondered what conversation the couple would have tonight and was more than happy to have slipped out early. She doubted there'd be a second time with Tina.

Chapter 4

Knock, knock. Alexis had covered her face with a pillow and had just managed to fall asleep, despite the sunlight streaming in her window, when the knocking started. *Knock, knock.* Pause. *Knock, knock, knock.* She pulled the pillow off her face and sat upright in bed, blinking in the golden light. Why couldn't it rain on mornings when she wanted to sleep in? She thought of marching over to Drew's apartment and kicking down his damn door. Their wall was too thin. The last thing she wanted to think about was Drew and Ben having rough sex with morning breath. Two more knocks, then slightly muffled moans. She hollered, "Who's there?"

Suddenly only silence greeted her, then a short ripple of nervous laughter came from the other side of the wall. Alexis was familiar with the knocking. Drew's bedposts banged against their common wall whenever he was bobbing around in the bed. She heard the sound often when he had a "friend" over, but she'd never called him out on it. With a tinge of jealousy, she realized that Drew and Ben probably had a very good first date.

Ben answered her finally with a stammered, "Um, sorry. Sorry to wake you. We were hanging pictures over here. Thin walls, I guess."

"So you don't have a knock-knock joke for me?" She could just imagine Ben-the-bread-man, naked and sweaty, caught red-handed on top of Drew, shyly staring at the wall.

Drew piped up, "Morning, Lex. How was your night?"

Alexis could tell by Ben's voice that she'd killed their mood. She thought of apologizing, but decided she was too pissed that they'd woken her at six a.m. "Just fine. Another rich married woman. Almost got caught by her husband who came home just as I was leaving."

Drew whistled. "See? Now that's why I don't go for the married type."

Ben seconded this with a grunt. Alexis heard him whisper, "So you wouldn't have flirted with me if I was wearing my wedding ring yesterday? Good thing I take it off when I'm bakin' honey loaves."

"Shut up!" Drew shrilled. "You're not married."

Ben only laughed in reply.

"Are you?" Drew gasped, in what Alexis guessed was an expression of feigned horror.

"Divorced. But I do still have the ring." Ben paused. "I like to wear it when I have to fend off a posse looking for tail."

Drew let off a string of swear words. Alexis crawled out of bed, deciding to leave the boys some privacy for their first argument, and dressed in a jog bra and a pair of Lycra pants. Her hands still smelled of Tina, and she wanted to start the day fresh, but the bath could wait. Although she complained about mornings, sunrise was her favorite time of day for a good long run. She left her apartment, pausing in the hallway to tighten her laces, and nearly collided with Darcy's front door as she headed for the stairs. Darcy popped out from the other side with a confused look on her face. She was probably wondering if Alexis had been hiding behind the door.

"Good morning," Darcy said. She disappeared down the stairs

before Alexis had a chance to respond. Had Drew's early morning make out session with Ben wakened her too? Or was she just an early riser? And what did she think of Alexis now?

Alexis tried to drive thoughts of Darcy from her mind as she followed her out of the apartment building. The crisp air charged at her face and she broke into a run, angling sideways to the wind. Her legs were eager for the stretch, and she trimmed her usual time down a minute after the first two miles. She finished the workout with some stretches and then stopped in at the corner market for a newspaper and a bottle of orange juice before heading home.

The paper didn't hold much interest until Alexis reached the classifieds section. There on the first column under Hobbies/Arts was a listing for a potter's wheel. And the price was right. Free. Alexis picked up the phone and dialed the number, hoping she wasn't too late. Free items went fast.

An old man with a thick accent answered the line, and Alexis immediately thought of the German mechanic that used to live at her old apartment complex.

"Do you still have the pottery wheel?"

"Ja, I do."

"And the price?" Alexis wasn't sure she could believe the Portland classifieds. "Free. Don't vork so vell, but maybe you fix it. You vant it?"

"Yes, definitely. When—where can I pick it up?" Alexis couldn't hesitate for a moment, and she guessed the old German man would hear the excitement in her voice. A broken wheel was still closer to a clay vase or a pasta dish than no wheel at all. And she really wanted to get her hands muddy. Maybe her mom could come up for a visit and help her with it.

"Tomorrow you come to my house to pick it up. I'm busy today. Have to vork in da garden."

Worried that someone else would call him about it and offer money, Alexis made him promise to hold it for her until tomorrow evening. He seemed pleased that she was so excited to get this treasure. As soon as she'd hung up, she realized she was going to need Paula's help with this. Lugging a wheel on the bus would be next to impossible. But Paula loved to get her Toyota pickup dirty doing "real work," and she wouldn't say no to Alexis. Of course she'd help her pick up the wheel. Alexis didn't mention to Paula that it was broken. Maybe it just needed a little finessing.

Giddy about the prospect of clay creations, Alexis was next on the phone with her mother—or rather her answering machine. Her mother was at some hippie revival weekend, according to the answering machine. Alexis left a long message, realizing she missed her mom's house, the smell of incense mingled with the earthen aroma of her pottery workshop, and she missed her laugh.

Alexis smiled as she remembered the last time she'd gone home for a visit. Her mom had come to pick her up at the airport, and as soon as they saw each other, her mother smiled, then started to laugh. She had a big laugh that startled others at first, and then incited more laughter, spreading like a dropped bag of marbles. First the corners of her lips would tug upward, then she'd stick out her tongue just over the tip of her teeth like she was going to tease you, and the sound would start. Then there'd be a jiggle in her belly and the laugh would gain volume. Others would turn their heads and smile, and then her face would redden and her sly dimples would deepen. She would end with a quick gasp of air, like she was coming up from an underwater sprint, and then she'd sigh and say, "Oh, my." She'd laugh when she was happy, or sad, and always the dimples would come.

As a child, Alexis had dreamt up stories that she was adopted. Although her mom used to tell her about her father, she'd never known him, and sometimes she didn't believe the stories. Since she didn't have dimples, had straight brown hair when her mom's was curly and red, and had a propensity to be inches taller and leaner than all her peers while her mom was short and wide, adoption seemed the most likely explanation. When Alexis was eleven or twelve, she found a picture that changed her mind. Under a stack of Kodak envelopes, she found a snapshot of a man who she knew from the writing on the back of the photo was her father, hugging her very pregnant mother. The photo was taken a few weeks before she was born, and her mother's belly, stretching the fabric of a tie-dyed tank top, seemed to threaten to pop at any moment. Her mother's dimples were fat jewels on her cheeks.

But the man was who she had focused on. He had a grin as big as her mom's, but his cheeks were as smooth as sanded wood. And he was lean as a birch, wore no shirt, a pair of Levi's, and had a wide-brimmed cowboy hat, tilted back on his head. She'd kept this picture of her parents, one of the few proofs she'd had that there'd ever been a father involved in her life, and thought of the man's smiling face often. He was so content that she just knew her mom had been laughing as the camera snapped the shot. Somehow the same features that she saw in this young man—her father—were in her own mirror. She wished she could have heard his laugh and used to pretend that pictures came with volume buttons just like TVs. Seeing her smile on a stranger's face made her long to have known her father for just a moment, maybe just to share a joke. Often she'd wanted to ask her mother about him, but it was a line she never crossed. Her mother had given no details about the man's life. She only explained his death. He'd been killed in a car crash a week after the picture was taken. He was driving too fast and hit one of the few trees in the area. "And that was that," her mom had said with a soft sigh. "Then you came into my life to help me remember what happiness felt like."

By mid-morning, Alexis was ready for a break from the newspaper crossword puzzle. She didn't want to admit it, but she was half expecting a phone call from Elana to explain her no-show last night. She'd given Elana her number and wondered when Elana didn't complete the exchange. But even if she had her number, or asked Ben for it, Alexis couldn't call now. She had to save a few shreds of pride. Rather than mope about being stood up, Alexis decided to call Sandy.

Sandy answered on the first ring. She was waiting for the call and didn't hide it. "I was hoping it'd be you."

Alexis smiled. "I didn't want to call too early. You had a big crowd last night, and I figured that would keep you working late."

"I like the big crowds. Good energy. But yes, it makes for a late night." She sighed.

"Tired?" But not exhausted, Alexis hoped.

"A little. I just need some coffee and I'll be ready to go. My one addiction. So what do you think about going for a hike today? The weather is so nice that I'd hate to stay inside."

"Definitely." It rained enough in Portland that the locals knew they had to take advantage of a sunny day. The hiking trails would have some traffic. And, Alexis thought, there'd be few opportunities for any close moments. "Maybe we could have dinner after the hike, if I'm not pushing things . . ."

"Sounds perfect. I know just the place."

As they arranged their meeting, it came out that Sandy lived in an apartment complex also, and as luck would have it, she was just two blocks west of Westside Apartments. They arranged to meet at the coffee shop between their apartments in a half hour. Sandy volunteered to drive, relieving Alexis from explaining that she had no car. She hung up the phone with a feeling of building excitement. Unlike many of her friends, specifically Paula and Moss, who both detested first dates, Alexis ate them up like an ice cream sandwich, eager to lick her fingers afterward and remember all the tasty details. She changed into a pair of loose khaki hiking pants, donned a tank top, then a long sleeve shirt and windbreaker, thinking layers, and found her old hiking boots.

It'd been a few months since she'd been out of the city, and her boots were still flecked with mud spots from the last hike. She tried to brush off the mud, but it held fast. Stubborn Washington state mud, she thought with a sigh, remembering the trip that had left her with the mud spots. She'd gone hiking somewhere with Paula, and all she knew for sure was that they'd crossed the state line into

Washington, driven for a bit, and then found a trail off the high-way.

Alexis was doubtful about the prospect of the dirt road that Paula picked, but she didn't argue. She wasn't in the mood for arguing at the time. She'd been casually dating a woman who worked as a receptionist in a dermatology clinic on her delivery route. They'd only been dating for a few weeks, and Alexis barely knew the woman's last name and thought she didn't really care until she got an, "I love you. You're inconsiderate, self-absorbed, and I'm done trying to make you love me. Have a good life!" e-mail. Her only memory of the trail was that once the dirt road crossed a few streams, it lost all semblance of road. She had a clear image of Paula's backside, which she followed doggedly, and a clearer image of the mud streams that enveloped their boots. Once she got into the swing of it, she'd tromped through the four-mile hike as happily as a Labrador retriever who'd been stuck in the city for too long. Paula had a way of knowing just what she needed. The hike had gotten the break up e-mail off her mind better than the delete button on her Internet mail account.

Alexis arrived at the coffee shop early. The place was filled with an assortment of folks, mostly young to middle-aged middle class urbanites, sleepy-eyed from the Saturday night party and eager for their first sip of the Fair Trade Dark Roast or the Light Organic Blend. Alexis sniffed the aromas and resisted the urge to buy a cup. When Sandy showed up, Alexis almost didn't recognize her. Her hair was pulled back, and a red bandana covered her head in a cute punk-kid style. Ripped jeans and a No War T-shirt with a flannel over shirt completed her outfit. Alexis couldn't help but smile. She loved the punk look and was happy to know it was Sandy's style.

"Coffee?"

Alexis shook her head. "I save that pleasure for the work week. But I think I'm getting high off the smell here."

Sandy nodded. "They make a damn good cup of joe. I'll be quick."

Alexis followed her with her eyes. Sandy stood in line, ordered "the usual," got a quick nod from a waitress, and then a minute later exchanged a dollar for a small cup of dark, steaming coffee. Alexis waited for her to add sugar, soy milk and then a lid. Sandy took a sip. "Ahh, now I'm ready." Her eyes seemed brighter with just the first sip.

They climbed into Sandy's car, a little black Honda hatchback that had seen better days, and headed east to get past the city limits. Sandy had turned on the radio, and they listened to three or four songs before she asked, "So I'm waiting for you to ask."

Alexis was puzzled. Was this a trick question? Was she hinting at dating questions? She decided to just admit ignorance. "What should I ask you?"

"Where I'm taking you."

"Oh." She paused. Really, she didn't care where they were going, so long as she got out of the city and had dirt instead of pavement under her soles. "Anywhere is fine with me. I'm easy."

"Is that so? Hmm, I'll keep that in mind." Sandy grinned. "You look different out of your uniform. I almost told you how sexy you looked last night, but then I got shy."

"Well, I'm glad you aren't shy all the time. And I have to admit, I like you out of your work uniform also."

Sandy glanced down at herself. "I used to play in a rock band. We never played any big gigs, but we had the clothes to prove we could rock." She laughed at herself.

"What'd you play?"

Sandy shook her head. "I sang backup vocals. Well, sometimes the band would let me add in a bit of harmonica so I'd get some limelight."

"Harmonica?"

"Oh, yeah. I play a real mean harmonica." Sandy laughed again. "I'll give you a private concert sometime if you'd like."

"I would." Alexis liked the flirt in Sandy's concert offer. She had a picture of Sandy in her head now that was so much different than the *Blue's Cafe chef*. And she had to admit, the new picture was growing on her.

They turned off the freeway, following the signs for the Multnomah Falls. Alexis had been on the winding waterfall route once before when she'd first come to Portland to check out the college, but she didn't remember how gorgeous the drive was. Her mind had been on other things—chiefly leaving her much-loved arid Arizona home for a soggy Northwest. Waterfalls hadn't impressed her much then. But now as they slowed the car, passing a few smaller waterfalls on their way along the Columbia River, Alexis caught her breath and stared in awe at the beauty of the shimmering light and cascading water. She was learning to appreciate Oregon.

The trail up to Multnomah Falls was thick with tourists and sun-starved Portlanders, as Alexis had guessed. Instead of going with the throng of people, Sandy pointed to an alternate route. "This trail will take us a few hours longer, but we won't have as much company."

Sandy had brought water and some fruit for their hike, more than Alexis had thought of, and with these items stowed in a little pack, they headed up a steep trail that threatened to drive them directly into a thick pine forest. The path had several switchbacks and a few openings through the trees allowed a view of the waterfall that they were hearing along the way. Multnomah Falls had a reputation for a good reason. The Columbia River, gorged with rainwater, was pipetted through a very narrow mountain ravine, sending water droplets careening downward in a chute that seemed to never quite reach the earth. The river quieted a quarter mile or so from the falls and carved through the middle of a perfectly flat greener-than-green valley. It was a stunning sight. And the green valley and descending water became even more beautiful as the trail gained perspective as they climbed in elevation.

Alexis found her attention divided between the landscape view and her view of Sandy. They'd both shed their outerwear, with Alexis in her tank top and Sandy in the rolled-up sleeves, No War T-shirt. It was unseasonably hot, and they were quickly lightening their water bottles. Finally the steep trail leveled off and the top of the waterfall came into view. The river seemed idyllic just a few yards from the rocky ledge, and a platform had been built out over the edge of the waterfall. Picture perfect.

Alexis headed toward the platform and then slowed when she realized that Sandy wasn't following her. "Do you want to stop here?" The trail ended at the edge of the platform, but Sandy had stopped several feet from this.

"I'm a little nervous of heights," she admitted. Sandy gazed at the river and then at the platform above the waterfall. The platform was five or ten feet above the water and stretched out like a tongue trying to catch the water before it fell into the green abyss below.

Alexis nodded. She had to stop a smile that threatened to creep over her face. Why had Sandy picked this trail if she was afraid of heights? "Well, it's beautiful right here." Alexis found her way to a flat rock, choosing one that had a very near neighbor, and started to take off her shoes.

Sandy joined her on the other rock and removed her shoes as well. Their knees bumped as they rolled up their pants legs and dangled hot, sweaty toes in the ice cold water. The river was a welcome chill. Sandy rinsed her hands in the water and then pulled her bandana off, soaked it in the water and retied it on her head. Water dripped down her neck and face. She wiped it away from her eyes, but let the other drops find their way to cool her skin.

Alexis didn't hide the fact that she was staring at the dancing water drops. It was more than a refreshing sight. Sandy glanced over at her. "What's that look about?"

She shrugged. "You're hot."

Alexis scooped her hands through the water and splashed it on her face a few times, loving the icy sting that replaced the feel of dried salt. She used the long-sleeved shirt tied around her waist to blot off the extra water and watched the water rushing past her legs. In a few yards, the water would be in for an exhilarating drop. "I'd love to dive in."

"Don't," Sandy said quickly. "I really am scared of heights and I'm not a good swimmer. You'd be over the edge in no time."

"But it would feel good while it lasted." Alexis smiled. "And I'd have a good view."

"What's wrong with the one right here?" Sandy asked. As soon as Alexis looked over at her, she blushed and then fought to recover with some line about how the river rocks and the swirls of water reminded her of a Portland postcard.

"Mm-hmm. The rocks and the little eddies aren't bad at all." Alexis reached out and caught Sandy's hand, noting that her cheeks were still tinged with red. Their fingers were wet from the river and cool. She stared at Sandy, wishing their rocks were closer. She wanted to kiss her, but for some reason she didn't want to move fast this time. "Not a bad view at all."

They finally left the waterfall and followed the trail deeper into the forest. The sound of the river soon gave way to chirping birds, buzzing insects and the snap of branches from little unseen critters making their way in the undergrowth at the side of the path. Just after three, Sandy suggested they head back. Alexis agreed, wishing she'd had more for breakfast and anticipating the dinner they had planned at the Multnomah Falls Lodge. Sandy had mentioned that she knew one of the chefs that worked in the lodge and promised that they would enjoy her friend's concoctions.

They both went to the bathroom at the lodge to wash up before dinner. Alexis rinsed her hands and face and then watched Sandy pull off her bandana, tilt her head under the faucet and rinse her short hair in the water. She came up looking quite refreshed and quickly dried off with the flannel. "You should try it."

Alexis glanced in the mirror. She felt dirty, but after a long hike, she didn't mind the feeling. Still, a cool rinse would be nice. She copied Sandy's technique. The water felt like a straight tap from the falls and she didn't waste any time under the faucet.

The hostess at the lodge restaurant seated them at a table with a perfect view of the falls. It looked like the best table in the place, and Alexis couldn't help but wonder if Sandy had called ahead to arrange this. Something about her was so endearing, almost innocent. And yet, that was exactly the type of woman that Alexis usually avoided. She seemed to attract and be attracted to the over-the-top women who knew what they wanted and weren't afraid to hunt her down to get it. She liked that. Yet, every time she caught Sandy looking at her, she got excited. Nervous almost. She was desperate to kiss her.

They ordered two dishes that came highly recommended by their server and then fell into the usual first date dinner conversation. "Have you lived in Portland long?"

Sandy nodded. "Since I was three-and-a-half."

Alexis wondered how old she was, but hesitated to ask. "You've lived in the same city since you were three? Ever thought of living somewhere else?"

"Well, I went away for college, got a job doing some activist work and spent a few years trying to save the world." She laughed. "I got too depressed fighting *the man* and never making a difference. One day, I remember seeing this cartoon picture of the earth snuggling under a big heating blanket and a caption about how we all love global warming . . . to death. I guess I should have been inspired to work harder. Instead, I suddenly couldn't save the world. Just burned out."

"So you became a chef?"

"I moved back to Portland and started culinary school. Always wanted to be a chef. Now my biggest worry is whether or not we'll have enough arugula for the mixed greens salad." She pointed at the kitchen, hidden from view by a pair of swinging doors. "My friend Rollins works here. We're in the same dessert classes. Working at Blue's is temporary. Eventually I'd like to have my own cafe. You know, some chill place that serves only fair trade coffee, organic produce and raspberry chocolate mousse. All vegan, of course. The Portland crowd would eat that up."

Alexis didn't know how to respond, but decided laughing wasn't the best alternative. Sandy really seemed committed to this. An activist in a No War T-shirt turned to a life as a vegan dessert chef? Fortunately she was saved from a response by the arrival of their meal, followed by Rollins himself. He had prepared Thai noodles with fancy cuts of vegetables in a spicy peanut sauce. The aroma of the dish was intoxicating, and after a quick greeting, Rollins left them to enjoy the food.

Rather than take the scenic route home, Sandy turned onto the main freeway, and they were back in Portland in a half hour. Too short, Alexis thought. Sandy parked her car just outside her apartment and turned to Alexis. Alexis reached out to catch her hand. She squeezed Sandy's fingers and glanced over at the apartment building. Was Sandy going to invite her upstairs?

"I had a good time tonight."

"Damn, I guess that means this is the end of the evening," Alexis said quietly. She tried a smile, and Sandy nodded in response. She mumbled something about an early morning class. "Maybe we could do this again sometime?"

Again, Sandy nodded. "I'd like that."

Ordinarily, Alexis thought, this is where I'd kiss you. And, she added, convince you that it's still early enough for a nightcap. But she realized Sandy was calling the shots and there'd be no kiss.

"Well, you have my number, so . . ." Sandy's voice drifted. She was watching Alexis's fingers as they played on her hand.

Alexis loved tracing the lines of a woman's palm. She covered Sandy's palm with her own and gripped her wrist, pulling Sandy toward her. Sandy shook her head and breathed, "Mmm, you're dangerous," before brushing her lips against Alexis's. She pulled back too soon. Alexis's head was spinning, and her lips tingled for another try. Sandy raised an eyebrow and then her lips turned up just a little.

"I didn't know if we were going there," Sandy said.

"Would you like to?"

A slow nod came in response, leaving Alexis to wonder just how much enthusiasm she was expecting. Maybe Sandy really only wanted a hiking partner. There was one way to find out. Alexis climbed out of the car and went to open Sandy's door. As soon as she stood, Alexis slipped her hands on Sandy's hips. "I'd really like to come up to your place." She felt her pulse quicken and hoped this wasn't going to be the one comment that ended an amazingly uncomplicated first date.

Sandy shook her head. "My place is a mess. The CDs aren't even alphabetized."

Alexis laughed. "I really wouldn't mind, but I'll respect your OCD tendencies."

"And I think you need to get up early."

Alexis nodded and started to step back, letting her hands drop off Sandy's hips. Sandy grabbed her hands and replaced them on her body, just at her waistline. "But I'm not ready to say goodnight yet."

They kissed again and their lips pressed longer. Alexis moved her hands back to Sandy's lower back, and she could feel her supple body moving toward her. She thought Sandy was still holding back, while her own body wanted to ask for more. Alexis's tongue touched Sandy's lips and she finally stepped away. She knew she would have to wait for another opportunity to push inside. For the first time in what seemed like forever, Alexis was more aroused than her partner. At least, that's what Sandy's kiss suggested. She was interested, but hesitating.

"I want to give you my number," Alexis said. "Do you have something I could write on?"

Sandy seemed surprised by the sudden halt to their making out, but didn't say anything. She ducked her head in the car and came back out with a slip of paper and a pen. "I'd love to call you for another . . ." She paused, watching Alexis print her number on the paper.

"Date?" Alexis asked. She wanted to be sure they were both chasing up the same tree, so to speak.

"I don't usually date. I mean, not often. Though I used to do it all the time. Too much, really. Too much dating, I mean. But that was years ago." She blushed and then finished with, "Anyway, I'd like to go out on another date with you."

Alexis kissed her again, just a soft brush of their lips. She wanted to tell Sandy to relax, but her nervousness was cute. She realized now that Sandy was indeed interested in more than a friendship. And maybe she'd rushed into too many relationships before. Alexis wasn't about to push her. They would take this slow and steady.

"I don't know if I can wait 'til our usual date on Friday." When she noticed Alexis's confused expression she added, "Your soup and salad special. Thinking of Friday's lunch menu has been my favorite part of the week for months now."

"Mine too." Alexis caught Sandy's hand and rubbed her palm. Her skin was smooth and warm. Alexis had to stop herself from thinking of where she'd like to feel Sandy touch her. They parted with a nod from Sandy and a grin in return from Alexis. They had tacitly agreed that there would be another meeting.

By the time she got home, Alexis was more than ready for a bath. After stripping out of the dirty hiking clothes, she started filling the tub and then went to find her waterproof vibrator. Dark clouds had gathered on her walk home, and she could hear the beginnings of another storm. It'd be raining soon. She lit a few candles in the bathroom and turned on a Norah Jones CD, then settled into the tub slowly. The one good thing about Westside Apartments was that there was no extra charge for hot water. The bathtub was steaming, and the smell of the lavender-scented candles filled the air.

Alexis soaped herself and then rinsed off. She leaned her back against the edge of the tub and spread her legs. Her fingers played with her clit, lazy and slow. She was thinking about Sandy, of course, and imagined what she'd like to do to her if they'd come home for the same bath. Finally she reached for her vibrator, hit the pulse button and slipped it under the water. The tip rested just below her clit, where she liked the vibration most, and she slipped her finger inside, moving in and out. Her eyes closed and she felt her body getting warm.

Alexis imagined Sandy's body on her, fantasized that the vibrator was pressing on Sandy's clit as her fingers pushed inside. She would love to watch Sandy come. Quickly the vibrations were moving deeper, and Alexis pulled the vibrator away from her clit. She tried to take things slow, but her body didn't want to go slow. The vibrator was back on her clit a moment later, and soon her own nerves had taken over, her muscles tightened around her finger and she gave one more thrust before her clit climaxed in a quick spasm. Alexis switched off the vibrator and relaxed her legs. Spreading her knees, she positioned each leg against a side of the tub. She rubbed the length of the vibrator between her legs and then tilted her hips up and pushed it inside. The thick plastic stretched her muscles and pressed deep. Alexis closed her eyes and pushed it a little deeper. Her thoughts were still on Sandy.

Chapter 5

Monday was hectic at work as usual. Alexis finished her morning deliveries and settled into the break room for a lunch of root
beer and a peanut butter and jelly sandwich, while the warehouse
guys made quick work of filling her truck with the afternoon order.
Unfortunately, she'd run out of bread last week and had forgotten
to pick it up at the store. Instead of a thick slice of winter wheat,
she'd substituted graham crackers, which didn't quite hold the jelly
as well, and she had to lick the edges to keep most of it off her fingers. Her weekend had passed in a blur with little thought for
things like bread. And though she really wanted to go over to
Blue's for lunch, she decided against it, knowing that it was too
soon to see Sandy again. Paula would have kicked her ass for not
following the lesbian dating code of the one day waiting period
after every first date.

Ace came into the break room and headed toward Alexis. She
glanced behind her, hoping he was angling for someone else. Ron,

the dispatcher, had been at the table behind her, but when she looked now, all that was left was his candy wrapper. The only other person in the room was Kate, seated on a stool by the coffee machine. She'd been elected coffee monitor and had to keep her post during all break times. It was Ace's way of preventing another serious cream and sugar heist. This seemed pointless since Moss was the perpetrator and she'd already left, along with the cream and sugar, but no one argued with Ace or Kate on the matter.

Ace paused when he reached Alexis's table. He jabbed his hands in his pockets. "How's it going today, Lex? Did you have a good weekend?" This was the "Monday Ace," trying to rally the troops with sweet talking so everyone in his understaffed, marginally-run company would pull their weight for the rest of the week. Then the Friday meeting would come, and he'd beat them all into submission so they'd fear losing their job all weekend. Ace positioned himself so he could look down on Alexis. Without waiting for her reply, he continued, "I'm sure you noticed that I've given you a wider delivery zone. Now that Mossinni is gone . . . well, I know you're the one on the delivery line that I can always count on to step up to a challenge."

"Yeah, so are you paying me more for doing twice the work?"

He shook his head. "I think twice the work is a bit of an exaggeration. I've just added a few more sites to your usual route. And you know, it won't be long until we have a replacement for Mossinni."

Alexis nodded. "Well, exaggeration or not, I don't mind as long as I get paid for the overtime." She wasn't about to let Ace win this round.

"Overtime? You won't need to work past five if you've got your running shoes on." He smiled down at her. "I'm sure you want to get a good workout and keep your good figure—"

"Ace, I think you'd better stop there." Alexis stood up and collected her trash. "Otherwise I'll have to steal the coffee pot so I can bang you on the head for that last comment."

Ace laughed this off and made some reference to overtime costing the company too much. "Alexis, you've got to understand that I've got too many guys with families working here. We can't pay anyone overtime, or someone else won't get paid. And just think about all of Ron's kids. He's got five little ones now. What do you want to do, steal their lunch money?"

"Ace, you gotta pay me to run two routes, like it or not. I'm charging overtime until you get someone to cover Moss's route." She really wanted to tell him to fuck off, but she needed the paycheck more than an ego boost.

"What are you trying to do, put APO Portland out of business? You know I can't run into overtime this week. We're over budget and—"

"I don't care. I'll run the extra deliveries if I get paid. Bottom line." Alexis tossed her paper bag in the trash and headed for the door. Ace let her go, and Kate gave her a subtle wink as she passed her.

Alexis really didn't mind the longer route. She was going to new businesses and she only finished a half hour later than usual. In between the deliveries, she spent most of the afternoon dreaming about what she'd make once she had the wheel in her apartment. She had too many ideas and decided to ask her mom's advice.

"Start with something small and useful," her mom had said, sage-like, when she called late Sunday night. Alexis could tell by her mom's voice that the hippie revival had left her tired and a little bit high. But she was just as excited as Alexis at the prospect of a new wheel, working or not. "In every wheel there is potential for greatness." She promised to send Alexis some good Arizona clay, and they finished the conversation with her mom describing her new crush—a guitar player with no hair but a big heart. They'd met at the revival and he was coming to her house next weekend so they could "make some music."

So a coffee cup was the first project on the agenda. Then she wanted to make a big vase with a waterfall streaming down one side. She had the design all set and made a sketching of it last night. If it came out well, she'd give the vase to Sandy. The coffee cup would be made out of Portland Art Supplies clay, but the waterfall vase would be out of Arizona clay.

By the time Alexis made it home, Paula was already parked outside of Westside Apartments in her Toyota. As soon as she spotted Alexis, Paula yelled, "Hey, girl, wanna get a move on? I'm half-starved and have been dreaming of a big pile of french fries for the past hour."

Alexis wanted to go up and change, but she knew she couldn't ask Paula to wait anymore. She ran over to the Toyota and passed Darcy just coming back from her run. She guessed that Darcy had gotten off work at her usual time and taken the earlier bus. Darcy waved to her then disappeared inside the apartment building. Alexis had stopped in the middle of the road to follow Darcy with her eyes, and Paula honked her horn to get her attention. "Hello? Lex, are you coming or not?"

"Coming." She jogged over to the passenger side and climbed in the truck.

"So who was that hottie that you were drooling all over?" Paula asked, starting the ignition.

"I wasn't drooling. Her name's Darcy. And to answer your next question, no, I haven't slept with her yet."

Paula laughed and slapped Alexis's knee. "You're right, that was the next thing on my lips. Put on your seat belt, Lex, you know what a mad dog driver I am in this truck." She waited for Alexis to fasten the belt and then continued, "So after we hit the burger joint, where are we headed for this damn pottery wheel? And why haven't you slept with her yet?"

"We need to head south for the pottery wheel. The old guy gave me directions, but I left them up in my apartment." She didn't want to answer Paula's second question.

Paula shot her a 'cut the crap' look. "No directions?"

"Sorry. I didn't count on getting home late. I'm taking over Moss's route, in addition to mine. So I had some overtime."

81

"Should we go back for the directions?"

Alexis shook her head. "No. I remember the address, and I can find my way just about anywhere."

"Since when?" Paula looked doubtful, but Alexis insisted they wouldn't get lost. Maps and driving directions were one thing she'd never had a problem with, and her job had given her a pretty good sense of the city. She could find just about any address if she drove around long enough.

After their stop for a fast food dinner, they headed south. Paula relaxed once she had a taste of her chocolate shake and a few fries. She turned up the music and rolled down the windows, though it was misting out and really too cold. "You know we ought to go on a road trip some time, for old time's sake."

They never had gone on a long road trip before, but Alexis didn't mention this. She made it a practice not to correct Paula on the *old time's* references. For instance, Paula insisted that they had dated for only a month, when in fact they'd been together for five months. And she always told people that their breakup had been mutual, when in fact it had been all Alexis's doing. She had slept with another woman and confessed this to Paula, primarily in order to convince her to move out of the apartment that they shared. In retrospect, she knew that she had wanted to break up with Paula several months earlier, but she had waited until another opportunity came along. Paula, of course, was pissed. After six months, they had somehow managed to become friends again. Now it seemed impossible that they had ever dated at all.

In less time than Alexis had predicted, they arrived at the address that the old man had given her. And they'd only had to stop to ask for directions once. The old man wasn't home, but he'd left the wheel with a note for Alexis on his front porch. Next to the wheel was a box filled with an assortment of pottery supplies, everything from lacquers to paints to miscellaneous carving knives. They gathered up the box and the wheel and Alexis left a note thanking the old man for the items.

"Maybe he didn't want to be here in case you'd tell him you didn't want the junk."

"Junk?" Alexis sent an indignant look at Paula. "Are you kidding? I can't believe how lucky I am. That box *of junk* would cost me a couple hundred bucks at the art store. A couple hundred at least." She unfolded the note that the man had left for her and read it aloud, "Thank you for giving my wife Helga's pottery items a good home. My heart broke when I found I'd let the wheel get a bit of rust. I fiddled with it some and it should work just fine for you now. My Helga will be smiling when she hears it spin again." Alexis folded the note and pressed it in her pocket. She had to glance out the window to keep Paula from noticing there were tears in her eyes.

When Paula finally spoke, she was whispering, "I'm so glad you have that wheel. What are you going to make?" Her voice was always husky and sexy when she whispered.

Alexis rubbed the moisture off her cheeks and laughed. "A coffee mug. My mom said I should start with something simple."

"Good advice." She let her hand drop on Alexis's thigh, rubbing it tenderly. "You know, I'm not doing so well."

"What's up?"

"Girl problems." She sighed heavily. "I'm going crazy waiting for Jen. And I'm beginning to think there might be no interest in sex at all on her end. You know, some women just aren't into sex."

Oh shit, Alexis thought, remembering what she'd learned about Jen from Bonnie. "Maybe you guys just don't click. You know, the wrong chemistry."

Paula shook her head. "I don't think so. I feel lots of chemistry on my end, and she keeps a hold of me like there's something she feels."

"Maybe you should buy her a teddy bear to hold and find yourself a woman that likes to get busy."

Paula laughed. They had reached Alexis's place already and she swerved into a parking place. Parking was a tight commodity after the commuters got home, and she knew better than to take her time angling for the best spot. They lugged the wheel and the box up the stairs to the apartment and set the things in the middle of the living room.

"Took me a while, but I knew I would find just the right thing for this place." Alexis grinned and smacked Paula's shoulder. "Thanks for your help. Wanna stay a while?" She still had to tell Paula the gossip about Jen.

"Sure. Got anything to drink?"

"How long have you known me?" Alexis joked. She always had a few beers in the fridge in case friends stopped by or she'd had a hard day at work. More often than not, it was the latter.

They sat on the kitchen counter, legs dangling, with a bag of pretzels and two beers between them. "So what's in the box?" Paula pointed to the unlabeled APO box sitting on top of the toaster oven. Alexis had placed it there to keep it out of the way. And prevent her from any urges to rip it open.

"I don't know. Not one single clue. I don't know who sent it or who I should have delivered it to. Well, someone here at Westside, but no one's claimed it yet. Ace gave it to me to deliver. It was one of Mossinni's extras, and she took off the label. Her last stand of defiance against APO was to deface a few packages and steal some sugar packets."

Paula arched her eyebrows. "Hmm. Well, Moss is a strange bird. You know, I can open it for you, tell you what's inside and then tape it up again. No one will ever know."

"No, I'm waiting for the owner to notice the sign that I posted. Eventually I'll deliver that damn thing, and it'll be in the same condition as I got it, so help me God."

"Neither hell nor high water shall keep the post girl from her Goddess-given duties of delivering every package, from printer cables to dildos to divorce papers." Paula laughed heartily at her own joke. Alexis shook her head. She had told Paula about her experiences with several of her early deliveries, a higher than expected number of which included sex toys, legal documents and computer parts. After a while Paula asked, "Something's on your mind, isn't it?"

Alexis took a sip of her beer. She nodded slowly. Yes, there was something on her mind. For starters, she'd been thinking of Elana since her lunch break because of the amazing Pink Lady apple that she'd munched on. With every bite, Alexis wondered why Elana had stood her up. Now she was considering giving the rest of the apples to Paula. She really didn't want to think about Elana now. Alexis also wanted to tell Paula about Sandy. She had such a good time with her, surprisingly so, but she still was unsure why Sandy was cautious. And then there was her evening with Tina, which had seemed fun at the time, but in retrospect, had left a bad taste in her mouth. She wasn't sure what she wanted out of the women she met, but Tina sure as hell wasn't enough. Too much sex and not enough . . . what? Which brought her to the final problem, Bonnie and Jen. "So I went out with this chick on Friday night. Don't know if you remember her or not. Curly red hair and big boobs? I know you and Jen were kind of, well, intertwined for most of the evening."

"Fishnet stockings, as I recall," Paula returned.

She grinned. "Right. Anyway, she knows Jen."

"No way? Well, Portland isn't that big of a town, I guess," Paula answered, crunching on a pretzel. "And what'd she say about her?"

After another sip of her beer, stalling, she replied, "She said she *knows* knows her."

"No way. Big-boobed Bonnie and Jen?" Paula scrunched her eyebrows in disbelief. She snapped another pretzel and shook her head. After a while the news seemed to sink in. "So she's been around, huh?"

"According to Bonnie, yeah."

"Then what's the reason she's holding out on me?" Paula glanced over at Alexis and held up her hand. "Forget that I just asked that. I really don't want an answer."

"I think you should ask her yourself. Maybe Bonnie was just

making up shit. Ask her if she even knows Bonnie and see what she says."

Paula nodded. "Lex, I'm too old for this crap. Shouldn't the whole dating thing be getting easier by the time I'm this age?"

"An ancient twenty-six?"

"Well, I feel old enough." She pushed off the counter and then turned to face Alexis. "And I think you should consider buying a couch. We're adults now."

Alexis smiled at the change in topic. Paula was an expert at shrugging off bad news. Her parents had disowned her when she'd come out to them. Instead of a birthday card, they had sent her a check for past due rent, eighteen years of it. She sent them flowers and a condolence card. "Why do I need a couch?"

" 'Cause sometimes I want to get drunk and crash here." She finished the last of her beer and opened the fridge to get another. "Like tonight. There's always your bed, I guess."

Alexis stared at Paula's back. Paula was leaning over the sink to make sure she didn't spill anything on the floor when her beer cap popped off. Alexis knew she was treading a dangerous line if she even agreed that Paula spend the night. They had maintained their friendship after the breakup with a pact to never sleep together. Alexis hadn't broken off things with Paula because of bad sex. In fact, they had no problem pleasing each other. "Maybe."

Paula turned to face her. "I think I better stop drinking now if I've heard you right. It's been a while since . . ."

The topic of fuck buddies had come up several times over the years since their breakup. Each time Paula had been the one to initiate the conversation, and Alexis had soundly nixed the idea. Now Alexis couldn't decide if she wanted Paula to stay the night. They couldn't sleep in the same bed without getting into trouble. Alexis reached up to touch Paula's face. She caressed her cheek and then moved down to rub her neck. "I think you heard me right."

Stepping forward, Paula wrapped her arms around Alexis's waist in a familiar grasp. Her arms didn't have the possessive hold that Alexis had once rejected. This time, Paula's hold on her was friendly, comfortable. They kissed tenderly at first, and then their lips pressed with more force, as if relearning the other's sensitive points. Paula's tongue brushed inside Alexis's mouth to play with her tongue and then disappeared as quickly as it entered. Letting go of Alexis, Paula sighed and shook her head. "Damn, girl, you still know how to get me going. Either we go to your bedroom for some hot and heavy, or I need a cool shower."

"No shower. We do have the sponge bath option."

"Oh, yeah, I forgot about your kitsch bathtub." Paula smiled. "Then I'll take the hot and heavy offer."

Downing the last of her beer, Alexis eyed Paula. "We're still just friends come morning?"

She nodded. "Don't worry. I promise I won't send you a dozen long-stemmed roses, even if you are as good in bed as I remember."

"Paula, I've gotten better than you remember," Alexis teased. She touched her toe on the inner side of Paula's knee and traced up between her thighs. Paula closed her eyes and murmured with approval.

As soon as her toe reached Paula's middle, she grabbed Alexis's foot. "So babe, what's your sign?"

Alexis smiled and pulled her leg back. "I'm sorry about Jen."

Paula nodded. "I'm glad you told me. It'd be hell to find out from anyone other than you." She stepped forward and slipped her hands around Alexis's waist. She glanced over her shoulder and nodded at the bedroom door. "For old time's sake?"

Alexis followed her lead to the bedroom. Originally, Paula was from Wyoming. She'd lived in several other states, but her family and her roots were in Wyoming, and it was nowhere as obvious as when she'd strip out of her clothes and stretch out in the bed, claiming every inch of the mattress and offering you every inch of her body. She had a rough-and-tumble tomboy attitude that was endearing beyond words, but she'd wait on a woman hand and foot if that was called for. Tonight, the rough-and-tumble was in order, and Alexis was feeling her own rambunctious tendencies flare.

As soon as they were both naked and had the comforter and top sheet stripped off, Alexis opened her top dresser drawer and found a bottle of body oil. "Why don't you roll onto your belly so I can give you a payback for your help moving in my pottery wheel?"

"I like the sound of that payback." Paula rolled over and stretched out her arms, waiting. Her naked back was beautiful with the strong, sculpted shoulder muscles befitting a rugby player, and her spine tracing a perfect line down to her smooth butt cheeks. Alexis straddled Paula's lower back, loving the feel of her hair as it rubbed over Paula's naked skin. She dripped oil between Paula's shoulder blades and watched it spread quickly on her warm body. With a little more oil in her palm, Alexis got started with the rubbing. She began at the shoulders and worked her way down the spine, then back up again to massage Paula's arms. A warm wetness had started between her own legs, and she noticed that the oil wasn't the only thing that was smeared over Paula's body. In no time at all, Paula had loosened up and was begging for a turn on top.

Alexis changed places, teasing her about always wanting the top position, and then forgot this argument of old as soon as she felt Paula's strong hands on her back. Few other women that Alexis had been with could give a massage to rival Paula's claim on hand strength. And Paula had a way with butt muscles that put all others massages to shame. Soon Alexis had relaxed into Paula's motions, and she hardly noticed when Paula's hands drifted off her lower back and down between her thighs.

"Roll over," Paula said, her voice whispered and husky.

Alexis started to argue, not ready for the massage to end, but Paula had her moving anyway. When she was finally on her back, she relaxed against the pillows and closed her eyes, ready to let Paula work her front side, just as she'd done with her back. This time, Paula started with her toes and inched upward, rubbing ankles, calves and knees until Alexis could feel a warm tingling sensation edging up her body. Paula had reached her thighs and was going to work on the inner muscles, then the hips.

Suddenly Alexis felt Paula's head push between her legs. Alexis's lips were already wet and ready to welcome the tongue that licked inside her. She spread her legs and murmured encouragement to Paula. Paula's tongue had moved from Alexis's inner thighs to drive inside her middle. She spun slow circles around Alexis's swollen clit and then sucked it between her lips and flicked deep inside. Alexis reached out to hold Paula's head, pushing herself into Paula's open mouth. Paula had her nearly over the top in the first minute, but she wasn't ready to come yet. "Keep going," she managed to say between moans.

Paula had no intentions of stopping, apparently. She tilted Alexis's hips up, sliding her hands under her butt and sucked harder on the clit, then drove her thumb inside. Alexis cried out and palmed Paula's head against her middle. She pushed herself once more into Paula's mouth and then felt a wave of warmth rush through her body. Paula eased off her, letting the aftershocks of Alexis's orgasm run their course. She wiped her face on the bottom sheet and then moved up to lie against Alexis's side.

Alexis started to climb on top of Paula but was stopped midway by a hand on her chest. "Lex, you know me. All I need is to see a girl come and I'm done."

Alexis sighed. That wasn't enough for her. She had hated their one-way sexual relationship and had hoped Paula would have changed. Alexis suddenly didn't want to get on top of her anyway. All of the frustrations that she'd felt so many years ago came rushing up afresh as Alexis stared down at Paula. "Come on, let me have some fun with you."

"Just relax. That's all I want right now."

Alexis collapsed back on the bed and stared up at the ceiling. Paula's arm curved around her chest, just under her breasts, and squeezed tightly, possessively. Yes, this was why she'd broken up with Paula in the first place, she thought. Paula was expert at getting her to climax, but she refused to let her return the favor. She listened for Paula's breathing to slow, knowing she'd be in her dream world in a moment. "We shouldn't have let this happen," she whispered. Paula was already asleep.

Chapter 6

On Tuesday morning, Alexis woke just before her alarm. She only woke early if she had company. Paula slept on as she slipped out of bed and went to take a bath. Alexis decided she wasn't upset about having sex with Paula, but she wasn't happy either. And she didn't want to face her this morning. After setting the alarm to wake Paula in a half hour, she dressed quietly and then left for work. She hoped the day's busy delivery schedule would keep her from thinking about what had happened. For the time being, she had decided to let it go as a lesson to remember. She and Paula were not meant to be anything more than friends. End of story. If Paula asked to spend the night again, Alexis vowed to call her a cab.

By midday, Alexis was filled with regret about sleeping with Paula. She tried to distract herself with thoughts of other women and decided to call Blue's Cafe hoping Sandy would be available.

Sandy had been in her thoughts off and on since Sunday. Her original plan had been to call her that evening, but suddenly she couldn't wait. Just after three o'clock, she phoned the cafe. Gillian, one of the waitresses, answered the line.

"Is Sandy available?"

"No, hon. Sandy's out on her half hour break."

"Can I leave a message?" Alexis asked. "Could you tell her to call Alexis Getty? And can I leave my cell number? Let her know that she can call anytime. No rush."

By a quarter to five the traffic was thick on the main roads, so Alexis took to the side streets to finish her deliveries. Only one package remained for the afternoon order, a medium-sized brown box about the size of a toaster. Alexis scanned the list for the package number and nearly rear-ended a white Honda hatchback when she read the name. "Elana Kingston" was printed next to the delivery address with a COD. stamp on the package. She'd have to face Elana to collect the charge. There was no way of escaping a one-on-one encounter unless Elana wasn't home.

Normally Alexis kept to downtown Portland for her delivery route, but since she'd taken on Moss's beat, her route was moving westward. The address on Elana's package was only a few streets south of the farmer's market and matched up with a corner grocer. Alexis double-parked on a side street and jumped out of the delivery truck with the little package in hand. She went to the front counter to confirm that this was indeed the address for Elana Kingston, hoping that dispatch had somehow mislabeled the package. It wouldn't have been the first time.

"Elana?" the grocery clerk asked, as if he hadn't quite heard her right.

"Yes, I've got a delivery for a . . ." Alexis glanced down at her list as if she needed to double check the name, "Ms. Elana Kingston. This is the grocery store's address, right?" She held up the shipping label for the clerk to see.

"Of course. Elana works upstairs. I'm not sure if she's in or not. Let me ring Mr. Kingston." The clerk reached past the cash register and picked up the phone. "Mr. Kingston, I've got a package here for Elana." He paused and glanced over at Alexis, holding his palm on the mouthpiece. "You need a signature?"

"COD," she replied.

The clerk spoke back into the phone. "Yes. Should I send the courier up to your office then?" He nodded at Alexis and hung up the phone. Pointing to a door marked Employees Only at the back of the store, the clerk gave her directions to find the store owner's office on the second floor.

Alexis made her way to the back of the store, passing several barrels of Fuji, Granny Smith and then Pink Lady apples, all emblazoned with the Kingston label, and then through the back door and up a narrow staircase to the second floor. She tried not to think about the barrels of apples, holding on to the idea that either the package was mislabeled, or there were two Elana Kingstons in Portland.

She tried a knock on the door officially labeled Office, straightened her shirt collar and exhaled slowly. After a busy day of running packages, Alexis knew she wasn't looking too fresh. And the thought of seeing Elana again, after being stood up on their first date, was testing the strength of her underarm deodorant. She waited, heard a creaking sound like someone was getting up from a chair and then heard the shuffle of papers. No footsteps. A minute ticked by and she knocked again, this time adding, "Delivery for Ms. Kingston."

The door opened after a moment and a gray-haired man with one gold tipped tooth and a very large belly that rippled over his pants and challenged his black suspenders, greeted her with a gruff, "Yes, I'm Mr. Kingston, and what's this now?"

"Delivery for a *Ms. Elana* Kingston." Alexis glanced at her clipboard to avoid having to make eye contact with Mr. Kingston. "I need to collect forty-one dollars for this and get her signature."

Mr. Kingston spat out something about hating CODs and then pointed across the hall at another door. The one he fingered was unmarked. "Elana's over there in her studio. Knock first! Don't just barge in or she'll have your head in some of them chemicals." He slammed the door before Alexis had even turned away.

Alexis went across the hall and knocked on the second door. Was Mr. Kingston Elana's father? The two bore less resemblance than a cucumber and a nectarine, but family ties were sometimes difficult to recognize. "Hello?" she asked after another knock. It was nearly five thirty, and she was ready to call it a day. Maybe she could pass off this delivery to someone else tomorrow morning. She'd have a good excuse if anyone asked. This wasn't her normal route. "Delivery for a Ms. Kingston," she repeated, thinking this would be her last attempt before abandoning the delivery.

Alexis turned and headed toward the stairs, somewhat relieved that she was avoiding this delivery after all. She heard a door open behind her and glanced over her shoulder. Elana stared at her with a dropped jaw. She closed her mouth, started to say something and then stopped herself. Dressed in a pair of loose jeans, a yellow T-shirt, darkened with some sort of liquid in a few spots, and a blue bandana to cover her hair, Elana was obviously in the middle of some sort of project. One of her hands rested on the door handle, and she seemed to be considering a retreat back into the room. "I, uh, did you knock?"

Alexis nodded. Pulling the clipboard out from under her arm, she found the last line and tried to sound official as she read, "Delivery for . . . Elana Kingston. COD." She handed the package to Elana. "There's a forty-one dollar charge."

Elana took the package and nodded. She pushed the door fully open and stepped to the side. "Can you come in? I have to get my wallet."

She wanted to say "No, I'll wait right here," but "Sure" slipped out instead. Alexis stepped into a small, dimly lit room. Three red bulbs cast a weak glow to the room, and Alexis shifted her eyes to avoid staring at Elana, who seemed like a ghost in the eerie red light. The smell of film chemicals permeated the air along with a more subtle scent of apple blossoms that Alexis knew belonged to Elana. Wash bins and lines of dripping photographs lined the edge of the two walls. There was one stool in the back of the room next to a slanted table, and other than that, the room appeared to be empty. Elana made her way over to the stool and pulled something out from under the table. After a moment she was back with Alexis, handing her a check for forty-one dollars. Alexis slipped the check into an envelope at the back of the clipboard and then held the clipboard over for Elana to sign.

"Where?" she asked.

Alexis pointed to the last line and watched the black ink swirl out of Elana's pen. Her signature seemed to fill the whole page. Alexis fought the temptation to say anything more and took the clipboard back once Elana had finished. She turned to leave and felt Elana's hand catch her arm.

"Wait." In a soft voice, she continued, "I was sure I wouldn't see you again."

Alexis stiffened under the hold. She didn't know how to answer. "I guess I could say I'm sorry to put you through another meeting. But it's just my job." She shrugged off Elana's hand and went for the door. Her heart was racing. What did Elana want?

"No, I want to apologize." Elana caught her arm again. "Then I'll understand if you never want to see me again. That's what I meant . . . that I didn't think you would want to see me after I . . ." her voice trailed.

"Look, don't worry about it." Alexis opened the door and stepped out into the fluorescent glare of the hallway. She could hear Elana following her but didn't look back now. She felt an odd sense of freedom mixed with her wounded pride. Elana had no hold on her, and Alexis knew she wasn't in the wrong by leaving without a full explanation. It was too late for Elana to win any points. She hadn't called and had made no attempt to smooth things over before this accidental meeting. Furthermore, Alexis argued, she and Elana were just two strangers who'd shared one moment of intimacy on some random Saturday afternoon. There was no reason to blow anything out of proportion. They should both just walk away and pretend they'd never even planned a date.

As soon as Alexis was out of the store, Elana stepped in front of her, blocking the sidewalk. She had her hands on her hips like she was readying herself for a shoot out. "Will you let me apologize now that I've chased you out here?"

Alexis glanced at the sliding glass door, noting for the first time that under the store's Open sign was a smaller sign that read Kingston Grocery and Fruit Distribution. She shook her head. What were the chances that she'd get Moss's route this week and end up facing the woman who'd stood her up?

"No? Does that mean that you aren't going to let me explain?"

Alexis realized that Elana had only seen her head shake and hadn't heard the rest of her mental conversation. "Um, you know, I don't mean to be rude. But I just don't think you need to explain. It's no big deal." She stood level with Elana and met her eyes for the first time, noticing again how beautiful she was. Alexis knew she was staring and said quickly, "I'm sorry. I've gotta go."

Elana shook her head. "My name was the last one on your list and it's almost six. Aren't you done for the day?"

Alexis tried to move past her, and Elana stepped to the side. Obviously she didn't intend to hold her hostage. Climbing into her truck, Alexis felt Elana's eyes watching her. She glanced back at the sidewalk.

"I'd like to take a picture of you," Elana said. "You have the right look for my next spread."

"What look is that?"

"You know that tough dyke attitude. Independent, sexy and take no bullshit. But still endearingly sweet when you look over at me." She laughed. In a quieter tone she continued, "I should have called Ben that night. Too much happened. Anyway, I'm sorry you waited for me."

"What happened?" Alexis didn't want to ask, but now it was too late.

Elana crossed the street and stood next to the truck. She folded her arms. "I got scared, I guess."

Alexis looked down at her. "Of me? 'Cause I'm a *tough dyke?*

You know, all you just described was a stereotype. People aren't stereotypes." She had a feeling there was something else that was bothering Elana.

"Ouch. Look, I know that there's more to you. And really, I'd like to know all the adjectives I left off. But it's bad timing now."

"Yeah. Bad timing." Alexis scoffed at this, thinking of how many times she'd said the same words to a girl she'd lost interest in. "Look, I understand. And speaking of timing, I'm still on the clock and I really gotta go."

"Wait. Just give me five minutes, will you?" Elana was obviously frustrated, and she gave Alexis a very pissed off look. "Give me a chance to explain. Then you can drive off and forget about me . . . I know I screwed up with you and I'm sorry."

Alexis settled back in her seat and took her hands off the steering wheel. "Okay. I'm listening."

Elana sighed. "I came up to Portland to spend some time with my family and forget about my ex. Mike and I had a rough break up, and well, I wanted to get my head back on my shoulders, you know?" She glanced at Alexis but didn't wait for an answer. "And I didn't think I wanted to get involved with anyone. Then . . ." She paused again and uncrossed her arms. "Well, I didn't think that I'd meet someone up here, let alone that the *someone* would be *a woman*."

Alexis thought of all the smart-ass replies she could make about men, straight women and *queers*, but she merely shook her head and started the truck. The best thing to do would be to drive away and forget Elana's signature ever existed. "You know, I should go. I think I've complicated your world enough as it is."

Elana gripped the arm hold on the side of the door. "I'm sorry about everything. I was stupid. Give me another chance?"

"Why?"

"I don't know exactly. There's something about you."

"Well, that's not the best pickup line that I've ever heard." Alexis wanted to accept her apology, but she wasn't ready to get involved with someone who had just broken off an engagement and wasn't sure she wanted to date women. Elana had her attention anyway, and Alexis could feel her resolve softening. "Look, what do you want to do?"

"I'm still new at this." Elana blushed. "How about going out for a drink? And I promise I won't miss our date. Tonight?"

"I don't know." Alexis wanted to keep the ball in her court this time and knew she should probably say no. Yet it was hard to ignore Elana's captivating eyes and appealing smile. She seemed so sincere. Alexis shook her head. "I really gotta get back to drop off the truck. I'll call you when I get home tonight."

It wasn't until Alexis had boarded the six thirty bus that she realized she didn't have Elana's phone number. She spent the bus ride home debating whether she should try to track down Ben in order to get Elana's cell number from him. Finally she decided that she didn't want to explain the situation to Drew in order to reach Ben. She guessed that Elana's parents' number was listed in the phone directory, or she could even call the store. But she wasn't in the mood to track anything down. She'd already had enough dating complications that week and decided on a quiet evening at home.

After a quick run and some weightlifting, Alexis finally had decided to ignore the issue of Elana for the evening. She settled in on the floor of her living room with a microwave dinner, complete with a brownie dessert, and a glass of milk. Helga's pottery supplies were spread out on the hardwood floor, and she delightedly examined every item, from the shapers, the ribs, the loops, the brushes and paints, to the slab of off-white clay, wrapped in cellophane and double-bagged in Ziploc. Helga had kept everything meticulously clean and sharp.

After she finished her dinner, Alexis nervously decided to try out the wheel. She had positioned it in the center of the room on a tripod stand found in Helga's box of supplies. A foot peddle controlled the speed of the wheel and a basin was positioned below to catch the mud splatter. Simple, yet daunting, Alexis thought. Helga's wheel was a much simpler design than her mother's and more elegant somehow. She stared at the precarious setup, thinking that it'd been a long time since she'd thrown any clay and reluctant to break her newly prized possession. Her mother wasn't there to give her any urging, but the bag of clay was enough enticement. With a pitcher of warm water in hand, she pulled a stool over to the wheel and resolved to make a mess of her living room, if nothing else. She cut a palm-sized chunk of clay and started working a little water into it until she had a thick mud pad. Patting and rolling it a few times, the mud warmed in her palms and she seemed ready for the wheel. She started working the foot peddle wheel and rounded the mud into a ball, eager to see the shape it would soon take.

The sound of the wheel reminded her of her mother's studio, as did the smell of the wet clay. When the wheel had reached an even speed, Alexis tossed the ball in the center plate and then moved in with her hands to shape a cone. She thumbed the cone down, built it up again and then flattened the cone to a shape resembling an ashtray. While the wheel spun under the foot peddle's direction, she increased the spinning speed and pinched the edges of the ashtray shape until she had the beginnings of a wall. She dripped a little water over the bowl that had formed, enjoying the spray of muddy water that flew off her hands. Her tank top and sweat pants were splattered with mud before long, as were her arms. She loved the mess that covered her hands. Soon the bowl was a little too oval shaped, so she stopped the wheel and scooped off the clay. After clearing the wheel and forming another clay ball, she was about to start again when the doorbell rang.

Probably it was Drew. Lost his keys again, she guessed. The bell was down at the front of the building, and he had a habit of ringing her whenever he ran out the door without his keys. As of late, he'd rung after going out for a walk with the puppy and realizing too late that he'd left his keys in his apartment. With the tip of her elbow, the only part she could find that wasn't too muddy, she hit the button to unlock the front door and then went back to the wheel.

Before she'd made much headway on the second clay bowl attempt, a knock came at her door. Alexis hated to abandon the clay, and guessing it was probably Drew just thanking her for buzzing him in, called, "Hey, Drew, is that you? I kind of have my hands full. What'd ya need?"

"Uh, I can come back if this is bad timing . . ."

Alexis stopped the wheel immediately and stared at the door. It was Elana. "Hold on a minute. I'll be right there." She dunked one hand in the water pitcher and grabbed a towel. She was filthy and there was nothing she could do about the mess. Why was Elana at her apartment now? At least this time she would be on comfortable footing, Alexis thought, heading for the door. Elana was the one taking the chance.

"Hi." Elana smiled. She rattled the key chain in her hand, and Alexis could tell she was nervous. "I know you said you were going to call, but I was in the neighborhood . . ."

"Oh, really?" Alexis doubted that Elana would have any reason to be in her neighborhood except this visit. And maybe that wasn't a bad thing after all. Elana slipped her key chain in her purse, shifted the strap on her shoulder and then glanced up at Alexis. Her eyes flashed, replacing the nervous air with a coy one. Maybe she was used to showing up uninvited. Of course, she'd probably only knocked on men's doors before tonight. Alexis wasn't going to worry about the straight issue now. When a woman as hot as Elana knocks on your door, you step aside and let her in. Asking questions was useless unless you wanted more than a one-night stand. And anything more could be dangerous. Tonight Alexis didn't want any complications. She was in the mood for a simple booty call. "Please come in. I've got mud everywhere, but if you don't mind the mess . . ."

"I don't mind. Thank you." Elana entered the apartment tentatively, almost as if she really hadn't expected an easy entry. She had exchanged her T-shirt and jeans outfit for a pair of form fitting black pants and a V-neck cream pullover. The bandana was gone now as well, and her hair framed her face, ending in a soft curl just below her ears. She eyed the living room and then the mud on Alexis. "You weren't kidding about the mess. What are you making?"

Alexis shrugged. "Nothing really. I'm just getting a feel for my new toy." She nodded at the wheel. "I just got it yesterday."

Elana went over to have a look, carefully stepping around the mud-splattered floor. "Looks like it was well used before you got it. And well loved." Elana touched the heart design carved on the base of the wheel.

"As any pottery wheel should be." Alexis brushed her hands over the wheel and then pushed at the clay bowl. One edge was sagging inward now. It too would have to be scrapped. She expected that and was looking forward to a lot of do-overs.

"That's how I feel about a good camera lens," Elana replied. She opened her satchel and pulled out a camera then uncapped the lens and pointed it at Alexis. "Don't move."

Alexis leveled her eyes on Elana, her hands still on the wheel. "Did you come just to take a picture?" She didn't want to sound upset, but she wanted to be sure of Elana's intentions. Why hadn't Elana called her before coming over? Alexis decided she didn't care. She was here now.

"I can't resist taking a shot when I see you looking so . . . in your space."

"Well, this is my house." Alexis smiled. She realized that she tensed every time Elana pointed the lens on her, and she tried to relax. Maybe she was still upset about Saturday night. She wished she could just forget that she'd been stood up, but the thought kept nagging on her conscience and warning her not to let Elana past her guard.

The camera snapped once, twice. Elana lowered the camera a few inches and finally answered, "No. But I can't miss an opportunity for a shot as good as this."

Alexis scooped up the misshapen clay bowl, rolled it in her hands and listened as the camera clicked another shot. She glanced over at Elana, more intrigued than upset now. Elana moved to the other side of her and took one more picture before replacing the lens cover.

"Will you let me start tonight with a clean slate?"

Alexis shook her head and tossed the clay on the wheel. She didn't want to be the girl who couldn't let something go, but she knew better than to admit she'd just forget about it. "I don't like clean slates. I like them muddy."

"Now that I believe."

"Can I get you anything? I was just going to break for a drink." Alexis went to the kitchen sink and started washing her hands. She needed a good scrubbing, but now wasn't the time.

"Sure, I'll have one of whatever you're pouring." Elana was over by the window, looking at the view of the intersection below. Alexis finished a rough cleaning and poured two glasses of apple juice. She was out of wine and beer, so milk or apple juice were the only choices on the menu. Elana had moved from the window over to the one decorated wall in the living room. There was a collection of framed eight-by-twelve black-and-white photographs of women that Alexis had taken when she was in college. For the photography class final project, she'd shot a series titled "Womyn with a Towel." Somehow she'd convinced a bunch of her friends to pose for her wearing only a towel, with each woman deciding how much or how little skin she wanted to bare. One of the pictures was of Paula in an Arnold Schwarzenegger bodybuilder pose, with just one towel wrapped around her head like a turban. Paula always laughed when she saw this one. Elana smiled at the image as well.

"Did you take these?"

Alexis nodded. She handed Elana one of the glasses. "Hope you like apple juice. And no, I'm not trying to keep us sober. I'm just out of beer, and wine, for that matter. Really, I'm in need of a grocery visit, but I think I'll be avoiding corner markets for a while."

"Can't say that I blame you after your last experience." Elana took a sip of the juice and then pointed to the pictures. "You know, you have a good eye. Each piece has a different voice, and you've caught it just right with a couple of these. So youthful and alive,"

Elana said. Her praise sounded like she'd given it honestly, and Alexis was pleased with the review, even if it had been a long time since she'd done any photography.

Elana moved to the last frame on the wall. It was a photograph of Alexis's mom working in her studio. Mud was splattered on her face and her hands were covered in it.

"That's my mom. She has her own studio."

"So you come by this habit of getting dirty honestly?"

Alexis grinned. "Yes, but my mom would kill me if I left my tools muddy."

"Nice work, really."

"The photos are all old. I sold my good camera when money got tight a few years ago. Now I use a damn disposable thing."

Elana covered her ears and feigned shock. "I'm going to pretend I didn't hear that." She arched her eyebrows. "But I know how these things go."

"I'd love to see some of your work. I'm a little embarrassed that a professional photographer is even looking at my stuff."

"Well you shouldn't be embarrassed about that. I would have been embarrassed to take all of those towel shots."

"They were friends, mostly. And I had a good time with the project."

"I'll bet," Elana said, eyes sparkling with the good-natured poke. She sat down on the stool and picked up the clay ball. "So you've given up a promising career in photography for a pile of mud?"

"I was just a girl with too many hormones. That college photography course got me enough action to appease my interests."

Elana blushed at this comment and looked down at the clay. She rolled it on the wheel, quiet for a moment. Worried that she'd said too much, Alexis tried to apologize. Elana raised her hand to stop her and then said, "You know, I was taken off guard this afternoon. Didn't expect to see you at my parents' shop. That's for sure." She laughed softly. "My dad would have another coronary and mom would disown me if . . ." Her voice trailed and she looked up at Alexis. "Normally, I'm better at this. I'm nervous tonight."

"Normally you're not with a woman?"

"Something like that." Elana didn't look up at Alexis. Her gaze was focused on the window while her hands worked the clay, rolling and flattening it like she had more experience with bread dough then pottery.

"Do you want to try?"

Elana's eyes shot up at Alexis. "What'd you say?"

"The wheel. Do you want to try throwing something?" Alexis went over to the wheel, close enough to touch Elana, but she didn't. She wouldn't make the first move. "It's really easy. The peddle's here." She leaned down to position the peddle under Elana's foot, and as she stood up, Elana's hand was on Alexis's hip.

"I really don't know how."

"It's easy," Alexis repeated. She picked up the lump of clay and then added a little warm water to it while she worked the ball in her hands. Elana was watching her intently. "Get a little water on your hands," Alexis directed. "It's one of those better when wet things." She smiled when Elana arched her eyebrows.

As Elana dipped her hands in the water pitcher, Alexis started the wheel and then passed off the ball of clay. "So first you throw it on the wheel."

"Throw it?"

Alexis nodded. "Yep, when it comes to pottery wheels, you just have to get on the wheel and work it. Not a lot of foreplay."

This time Elana laughed, and Alexis could tell she was starting to relax. "Okay, tell me when to throw it."

"Whenever you're ready. As long as the clay's wet and the wheel's spinning, you're ready to aim for the center."

"Is it safe to assume that you apply that rule of thumb to situations beyond pottery class?" Elana taunted. She tossed the clay on the wheel and then eyed Alexis. "Okay, what next?"

Alexis took Elana's hands in hers and set them on the clay. The wheel spun under their fingers, and she adjusted the foot peddle to slow the speed as they started to shape the clay in a cone. She loved the feel of Elana's hands in hers, both covered in mud and wet with anticipation. Elana's hands had left muddy fingerprints on the pockets of her sweats where she'd touched Alexis, and now Alexis couldn't help herself from imagining the places on Elana's body where she'd like to place her own muddy prints.

After they had made a few attempts at perfecting the base and centering the clay, Alexis started forming the sides. Elana latched onto the pinching part of the job, and before long a vase had formed on the wheel. Alexis picked up one of the wooden ribs—a shaping tool from Helga's collection—and trimmed the walls so the thickness was closer to even. The vase certainly wasn't perfect, but with a little colored glaze it could have definite charm.

"Well, would you look at that? Not bad, huh?" Elana pulled her hands off the clay as Alexis stopped the wheel. "You'd think we were professionals!"

Alexis smiled at the pride in Elana's eyes. She leaned down and kissed her, suddenly unable to wait for Elana to make this step. Elana's lips were warm and not as shy as Alexis had expected. She pushed her mouth forward, and Alexis let her tongue slip in just enough to taste . . . tart apples. They kissed for longer than Alexis would have planned, if she'd thought to plan this, and neither seemed quite ready to stop. As they separated, Alexis caught a look of surprise on Elana's face. Apparently she hadn't planned on feeling so uninhibited either. "It's not bad at all. Damn good for a beginner in fact."

Elana covered her mouth with her hand. "I have to admit you're good at that. I usually don't like kissing so much."

"Maybe you're not kissing enough women."

"Maybe not," she agreed quietly. Her index finger traced along the top edge of the vase.

Alexis could tell Elana was tightening up her guard. She'd softened for a while, but now they were back to square one. With her obvious experience flirting, Elana didn't lead past that stage. Alexis guessed this was because she was used to guys who would take over. Turned on by the fact that Elana had shown up at her place basically as a booty call, Alexis was disappointed that she wasn't following through with things. Elana seemed to expect someone else to take charge, while Alexis wanted a more aggressive partner tonight.

Elana stood up and faced Alexis. "You know, I didn't get the full tour. Where can I wash up?"

While Elana was in the bathroom, Alexis carefully removed the vase from the wheel and started cleaning up the equipment in the kitchen sink. Just as she realized the bath water was running, she felt a hand on her shoulder. Alexis turned, and her jaw dropped when she saw Elana standing in only a bra and black underwear.

Elana laughed and reached a hand up to cover Alexis's eyes. "You're going to make me lose my nerve if you stare like that."

Alexis caught her hand and pulled it away from her face. "How can you expect me not to stare when . . ." She paused. Seeing Elana nearly naked in the middle of her kitchen literally took Alexis's breath away. Her impulse was to pull Elana close to her, finish undressing her while she nibbled on her neck and then take her to the bedroom so she could investigate every inch of her body, especially under the black panties. But she knew she couldn't go that fast with Elana. "You've really got a nice way of just standing there, you know. And damn, girl, you've got some nice curves."

Elana blushed and shook her head. "I've always felt a little out of place in my body. A little too curvy. My hips are too wide and my breasts are, well, more than a handful." She sighed. "That doesn't mean nice curves. I was shaped like this by the time I turned thirteen and haven't really ever felt happy with the size of anything. And now, my belly—"

Alexis stepped forward and kissed her. She hated to hear a beautiful woman deprecating her own body. As she pulled back she whispered, "Your body is perfect, and I love that you caught me off guard here."

Elana slipped her hand under the strap of Alexis's tank top. "I came to ask if you'd take a bath with me."

"I am a little dirty," Alexis admitted, wiping her hands with a dishcloth and watching Elana intently. She could still feel Elana's tension, and it made her feel a little uneasy too. Alexis pulled off her tank top and sports bra. She took Elana's hand and kissed her fingertips then stepped closer and kissed her lips as her hand caressed Elana's neck.

"You know," Elana said, pulling away from Alexis, "the answer to your question—how many times with a woman—well, tonight brings the total up to two. And the first one didn't go so well."

Alexis knew this was Elana's way of telling her to take things slow. She clasped Elana's hand and said, "Just a bath, for now. And maybe a little more kissing because we make a good team at that part." Alexis slipped her watch off and watched Elana begin to undress. It was already half past eleven. The alarm clock was going to wake her up way too early tomorrow.

Chapter 7

The alarm, as predicted, rang much too early. Alexis turned it off, crawled out of bed and turned on the stereo. Melissa Etheridge's melodic voice drifted out of the speakers as Alexis did a few morning stretches. Last night had gone better than she'd expected, though Elana had left immediately after their bath. The bath had definitely gone beyond a PG-rated experience, and she'd ended it more wet than when she'd started. The image of Elana, buck naked, toeing the water to test the warmth kept replaying in her mind. She had several other nice images to reflect on the next time she took a bath alone. Even if they soaped their own back-sides and touched nothing more than lips, she had enjoyed sharing the space in the dirty bath water.

After dressing for work and making a quick breakfast, Alexis headed out to start her day. She met Darcy in the hallway again. Darcy was dressed up in a slick-cut beige suit and a pair of heels. Her usual authoritative presence was nearly doubled in this outfit, and Alexis had to forcibly stop herself from staring.

"Good morning," Darcy said cheerfully.

Alexis nodded and murmured something close to a reply. "Hmm, oh yeah, morning."

"You look like you could use some coffee," Darcy suggested as they started down the stairs.

Say something intelligent, Alexis pleaded silently. Instead she said, "Yeah, guess so. Running late though."

They stepped off the last stair and Darcy handed Alexis her thermos. "Here, have a sip. I make a mean cup of java that can combat any level of sleep deprivation." When Alexis gave her a hesitant look, she insisted. "It'll at least get you started. I wouldn't want any packages to be late just because of a late night and a caffeine shortage."

Alexis took the thermos and had a sip, wondering how Darcy knew that she'd had a late night. Maybe she'd seen Elana leave? The coffee was good, strong and not a bit bitter. "Thanks. That's perfect."

Darcy nodded. "No problem. I'm driving into work today, so you'll have to keep the bus driver in line without me." She waved good-bye. "Have a good day."

Alexis watched her head for the parking garage, thinking that they had come very close to a real conversation. Maybe there was hope. She saw the bus pull up across the street and had to run to catch it, stopping the train of thought that was examining her interactions with Darcy. She wanted to get to know Darcy, but the damn crush had her too intimidated to even enjoy a sip of coffee with her.

"Are you in line?"

Alexis shook her head and stepped aside to let a brunette woman with tight curls step up to the counter. The hair salon was busy this afternoon. She'd hoped to just drop off the delivery and run on to the next one, but the manager who normally handled the styling product orders was out on a break. "She'll be back in five," the receptionist had chirped. The main reason Alexis had wanted to make this a quick stop was to avoid another meeting with Tina. She'd met Tina here for the first time two weeks ago, same day, and about the same time. She had no idea how often Tina came to this salon, but her instincts told her to be quick. Alexis was dreading another meeting.

Finally the manager approached the salon, complete with a protein shake and box of cigarettes in hand. Alexis propped open the door to let her in, anxious for any way to speed up this delivery.

"Oh, it's my products. Late as usual. You know, I ran out of the super hold color-safe gentle gels and the vitamin A enriched detanglers three hours ago. Why can't you get here earlier?" The manager was huffing now and had to pause in her tirade for a breath. "And when you're three hours late, honey, it's my money!"

"Sorry, *ma'am*. Busy schedule, you know," Alexis replied, adding emphasis so the old hag would know how she really felt. She even considered telling her to lay off on the smoking so she'd have more wind power to really chew her out when she was late again next week. Every week, she tried to get to the salon as early as she could, but the products came with the afternoon orders, and the manager knew this. Alexis had explained the delivery process to her several times, but she repeated it again with, "You know, it's only five dollars more for a morning delivery."

The manager grabbed Alexis's clipboard, found the order line for the hair salon and scribbled her name. "Stack the boxes in the staff room, just like always. And watch what you're doing back there. I found my coffee mug in pieces after *someone* was throwing things around with the last order."

Ordinarily Alexis would have defended herself against such a charge, but she didn't want to create any more of a scene than she already had. "I'm always very careful, ma'am. If you have any problems with APO's service, please feel free to contact my supervisor. In fact, I can give you the number for the distribution center if you'd like."

"I don't have time for any of that." She waved Alexis off indignantly. In a lower voice, she concluded with, "Look, honey, I don't have time for your pert little attitude either. Move the order into the back so I can get back to running my business, if you don't mind."

Alexis tilted the dolly back and rolled the three boxes between the line of stylists and fluffy-haired women. After placing the boxes in the staff room, Alexis left the salon, conscious of the dozen pairs of eyes watching her back. Tina was just parallel parking her hot rod in front of the salon. Alexis knew that she'd spotted her. It was inevitable. She waved and then continued pushing her dolly up to the truck.

Tina called, "Hey, Lex! Babe, you and I have gotta talk."

Alexis closed the back of the truck once the dolly was strapped in. She turned to face Tina, who'd followed her. "About what?"

"Joey saw you getting into your cab. Talk about a close call. He came home early."

"Good thing I left when I did. I bet he'd have been a little upset if he saw us together."

"You could have handled him." She smirked. "But, God, did he grill me."

Alexis wished suddenly that she'd never gone to Tina's place that weekend. "What'd you tell him?"

"Everything! Let me tell you, I shot it all back in his face." She pushed her hair out of her eyes and then continued, "And he deserved it. I told him everything you and I did. Upset? He was livid!" She snorted, and her hair fell in her eyes again. She whipped it back with a vengeance. Tina was in rare form. "I even told him I went down on you, and I never give him any blows." At this point her hand grabbed onto Alexis's belt.

Alexis shifted uncomfortably under the hold. "You didn't have to tell him everything."

"Of course not, but I wanted to," she puffed. "He's been planning on leaving me, and I want him to get on with it. I know he's got his affairs, and now I have mine as well. When he finally cuts me off, I'll really be able to have some fun. Speaking of fun, when do I get the pleasure of you again?"

110

"Again? I don't think it'd be a good idea." Alexis had no intention of another round with Tina, especially now that she knew there was a pissed off husband to contend with. "We don't want to risk your relationship with Joey, you know? Guys can get crazy."

"Relationship? Lex, there's nothing between Joey and me except a pickle-sized dick." Tina loosened the belt buckle while Alexis squirmed. Alexis moved back until she was against the truck. "I'd rather have my own selection of hard-ons, and the ones I buy are always *up* when I need them to be."

"Tina, I'm just not comfortable with—" Alexis stopped mid-sentence as Tina's hand slid under her waistband. She had always appreciated the comfort of her loose-fitting uniform cargo pants, but she suddenly longed for a pair of tight-ass jeans. Tina's fingers were under her boxers now and spreading open her lips to get a feel of her clit.

"Oh, yeah," she whispered in Alexis's ear. "As I expected. Your clit is ready for another night with me. You can try to avoid it, girl, but you know you want another go. I can get you wet and ready with one little massage. Imagine what we can do with a couple hours to ourselves."

Alexis didn't want to imagine anything with Tina now. She shifted her legs and pulled Tina's wrist. "Tina, I don't think I'm ready for that."

"Lex, you're ready all right." Tina put her wet fingertip up to Alexis's lips. She kissed her, turned on her heel and crossed the street toward the salon. Over her shoulder she called, "Call me."

Alexis sighed in relief. She wondered how many heads would turn when Tina sauntered in. No doubt the manager had watched the scene. Fortunately, she didn't really care. Alexis planned on trading with another driver to get the salon off her route for good. Besides, Ace wouldn't fire her over a late delivery, or kissing a woman in the middle of the street, even if the manager reported it. But she'd have a headache trying to ignore the gossip buzz at the DC.

≈≈≈

111

Ron congratulated her as soon as she jumped out of her truck. She handed him the keys and her clipboard. "What'd I do to earn your congrats? Show up to work on time or something?"

"Employee of the Month. Didn't you see the bulletin?"

Alexis shook her head. The last thing she wanted was to be the Employee of the Month. All it meant was a coupon for a free meal at Blue's Cafe and a guarantee that the rest of the drivers would be on your ass for showing them up. Worse yet, she had no idea why she'd earned the ominous award. "Is Ace still around?"

Ron nodded. "In his office, of course. You can count on him being there until that little clock," he pointed at the huge wall clock above the red and blue APO Distribution Center sign, "points to five-o-one."

Surprisingly, Alexis had managed to finish her bloated delivery schedule on time. She'd stopped flirting with the hotties on her route, and the difference in time saved was amazing. The door to Ace's office was open, and Alexis poked her head in, finding Ace dozing at his desk, feet up in the air, magazine on his lap and a Diet 7UP in hand. His secretary's desk was too neat, and Alexis guessed she'd already checked out for the day. "Knock, knock."

Ace's head twitched like he was about to have a convulsion, and the soda can crackled as his hand squeezed. "What's wrong?" he mumbled. His gaze shot to the door and he scowled at Alexis for a moment. "Oh, Lex, it's just you." He pulled his feet off the desk, closed the magazine and rubbed his hand over his face like a toddler who'd just risen from nap time. "What time is it?"

"Almost five. Didn't want you to miss quittin' time. Good article in that magazine?" She smiled, happy to have caught her boss in this compromising situation. The magazine she recognized from Paula's house—an upscale collection of soft porn. Paula actually read the articles, though she wouldn't admit it in mixed company.

Ace blushed with this comment. He turned the magazine face down and shook his head. "Uh, no. I wasn't really reading it. I mean, I think I just grabbed the wrong magazine. This one must

112

have been one of the boys' down in loading." He stumbled through some excuse about wanting to read a news article and picking up the wrong thing, but then finished with, "You know, Lex, I didn't even notice what this magazine was about. Didn't read the articles at all." He stopped as soon as he realized what he'd just admitted, and his cheeks and neck turned red again.

"Relax, Ace. I never read those magazines either."

He sighed. "Shit. I'm going to stop digging my own hole. What'd you need, Lex?"

"Why'd I get Employee of the Month? You know I don't want the award. Can't you give it to Kate for protecting the coffee or something? How 'bout Ron for changing the dispatch lists so quick now that Mossinni's gone?"

"Lex, all it means is your name in the bulletin and a dinner at Blue's. Why the hell don't you want the damn thing?" He shook his head. "And no. I can't give it to someone else now that I've put your name in the bulletin." He opened the top drawer of his desk and handed her the gift certificate for the restaurant.

"Fine," Alexis grumbled. "But why'd I get it anyway?"

"For delivering the unlabeled package. Word got around to corporate about what happened, and I told them that one of my best drivers got everything settled and even took on the extra route. They're the ones that told me to give you the award. Like hell am I going to change it now."

Alexis shook her head and shoved the certificate in her pocket. She turned to leave and glanced at the big wall clock. "Five-o-one, Ace. Better get your ass outta here or Ron will think better of you for working up here."

"Hey, Lex," Ace called to stop her. "About the magazine . . . Well, thanks for not reading the articles, you know."

She glanced over her shoulder. "Yeah, I know." The planets had aligned in her favor, Alexis thought smugly. Even if the bitchy manager at the hair salon called over to issue a complaint, Ace wouldn't touch Alexis for a long while to come. She was also lucky that she didn't have to admit that the last box hadn't actually been delivered. If someone didn't call her about it soon, she'd have to open the damn thing.

Alexis caught the five thirty bus and found a seat in the rear. One of the other commuters recognized her and gave a tired nod. He was a forty-something businessman who got off on the stop before Westside. She never knew where he worked or what he did. They'd never exchanged a word though they'd shared the same bus route for weeks now. The muggy air, muffled traffic noises and familiar jostling of the bus shocks lulled Alexis asleep. She woke to the feel of someone's hand on her shoulder. "Hmm?"

"This is our stop, Alexis." Darcy was smiling down at her. "I hated to wake you, but . . ."

Alexis was completely awake now. Darcy had not only shared her coffee with her that morning, but was now resting a hand on her shoulder. She'd have to tell Drew about this progress. "Thanks." Of course, progress had its limits, and Alexis wasn't ready for full sentence conversations. Why had Darcy driven to work but taken the bus home? If Alexis could have managed a normal interaction with her, she'd have asked about this. As it was, she decided to let the issue drop.

She silently followed Darcy off the bus and up the walkway to the apartment building. They both headed to the mailroom, with Alexis pausing by the message board to make sure her posting was still up. She'd gotten no new leads on it. Darcy left the mailroom with her pile of envelopes, and Alexis went to unlock her box. Empty. Not even credit card companies or window repair and carpet cleaning services wanted to send her junk mail. Staring at the empty mailbox, she mumbled, "Well, guess I don't really need love letters with all the loving I've been getting this week. Wham, bam, thank you, ma'am." She kicked the door closed and turned to leave, freezing as she noticed Darcy standing in the mailroom doorway, grinning.

They watched each other silently for a moment and finally Darcy spoke up, "You know, I was going to ask if you've been having trouble sleeping. Drew Riverton's new puppy had been keeping me up until I got a pair of earplugs. Anyway . . ." She smiled almost coyly. "I thought it might have bothered you also. But now I know why you looked so worn out this morning, and I see it has nothing to do with a shortage of earplugs."

Alexis felt her skin blush. "Uh, no."

Darcy waved the assortment of letters in her hand. "You know what's worse? Waiting for love letters and finding only bank notes. There's nothing as nice as a little real lovin' that keeps you up late." She winked and added, "I'd trade that for an empty mailbox."

As Darcy headed up the stairs, Alexis sank against the wall of mailboxes. She couldn't really decide if this was a good type of progress or not. Darcy had used her name, and her full name at that, which no one ever did. But she insinuated that she was waiting for a love letter, which suggested that Darcy had a romance with someone, albeit not a prolific correspondent. And what was worse, Alexis had revealed that she was basically a slut. She hated the "Wham, bam, thank you, ma'am" expression and didn't even know why she'd said it aloud.

Drew entered the mailroom a moment later, dressed in his expensive Italian suit and looking dapper as always. He was just getting home from work as well. "Hey, Lex. You know, you're just the person I was looking for. Ben asked me to meet him for dinner tonight, and I'm running a tiny bit late." He opened his mailbox and pulled out an armful of mail. "So can I ask you a favor?"

"Let me guess, the puppy needs a walk?"

"You're amazing, you know that? I knew I could count on you. By the by, I heard a rumor that you had company last night. True?"

"Yep, Elana. And I'll cut to the chase since you're running late and I know how you think. No, I didn't get any." She didn't ask how Drew knew, guessing it was the thin walls again that had outed her.

"That's not what I was thinking at all! Well, I mean, I would have if you'd given me enough time." He laughed. "So you forgave her for Saturday night?"

"Sort of. We made a truce."

"Well, I say we plan another double date. Maybe we could cook dinner at my place or something. Ben's absolutely fabulous naked in the kitchen."

"What'd you say? A naked baker?"

"You heard it, honey. Just the way I like my men: barefoot, big-balled and baking in the kitchen." He chuckled then fanned himself with an envelope as though merely the thought of Ben in the kitchen had gotten him hot.

"You know, I'm glad you boys are having fun, but I really don't want to imagine Ben's privates wagging around in your kitchen."

"Lex, don't be such a prude," Drew chastised. "I know you don't have any problems with a sex-positive environment."

Alexis didn't want to get Drew going off on one of his tirades about sex. "Aren't you late? I'll take care of the puppy tonight."

"You're such a good auntie," Drew gushed. He wished her a good sex-positive night and then headed for the garage. As soon as Drew had mentioned a double date for cooking, Sandy had popped into her mind. It seemed like a long time ago since they had gone out to the waterfall, and she wanted to call her now. The phrase "Too many girls, too little time," rattled in her head as she took the stairs two at a time.

There was a message on her answering machine from someone named Dave in Apartment 7. He wondered if the box was from a computer company, as he'd been expecting a new printer. Alexis had to call him to say that the package was too small and too light to be a computer printer. Besides, the company's label would have been printed all over the box. She pulled the box down from the refrigerator to shake it around and look it over once more for any clues. It was hard to resist opening it.

On a whim, she'd called Blue's Cafe. Unfortunately, it was Sandy's night off. Satisfied with a night alone, she changed into running clothes and grabbed Drew's spare key. The puppy started peeing as soon as he saw her, too excited to contain himself. She tossed paper towels on the urine puddle and headed out to the park. Before long, the pup had tired, and she ended up carrying him for the better half of her jog. Although she had planned to leave him at Drew's for the rest of the night, he started whimpering as soon as she went for the door. Feeling softhearted, she brought the puppy back to her apartment and shared her dinner with him. Alexis gave the puppy a plastic water bottle to play with, or otherwise destroy, and went to the pottery wheel to consider the next clay challenge. She settled on making a coffee mug and had just started the wheel when her phone rang.

"Hey, it's me," Paula said. "Mind if I come over and hang out at your place? I've got a bottle of wine that needs to be shared."

"What's up?" Alexis asked. Paula sounded like she'd been crying. Maybe she'd finally talked to Jen.

"Nothing. I just don't want to spend the night watching sitcoms. I hate people who have rockstar salaries, perfect hair and fake loving relationships." She sniffled. The sound of a muffled nose blow followed. "How many hours do you think they spend in the gym? It's just plain narcissistic to have a perfect body."

"Some people would call it healthy." Sounds like she's single again, Alexis thought.

"Load of crap!" Paula shot back. "I'll be there in an hour. You're alone, right? I mean, I'm not stepping in on a hot date, am I?"

"Not exactly. I've got Drew's puppy over here for company. But he won't mind." Alexis glanced around the room to find the puppy. Earlier, he'd been lying next to the stool playing with the plastic bottle, but now he was missing from the room. Paula was saying good-bye now and she mumbled, "Yeah, see you soon," while looking for the puppy.

She found a mess in the kitchen and the puppy in the middle of it. Somehow, the puppy had grabbed the tablecloth and pulled it, as well as two candles, a saltshaker and the unclaimed APO box, off the table. Then he'd proceeded to tear apart the box. Infuriated that he'd opened the box, Alexis scooped up the puppy and tossed him in the bathroom before investigating the damage. The candles suffered a few teeth marks, and the tablecloth only had a few

117

patches of saliva on the lower hemline. The box, however, had not fared well. He'd gnawed through the top corner and then found a way to pull out the newsprint stuffing.

Alexis started cleaning up the mess and noticed a small envelope on the floor amongst the slobbery newsprint. She caught her breath as soon as she saw the name handwritten on the envelope. Darcy. Who had sent Darcy this package? Obviously she hadn't been expecting anything since she'd seen the posted signs and knew Alexis had the mysterious box. Staring at the half-open package with renewed interest, she debated whether she should deliver the package now, take a quick peek inside the box first, or read the note in the envelope. Ordinarily, she wouldn't consider any decision other than delivering the box, but Darcy made her curious. And the envelope wasn't sealed. Alexis unfolded a single-sided note and read, "My Love," at the top of the page. That was enough. She folded the note and replaced it in the envelope, careful not to make any new creases, then pushed it back into the box.

So Darcy had a lover. There really wasn't anything more to do than deliver the package. And for the first time, she didn't feel at all nervous about the idea of an interaction with Darcy. There was nothing she could do but get over her crush. Alexis went to change out of her running clothes, deciding that she didn't want to face Darcy or Paula in old sweaty clothes. With the puppy watching her, acting contrite after the scolding he'd gotten for ripping open the box, she rinsed off in the bathtub and then changed into clean jeans and a T-shirt.

Darcy didn't seem surprised to see her. She opened the door and invited her in, then asked, "So to what do I owe this visit from my quiet neighbor?"

Alexis never thought of herself as the quiet type but knew she had been around Darcy. She handed her the box. "I think this is yours, and let me apologize right now for the teeth marks."

Darcy took the box, obviously surprised. "This was the package that you posted the note about, isn't it?"

"Yeah, Drew's puppy got a hold of it and ripped the thing open. Probably for the best, though, 'cause I didn't know it was yours until the puppy pulled out the card." Alexis was pleased at how easy this seemed. She could even look directly at Darcy without feeling stupid.

"Huh. I really wasn't expecting anything." Darcy glanced at Alexis and then at the box.

"Well, I'm pretty sure it's yours. The address label was torn off the package, but our dispatch said the package was to be delivered to someone here at Westside." Alexis pointed to the place where the remainder of the label was. "And the only clue that I had was the name on the envelope inside."

Darcy opened the box and took out the envelope. She pulled out the note and read it silently, then folded it and replaced it in the envelope. There was no sign that she was happy to get this package. In fact, Alexis sensed that the note had disturbed her for some reason.

"Well, thank you. You've gone above the call of duty in delivering this."

"Oh, it was no problem, I'm only sorry it was late, and well, a little damaged." Alexis wanted to ask if Darcy was upset or if the note had contained bad news, but she felt out of place staying any longer. "Anyway, have a good night."

"Yes, thank you."

Once Alexis was back in her apartment she breathed a quick sigh of relief. Now that the box was out of her hands, finally delivered, she felt relieved. Yet, finding the owner had not ended the mysteriousness of the box. She was intrigued by Darcy's response but decided she'd probably never know any more about it.

The puppy heard her come in and whined to be let out of the bathroom. Apparently, he'd already forgotten about his previous scolding, and in the short time she'd left him, had pulled half of the toilet paper off the roller. Alexis grabbed the plastic bottle that he had been playing with earlier and tossed it for him. He wasn't the brightest beagle and hadn't managed the concept of fetch, but it was fun to watch him waddle around the room trying to get the toy.

A knock sounded at her door, and Alexis glanced at the clock. Someone must have let Paula in downstairs, she thought. It'd been exactly one hour since Paula's call, and she was almost annoyingly punctual. Alexis knew that Paula's father had been in the military and had indoctrinated her with the concept of being on time. The puppy had latched on to one end of the plastic bottle and was engaging Alexis in a fierce game of tug of war. She continued to pull on her end of the bottle and hollered, "Come on in. The door's unlocked."

After a moment, the door opened and Darcy stood in the entry-way. She smiled but her reddened eyes belied the expression. "I don't suppose you'd be interested in a drink? I was going to open this bottle of vino, but I hate not to share a good year of a Napa Valley cabernet."

"I never turn down a good year." She stood up, letting the puppy finally win the plastic bottle, and approached Darcy. For the first time, Darcy didn't look put together. She was clearly upset about something, and Alexis guessed it had to do with the package she'd just received. "Is something wrong?"

Darcy shook her head then sighed. "That package was from my ex. She wanted to get rid of all the photos we took together. I wasn't smiling in half of them anyway." She laughed, and a note of bitterness tinged her voice. "It was one of those break ups where one of us was ready and one of us kept holding on. I was hoping she'd finally let go, but her note didn't sound like it."

"I'm sorry. Sometimes I hate being the messenger."

"Don't worry. I promise not to take it out on you." She lifted the bottle. "So after my admission, are you still up for a drink? I'd love to get my mind off things."

Just then the doorbell buzzed. Must be Paula, Alexis thought. God, her timing sucked. She hit the button to let her in, avoiding

Darcy's eyes. This could get sticky, she thought, wondering how Darcy and Paula would interact.

"You're expecting someone?"

"Just a friend."

"Oh." She glanced at the bottle and then at Alexis. "You know, I don't want to interrupt your visit. We can do this another time." Darcy turned to leave and Alexis reached for her arm.

"Wait." Now that she had Darcy this close, her heartbeat was pounding in her chest, and she knew her cheeks were reddening. She didn't want to let her go. "My friend was actually just coming over to have a drink. She just broke up with a woman as well. Strange timing. Anyway, she also wanted to get her mind off things. If you don't mind the added company, we can just make a night of forgetting our exes."

Darcy smiled. "Maybe . . . But I'm sure she'd rather not—"

"Please stay," Alexis interrupted. "I know she'd love it if you did." The way Darcy looked at her made Alexis feel like she'd been caught admitting it was her own interests she was looking out for and not Paula's. "As my mom says, good wine and good company help you forget debt and heartbreaks. Always works for me."

"And how many heartbreaks have you had? I'd bet you're more often the cause of a heartbreak."

Alexis shrugged. "I've had time on both sides."

Without a knock, the door swung open, narrowly missing Darcy, who was still in the entryway. She stepped quickly to the side to avoid being hit by the door and then stared at Paula. Paula stood in the hallway shaking water off her jacket. She kicked off her boots and finally glanced up. "Oh, hi." Her cheeks, already red from the cold, reddened more as she noted Darcy standing next to Alexis. "Um, should I have knocked?"

"No, of course not," Alexis said quickly. "Come in." She glanced over at Darcy who was staring at Paula with obvious appreciation. Wearing her old jeans, a plaid workman's shirt and a knit cap, Paula could have been the poster child for a tree-hugging granola dyke. She pulled off her cap, and her spiky wet hair underneath furthered the image of a tough, Northwestern lesbian. On her side, Paula wasn't shy about giving Darcy a once over either. Darcy was wearing black dress slacks with a stylish gray sweater, cut low to expose her collarbones and the pearl hanging at her throat.

Alexis suddenly realized that these two apparent opposites would make a great couple. After all, they were both single, attractive, goal-minded professionals, and of course, lesbians. What more did you need? She almost blurted this out, amazed by the discovery as she was. Instead, she stumbled through introductions and then invited the group to leave the doorway. Sadly, she realized that Darcy wasn't really meant for her, and she forced herself to ignore her feelings of attraction in deference to Paula's possible interests. She resolved to suffer through one night more to help her best friend discover what a great match she had handpicked for her. For whatever reason, she had decided Darcy and Paula were definitely meant for each other. Maybe life partners even. Now she just had to convince them of this, and with the looks the two women were exchanging, she guessed it wouldn't be hard. Three wineglasses and a bottle opener in hand, Alexis directed Darcy and Paula to the seats at the kitchen table.

When Darcy heard Paula's last name, she immediately asked if Paula's family lived in the Midwest. As it turned out, they had both grown up in the same town. Paula's distinctive last name—Baldercanton—gave Darcy the hint. And though they hadn't met each other, they both knew of the other's family. Small town, they kept saying. Alexis opened the wine and let the two women chat about their old hometown. They both had plenty of stories to share, including bits from the high school they'd both graduated from, four years apart. Darcy was four years older than Paula, Alexis thought, and completely smitten. Paula seemed to have come alive in a way that Alexis had never seen. She obviously missed her old home, and Darcy's invitation to talk about the past was exactly what she needed.

Strangely, two hours ago, Alexis had been battling a crush on

Darcy and would have never forgiven Paula for moving in on this catch. Her feelings had changed in such a short time that she didn't really know what to think. All she knew was that Darcy and Paula would end up falling in love, unbelievable as this would have been until she'd seen them together. And she wouldn't deny that she was sorry to take a back seat to these two. Darcy was a very attractive woman, but the more she knew of her, Alexis realized she wasn't her type. The safe, almost motherly appeal, the air of conservatism and the gentle personality that Darcy seemed to possess were endearing. Yet, Alexis knew these qualities fit Paula's desires more than hers.

After a while, Paula suggested they play a game of cards. They settled on Hearts and played a few hands, slowly because Paula seemed to have forgotten half the rules, or more likely, wanted the excuse to talk to Darcy. She still wondered what had been inside Darcy's package and what news the note had carried. If it hadn't been for the damn puppy, now asleep in the middle of her bed, she might have never known about Darcy's lover. And now the question was, should she warn Paula?

They finished the bottle that Darcy had brought and were ready to open Paula's wine when the phone rang. Alexis excused herself from the table, happy to leave a discussion about the true point value of the jack of diamonds, and went for the phone in her bedroom.

"Hey. I hope I'm not calling too late."

It was Elana. God, she had a good phone voice. Deeper toned than most women with a slow, sexy pause at the end of her sentences. Elana could make a killing if she started a career in lesbian phone sex. She'd have tortured women on call waiting all over the country. And Alexis was quite pleased that Elana had called her back so soon. She sat down on the bed. "No, it's not too late. How are you?"

"I'm okay. I've been fighting the urge to call you all night. Finally broke down." She chuckled. "I'm feeling a little foolish about everything."

"Foolish? About last night?"

"A little," Elana admitted. "And . . ."

Alexis loved the silence. She could hear Elana's soft breathing. "And what?"

"And foolish about wanting to come see you again tonight."

She sighed. Elana was going to get her in trouble. She could feel it coming. "I can be at your place in a half hour."

"No. Remember, I'm staying with my parents." Elana paused again. "I don't know what I want from you, Lex."

"I rarely know exactly what I want. And then half the time I change my mind." Alexis thought of Paula and Darcy in the kitchen together. At one time, she'd had a crush on Paula about as bad as the crush she'd just gotten over with Darcy. And now she didn't want to be with either of them. "We'll just have a good time together and not worry about it, okay?"

"Can I sleep in your bed tonight?"

Shit, Paula is going to kill me for this one, Alexis thought. "I have to warn you, my alarm goes off before dawn."

"Can we push it back a little if I give you a ride into work?"

"A little." Alexis was impressed that Elana remembered she took the bus to work. She'd only mentioned it on their first walk together Saturday, just as an aside to a conversation about urban smog. She liked that Elana paid attention to details. Soon, Alexis hoped, she would pay Elana back with a little of her own attention to details.

"Good. I'll be there as soon as I can."

After hanging up the phone, she picked up the puppy and headed to the kitchen to face Paula and Darcy. Considering all of her options, she decided to just go with honesty. "Hey, Paula, I've got a little problem. About your sleeping here tonight, well—"

Paula raised her hand to interrupt. "Let me guess. That was a booty call?"

Alexis sighed. Paula made *subtle* impossible. "Well, not exactly. Well, yes."

Darcy laughed. "You're not serious?" She looked from Paula's face to Alexis's. "Wow, now I'm impressed. I've never had any friends that got booty calls at eleven at night."

"Maybe they just didn't admit it," Paula volunteered. "Or maybe you haven't had a friend like Alexis who's slept with half the lesbians in Portland."

"Ouch." Darcy laughed again. "That rang of a little jealousy."

"Not at all, it's just the truth." Paula smiled. She patted Alexis on the back and then added, "Although I don't condone my friend's behavior, Ms. Darcy, I will say she's got herself a damn good reputation."

"Well, cheers to a girl with a good reputation." Darcy laughed and held up her glass.

Paula winked at her and toasted Darcy's glass. It was obvious that they had both drunk more than a good amount of the wine. In fact, the second bottle was almost empty.

"Well," Paula stood. "I guess it's time to let my friend get to work."

Before Alexis could argue, already feeling like a heel for kicking Paula out, Darcy interjected with, "You know, I've got a sofa bed. And another bottle of wine."

Paula glanced at Darcy and arched her eyebrow. "Hmm, I like your offer. But I don't want to impose when we've only just met. I can take a cab home."

"No, please stay. I insist." Darcy stood up, staring directly at Paula. They were eye level and each would have been daunting, if they weren't both exactly the same height and made of the same Midwestern strength. "I'd like the company."

Alexis had to stop herself from laughing at their flirting tactics. She was a little too intimately aware of what a raised eyebrow from Paula meant and could already guess what Darcy intended with her sofa bed.

"Fine. Then it's settled," Alexis said. "I owe you both for this one." Even as she said this, she couldn't help but think that the debt was really on their side. After all, she'd brought two heart-heavy women together, and now the rest was up to them. Surely the sofa bed wouldn't get any use tonight.

After Darcy and Paula left, Alexis cleaned up her kitchen and then took the puppy back to Drew's place. Elana showed up only a few minutes later. She was wearing a dark blue baseball cap, a blue sweater and a pair of beige cargo pants. Alexis smiled when she saw her. It was obvious that she hadn't gotten dressed up. She'd probably come in the same clothes she was wearing at home, and that made every inch of her more attractive. She acted much more comfortable even just stepping into the apartment. She also had a backpack on her shoulder, suggesting that she still planned to spend the night.

"So you really don't mind that I'm here?" she asked first thing.

Alexis grabbed her hand and squeezed it. "I really like it, in fact."

Elana took off the baseball cap and combed her fingers through her hair. "I've been thinking a lot about you . . . wanted to bring you something." She set the bag on the ground and then fished through it. "Here."

Alexis took a large manila envelope and opened it. There was an eight-by-ten photograph inside. She pulled it out and stared at the picture of herself. She was standing next to the pottery wheel, her hand filled with wet clay and her skin splattered with mud. The detail was amazing. "Well, I think you could have picked a better subject, but I have to admit, this is a beautiful print."

"I don't know what you're talking about. I picked the perfect subject." She smiled. "In fact, I've always had a good sense of knowing who belongs in a scene. And this one had to have you." She traced the curve of muscles on Alexis's arm. "I had some time to appreciate your arms while I was playing with the technique on this print. I must admit I like how much you work out."

"I lift a lot of boxes." Alexis stepped toward Elana. She was tired of talking and wanted to do something else with her lips. "So what's off limits tonight, Ms. Kingston?"

"Off limits?"

126

"I just want to know what you're comfortable with." Alexis paused. "You know, what your limits are." She leaned close to kiss her, pressing gently at first and then opening her mouth to invite Elana to slip in her tongue. And Elana took the cue. When she pulled away, Elana's eyes were closed. After a moment, she was staring at Alexis.

"You could corrupt me." Elana shook her head. "I usually wouldn't dream of having sex with someone before dating at least a month. I don't even know your last name or your birthday."

"Getty. March second. And you'll want my Social Security number as well, right?"

"Oh, that's a good idea." Elana laughed when Alexis started to recite it. She held her hand up to Alexis's lips to stop her. "Relax, I was kidding. I'm really not a freak. I'm just used to being more cautious. Dating men is different, you know."

"I can imagine." Alexis couldn't remember ever waiting as long as a month to have sex with someone she was dating. But she'd only slept with women. "But I don't want to push too fast. Just kissing tonight?"

"Try a few other things, and I'll let you know when to slow down."

Alexis pulled off her own T-shirt and then took Elana's sweater and bra off. She couldn't wait to feel Elana's skin on hers. She kissed each of Elana's nipples while cupping her breasts, loving the weight in her overfilled hands. Elana's lips met her again and again, with murmurs of contentment in return. Alexis led her to the bedroom and pulled down the comforter. She slipped a CD in the stereo and skipped to her favorite track, a melodious guitar and piano duet, no words. Elana went over to the window as the music started. The sky had cleared after the earlier rain, and a nearly full moon shone its light through the window, outlining every curve of Elana's body.

Alexis moved behind Elana. She caressed the line of her shoulders and then moved down her back, pausing at the waistline of her jeans and massaging her lower back. Elana turned to face her and they kissed again. Alexis had to admit that in spite of her professed lack of experience with women, Elana was a great kisser. She knew exactly when to add a little extra pressure and when to pull back her tongue. Alexis took off her own pants and then started unbuttoning Elana's. She moved slowly, expecting to be stopped after each button was unfastened, yet Elana kept her hands on Alexis's shoulders and kissed her intermittently. They swayed ever so slowly with the drifting tones of the guitar, dancing as though they were drugged.

Once she had them both naked, Alexis pulled Elana toward the bed. Elana resisted, glancing back at the window. "You want to keep dancing?"

"Maybe." Elana's skin prickled with goose bumps. "Can we just keep dancing under the covers?"

"I've heard that euphemism for a lot of things that we could do." Even in the dim light, Alexis could tell that she'd made Elana blush. She added, "We'll take it slow."

Elana finally nodded and went to the bed. They stretched out on the sheets and then pulled the comforter up around them. "Can I get on top?"

Alexis grinned. Elana seemed so sexual and yet, her inexperience was obvious. "Anything you want tonight." Alexis shifted under Elana's body. She lifted her hips, guiding Elana's leg between hers and then showing her where she wanted a knee placed. Elana caught on quickly and moaned with pleasure as her middle slid over Alexis's pubic hair. Alexis slid lower in the bed and started nuzzling Elana's breasts. She had one nipple between her fingers and the other between her lips, alternating between gentle bites and sucking. Elana continued to grind on her body, with her wetness coating Alexis's thighs and her skin glistening with sweat. Alexis moved her legs between Elana's and then shifted lower toward the foot of the bed. She made a line of kisses from Elana's breasts, down to her belly and past the line of pubic hair. Her face was now between Elana's legs, and she lifted her chin to fill her mouth with Elana's warmth.

Elana gasped and arched her back, pulling her groin away from Alexis's mouth. She stared down at Alexis. "What are you doing down there?"

"Testing your limits. Did we reach them?"

Elana didn't answer. She let her back relax and her middle came close to Alexis's face. She reached down to wipe Alexis's lips. "Go slow. I want to feel everything you're going to do to me."

Alexis had no problem with that request. She shifted back into position, her head between Elana's knees, and reached her arms behind Elana. She needed to have her hands on Elana's butt so she could direct the grinding movements when she went down under. After a few kisses on Elana's thighs, she nuzzled Elana's hair and slipped her tongue between her legs. Elana immediately started pushing into Alexis's mouth with forward thrusts. Her clit was swollen already, and Alexis circled it with tongue licks and then sucked on it, just as she had the nipples. Elana moaned when Alexis caught her clit. From the clit to the wet hole beneath it, Alexis made certain her tongue reached every spot. She found a few points that made Elana's moans gain in volume and lingered there a little longer. Elana's forward thrusting action increased in speed, and Alexis had to direct her pelvis back down toward her mouth more than once.

Slowing Elana down was next to impossible. Alexis tried for a good grasp on the point that Elana seemed to like the most, but she was moving too much. Finally, Elana pressed herself down on Alexis's tongue once and then stretched back, squeezing her legs tight and groaning. Her muscles trembled, and she sat down on Alexis's chest, shaking. She pushed her hips forward, begging for Alexis to touch her again. Now. Come was smeared on Alexis's chin and cheeks. Just as she drove her tongue over Elana's swollen clit, she heard Elana cry out and felt her muscles tremor with the rush of an orgasm.

After a moment, Elana collapsed on Alexis. Her body filled with firing nerves only seconds before, relaxed completely now. Covered in sweat and come, she smelled exactly the way Alexis wanted. With a sigh, she shifted her legs and rolled off Alexis. "God, that felt good." She laughed softly.

Climbing on top of her, Alexis said, "You know, you'll give a girl a complex if you laugh after sex." She caressed Elana's face, loving the feel of the slow rise and fall of her breaths in her spent body.

"I was just thinking . . . I always knew I'd like it better on top, but I never had the guts to try it. Damn, was I missing out."

"You just needed the right partner, honey." Alexis winked. She liked the fact that Elana wasn't shy about her orgasms.

"So since I don't know all the rules here, I have to ask, do I get a chance to have my way with you now?" Elana asked, combing her hands through Alexis's hair.

"Yep, that's the way it works." Alexis kissed her neck, then her ear and finally her lips. She stared at Elana, who no longer seemed shy at all. "Whenever you're ready."

Chapter 8

Alexis heard the alarm go off, but it was only a few hours after she'd fallen asleep, so she turned it off, not thinking very clearly, and went right back to sleep. Elana was the one to wake them both, shaking Alexis's shoulder and asking, "When do you have to be at work? Can you call in sick?"

"What time is it?" Alexis sat upright and eyed the clock. Five after eight. "Shit! An hour ago, and no, I used up all my sick days playing hooky for a—"

"Hot date?"

Alexis stifled a yawn, already dressing. "You did know my reputation, right?"

Elana sighed. "Yeah, I knew what I was getting myself into. What about your underwear?"

Alexis had her work slacks on and was finding her socks when the lack of underwear was pointed out to her. "You know, I'm out of clean underwear. And I need a bath, but I'm already late."

Elana whistled. "Now that's something I didn't need to know. It's been nice, but, uh, I think I better go."

"At least this will stop me from flirting with the women on my route." Alexis grabbed her and kissed her lips. Elana pushed her away playfully. "So when's our next date?"

"When are you doing laundry?" Elana shot back.

"Tonight?"

"Can't. How about Saturday?"

Saturday was two days away. Too long to wait, Alexis thought. But she didn't want to push things. Last night had gone well, and she knew Elana would be wanting another date as much as she was. "Saturday is perfect. Maybe we can go dancing first. You know, a little warm-up exercise."

"Warm-up?" Elana shook her head. "We'll see. By Saturday I may have come to my senses about dating such a player."

"Player? Me?"

"Don't even try to deny it, 'cause whatever you're thinking, I'm not buying your excuse." Elana shook her head when Alexis started to argue against the title. "Besides, I kind of like that you're a player. I know you won't get serious on me."

Ace didn't notice what time Alexis finally clocked in, though Ron did, and he grilled her for the tardiness. She couldn't believe how busy the morning delivery schedule was and thanked Ron sarcastically. Not only was she going to have to skip her morning coffee, a lunch break was out of the question. As soon as she left Ron at the dispatch desk, she noticed the second delivery on her list was for Anderson Computers. After her evening with Bonnie, she'd asked Anderson Computers to be removed from her route, but apparently her request hadn't made its way off Ace's desk. She was uncomfortable about another meeting with Bonnie but decided it'd be best to get it over early.

Bonnie didn't get up from her desk when Alexis entered. She was on the phone and seemed a little harried by the caller. Alexis pointed at three boxes positioned on her dolly and then at the back hallway where she usually left deliveries. Bonnie nodded at her and then said into the phone, "Well, yes, sir. Of course we want you to be satisfied with our service." She paused, took the phone away from her ear and covered the mouthpiece. "Can you wait a minute? I've got a package to send out."

Alexis nodded. She rolled the dolly past Bonnie's desk, hearing fragments of the irate caller's complaint about a malfunctioning hard drive, and unloaded the boxes. She handed the clipboard to Bonnie, pointing to the line for her signature.

Bonnie was still in the thick of it with the caller. She scratched out her signature and then said into the phone, "And we here at Anderson Computers understand that completely, sir . . . Yes, sir. I will tell them . . . Yes, in fact, I'm typing up the memo right now. Thank you, sir, and have a nice day." She slammed the phone down and shook her head. "I hate guys like that."

"Rough morning?" Alexis asked.

"Yeah, you could say that. Sometimes I don't feel like picking up the phone at all. And I've considered swearing back at some of those SOB's who get off screaming at me." She laughed sourly. "Unfortunately, that's a bad trait for a receptionist. Hold on and I'll grab that other package for you." Bonnie disappeared down the back hall. She came back carrying a small box. "Here it is."

"Do you need a shipping label? Where's it being sent?" She had her clipboard out and had flipped to the page for outgoing shipments.

"It doesn't need a label," Bonnie said softly. She had a smirk on her face and was spinning a pen in her hand.

Alexis eyed her, full of suspicion. "Do I want to ask what's inside?"

"I think you could guess. Or you could open the box now and we could have a little fun. I could use something to improve my morning."

"You know, I'm running really behind schedule." Alexis didn't want to guess, and she definitely didn't want to open the box. She figured it was some sort of sex toy. Maybe handcuffs or some leather item, judging by the light weight, but since it was from Bonnie, she wouldn't assume anything. "My boss will be on my ass if I don't have every name on this list signed off in three hours."

"Well then, you'll have to open it later. Alone." Bonnie clicked her pen and reached out to grab Alexis's belt. Her hand slid down from the buckle, along the zipper of Alexis's pants and then pressed up between her legs. She moaned softly. "Oh, the things I'd like to do with you . . ." The phone rang just as her voice drifted. "Another time, I guess." She answered the line and Alexis made a quick exit.

Despite the busy schedule and the uncomfortable delivery at Anderson's, she had plenty of time during the rest of her morning route to reflect on the past night. She wondered how Paula and Darcy had spent their night, guessing they hadn't slept in separate rooms. Although she was still certain that Paula and Darcy would make a good couple, it was hard to ignore her own pangs of jealousy. Paula would doubtlessly call her, and she'd be eager to share too many details, being the kiss-and-tell type. Paula had a tendency to make a relationship serious very quickly. Since Darcy seemed such a good match, it was possible that they'd be exchanging rings before long, and the thought of that made Alexis cringe. She wasn't ready to lose her best friend, and part of her hoped that Darcy wasn't as great as she seemed.

The other thought that plagued Alexis had to do with her conversation that morning with Elana. She hated the term "player," at least when it was applied to her. And while she admitted that she dated plenty of women, a player was often used to describe someone dishonest with her lovers and who used women to fulfill personal interests.

Her cell phone rang just as she'd backed the truck out of the DC to start her afternoon deliveries. She glanced at the screen as Paula's number flashed. She'd expected to hear from Paula first thing in the morning with an update on her night. "Hey, Paula, what took you so long to call?"

"I was sleeping in. Caught a cold." She faked a couple coughs and then laughed. "Damn, what a night."

"That good?"

"Darcy had me in bed five minutes after we left your place. That woman knows her way around, if you know what I mean."

"Okay, I don't need details. It's too soon after lunch." Alexis wondered if Paula let Darcy do much more than lay back and groan while she went to work pleasuring her. Of course, Paula's own boundaries might be different with another lover. But stone butch seemed to be part of her DNA.

"Hey, you're the one who kicked me out last night," Paula defended. "And why are you in a bad mood? I thought you had a *friend* over last night yourself. Didn't that work out in your favor?"

She didn't want to answer the second question. "I'm not in a bad mood. Look, I'm happy you and Darcy had a good time. Is there a second date on the horizon?"

"Well, we're having a real first date tonight. We decided that we had more than a hormonal interest in each other. I know it's too soon, but I really think this one might work out, you know?"

"I hope so." She kept to herself her reservations about sharing Paula with Darcy. "You deserve someone like Darcy."

"Thanks, Lex." She sighed the way someone does when she's too happy to be thinking clearly. "So are you gonna tell me what happened at your place last night?"

"Paula, would you call me a player?"

"Absolutely."

Alexis was a little miffed by the quickness of Paula's reply. "You know what? Forget it. I gotta go."

"Whoa, look who's in a pissy mood. Watch out!"

"I'm not pissy. Look, I gotta go. This traffic is hell." Alexis swerved to miss a car that had pulled out unexpectedly in front of her. "I hate bad drivers."

"You're the one who's talking on the cell phone while driving,"

Paula chided. "So what happened? Didn't your *friend* give you any loving last night? Did she find out you were a player and head for the hills?"

"Paula, hold on for a second." Alexis had noticed a patrol car coming up on her left, and she quickly dropped the phone on the bench seat. No reason to attract a cop's attention, she thought. The patrol car turned at the next intersection, and Alexis grabbed the phone. "Sorry about that. I'd be in hot water if I got a ticket while talking on the phone."

"Lex, call me back later. I'd kill you if you got in an accident talking to me on your damn cell. And about the player thing . . . I really wouldn't worry. It's not like you're looking for a serious relationship. As long as you're getting what you want and satisfied the morning after, then who gives a damn?"

"Yeah, I guess." Alexis sighed. "I don't even know why I'm letting it bother me." Maybe she wasn't satisfied with every morning after, but overall, she was happy. And though she'd often hoped that one of her relationships would last, she couldn't imagine herself with just one lover.

After Paula hung up, Alexis tossed the phone in the glove box and concentrated on the road. The first drop off on the afternoon list was on 14th Street, but the main thoroughfare was choked with traffic. She'd been listening to the radio, and her favorite afternoon DJ, Mel, hadn't mentioned anything about the traffic. Sometimes she wondered if the radio DJs didn't just plug in a few CDs and leave for the afternoon. When Mel's sexy voice did come on to give the introduction to a commercial break, Alexis considered calling the station to find out if the reason for the bad traffic had been reported. She loved the music that Mel played, as well as the innuendos to being a dyke that she dropped, but the station's traffic detail was lacking.

Finally, blaring sirens declared the reason for the traffic. Alexis craned her neck out the window to get a look at the lanes ahead. A fire truck and an ambulance were making their way to the scene of a multiple car pileup. As the parking lot of cars slowly inched forward, Alexis knew it'd be faster to circle around half the town than to wait for the road to clear. She glanced at the delivery list to see if she could change her route and make the deliveries on this side of town later.

Blue's Cafe was listed near the bottom of her sheet. She hadn't made any deliveries there before and guessed that the cafe must have been part of Moss's route. With the traffic at a near standstill and her stomach growling, Alexis radioed in to DC to let Ron know about the schedule change. For once, he had no problem with the plan. Apparently, the multiple-car collision ahead of her was only one of three accidents that had simultaneously shut down the city. Ron was pulling out his hair trying to reroute a half dozen trucks, and he was happy to let Alexis change her own schedule this time.

Alexis found the package for Blue's Cafe, a five-pound box with a return label from a chocolate company, and then checked her reflection in the rearview mirror. Her hair needed a comb and her uniform was a little disheveled, but with a little smoothing down she looked fairly presentable. She had no idea if Sandy was working today, but Alexis was certainly hoping to see her.

"How's it going, Lex? You're running a little late for lunch. Or maybe you came for a reason other than eating?" Gillian, the waitress, asked the question as if she were in on a secret.

"Well, I was hoping to get a quick bite and some coffee, but I really came because of this." She handed the box to Gillian.

"Work comes before play?"

Alexis ignored her innuendos. "Can you sign for this?" After months of eating here, Alexis knew that Gillian and Sandy were good friends, but she wondered how many others on the staff also knew about her and Sandy. There wasn't much to know anyway. They'd only gone out once, and Sandy hadn't called or returned her message. Alexis grudgingly admitted she was a little surprised that she hadn't heard back from her. Of all her dates that week, she'd been most interested in having a second date with Sandy. For some reason, it just felt natural to walk with her, natural to dream about her, perfect to kiss her. So it only figured that Sandy wasn't as interested in her.

Gillian took a look at the package label, then shook her head and handed it back to Alexis. "You know, I better let you take this back to the kitchen. I know Sandy is gonna want to see this. Might as well let you get some credit as the messenger." She pointed to the back double doors as if Alexis didn't know by now where the kitchen was, and then smirked, adding, "And I know she'll be happy to see you. Go on." The phone at the front desk rang, and Gillian waved Alexis toward the kitchen, mumbling, "I need to get back to work anyhow."

With the package under her arm, Alexis pushed through the doors to the kitchen and glanced around the place, fighting a sudden bout of butterflies. Vegetables were sizzling on a skillet, and the smell of garlic permeated the air. She recognized Juan, one of the line chefs, and gave him a nod. He was busy trimming chicken breasts and raised his knife in salute before scooping up the pink flesh and tossing it on the grill. Just relax, she coaxed, and pretend you're just working. "Is Sandy around? I've got a delivery for her."

"In the back," Juan replied, pointing to the exit door at the back of the kitchen. "She's on her break."

Alexis followed Juan's directions outside and spotted Sandy sitting on a picnic table behind the building. There was a small grass area and a big sycamore tree that was fast dropping all of its leaves. The picnic table and most of the grass were covered in a clutter of crinkled brown. Sandy glanced up from a paperback as soon as the door closed behind Alexis. "Um, I've got a delivery for you. Gillian told me to find you in the kitchen, then Juan sent me out here. I'm sorry to interrupt your break."

"Don't be." Sandy set the book down, dog-earing the page where she'd stopped, and then turned to face Alexis. "A package, huh? Who's it from?"

"A chocolate company." Alexis handed the box to Sandy, noting the smile that spread over Sandy's face.

"I've been waiting to hear back about a couple recipes I'd sent in to this company. They make this amazingly smooth baker's chocolate. My mom's the one that sent me the information about this contest for new chocolate desserts." She tried pulling open the lid and then accepted the pocketknife Alexis handed her. From out of the mess of Styrofoam packing pellets, Sandy pulled a shiny new cookbook emblazoned with the title *Chocolate Passion and 100 other Desserts for Lovers to Share.*

"You have a recipe in this book?" Beneath the title was a photo image of a row of chocolate dipped strawberries, a vat full of chocolate syrup and a scantily clothed model licking chocolate off her fingertip. "Does your mom know what sort of book this is?" Alexis teased.

"It's not like this is a smut book." She flipped to the first page and swept her finger over the list of contributing chefs. As soon as she reached the name Sandy Webster, she slapped Alexis on the shoulder and nearly shrieked with excitement. "Right there. Look, there it is!"

Alexis congratulated her, and Sandy quickly found the index and the two recipes of hers that had won a spot in the book. One of the recipes was a complicated blackberry chocolate tart, while the other was a fairly simple rocky road-style cookie with chocolate chunks and almonds. "I can't believe you can make something look that good and still be vegan. God, that would be good crumbled over some ice cream," Alexis said, pointing to the pictured cookie.

"Soy ice cream, of course." Sandy smiled. "Or it's perfect alone, fresh and moist and just out of my oven." Sandy leaned over and kissed Alexis on the cheek. "Thank you for the delivery. You've made my day."

Alexis had plenty of experience with excited people, especially when she delivered birthday or holiday presents. But this reaction from Sandy was better than any she'd had in a long time. "So how is it that I've been eating at Blue's for months now and never had a bite of any chocolate? Not even a brownie. And by the way, I need a signature for that." She handed her clipboard to Sandy and pointed to the X-marked line. "Not that I'm upset, but I do think you've been holding out."

Sandy blushed and averted her eyes from Alexis. After signing the delivery form, she set down the clipboard. "I got your message, by the way."

"And you were waiting for a good time to call me back? Your phone wasn't working?" Alexis joked, realizing by Sandy's note of hesitation that this wasn't the real reason she hadn't called. She knew by the fact that Sandy wouldn't look up at her that she'd been avoiding her all week.

"I wasn't going to call you back."

"Ouch." Alexis sighed. She hadn't been expecting such a sharp answer. "Well, those are the breaks. For the record, I had a good time with you on Sunday. Sorry the feeling wasn't mutual." She picked up the clipboard and stood up. "Congrats on the recipe book. I'll look for it in a bookstore someday when I finally find a lover I want to bake for." She laughed, trying not to let on how much Sandy's honesty had stung.

Sandy was at her side before she reached the door. "Wait, I wasn't finished."

Alexis tried to ignore the grumbling, "Oh, here we go again" in her head and stared silently at Sandy. Sandy's eyes, amber brown and clear, were locked on hers.

"Look, I'll be honest," Sandy started, "Gillian told me a little about you, and I wasn't sure I wanted to get involved. I usually only date women if there's an interest for, you know, something longer than a one-nighter."

"I don't even know Gillian. What does she know about me?" Alexis wondered aloud. She hadn't seen Gillian at Decker's and would have guessed that Gillian was straight. How would this waitress know rumors about her? And what rumors did she know?

"Gillian has a lot of friends. And more than one of them have slept with you."

"Damn." Alexis shook her head. "You know, people say things about exes that aren't always true." She paused, unable to meet

140

Sandy's eyes now. She was pissed and struggled to keep her voice even. "Well, like I said, I had a good time on Sunday. And I'm sorry about my reputation. See ya around." She pulled open the door and brushed past Sandy's hand. The last thing she wanted was to walk through the cafe and see Gillian again, but she had no choice. She wanted to run out of the cafe.

"Did you find Sandy?" Gillian asked.

"Yep. And you were right, she was happy to get the package." Alexis forced a smile and then continued to the front door.

"No time to have a bite?"

"Not today," Alexis replied. Nor ever again, she finished silently.

By the time Alexis had reached her truck, kicked the back tire and jumped into the front seat, her anger had started to evaporate. She never stayed mad for long. Her frustration with Sandy was quickly replaced with an intense loneliness, which she hated more than the anger. She grabbed her cell phone out of the glove box and punched in her mom's number. Before the first ring, she saw Sandy coming up to the truck. Her mom could wait, she decided, ending the call.

"Can I get in?" Sandy asked.

Alexis sighed. She really wasn't ready to talk yet. Sandy's eyes met hers, and she could see the moisture in the corners. She leaned over to unlock the passenger door. Some of APO's newer trucks didn't even have a door on the passenger side and only had one seat for the driver. Alexis's truck was an older model with a bench seat big enough to sleep on, as she knew firsthand, and fully function-ing doors on both sides of the cab. "Sorry. I think I was a little harsh back there."

"I'm the one coming to apologize," Sandy said. She set a small paper bag on the dash. "Chocolate chunk peanut butter cookies. They're not warm, but I figured you'd at least get the idea. If you come by in the morning sometime, I'll have a warm one for you to try."

"I don't think I should come around anymore. But thanks for

the cookies." Alexis crossed her arms and stretched her foot out to tap the gas pedal, wishing she'd sped out of the parking lot when she'd had the chance. She wasn't in the mood to have a polite conversation and wanted Sandy out of her truck. Sandy extended her hand across the bench toward Alexis. "We're shaking hands now?"

"I'm saying good-bye," Sandy answered. "You obviously want me to get the hell out of your life, and I don't blame you. Not at all."

"You were the one who already decided not to call me again." Alexis knew she shouldn't argue with Sandy. She was still angry, and more than she should be about a little poke at her being a player. If Sandy really didn't want to hang around because of a stupid rumor, then it would be better to let her go. And if she was a player after all, losing Sandy wouldn't hurt her. Bonnie or Tina certainly wouldn't mind if she called them, and things with Elana were starting to heat up. She didn't need to juggle another ball. And yet, Sandy was the one on her mind all the time. "Look, I don't want you to get out of my life. We still barely know each other." She paused, taking Sandy's hand in hers. "Why don't you give me a chance? Forget about everything you heard about me and make your own judgment. I'd do the same for you, except I haven't heard any bad rumors."

"I've been good at staying out of the Portland lesbian circuit. Keeps the rumor mill quiet." Sandy kissed Alexis's hand. "So does this mean you aren't seeing anyone else?"

"I've been out on a few dates lately, but nothing serious."

"Are your relationships ever serious?" Sandy's criticism was mitigated by an understanding smile as soon as Alexis shrugged.

"I keep trying."

Sandy laughed. She shifted across the bench and kissed Alexis on the cheek. "Then why don't we try just getting to know each other. I need more friends anyway."

"Just friends?" Alexis clarified. "I'm okay with that, but I want to know the rules so I don't get kicked out of the game."

"Just friends. I don't casually date and you don't seriously date, so I think this is what we're left with."

"Kind of a shame, you know? We've been flirting for months, we finally go out and find that we like each other for more than our looks, and then we're calling the whole thing off because . . ." Alexis didn't finish her sentence. She really had never had much luck being friends with a woman she was attracted to and doubted it would work out well with Sandy.

"Because we might make good friends," Sandy said, finishing Alexis's sentence. "You're upset?"

"I've had a long day and it's not over yet. And I'm hungry. Fortunately, I have cookies." Alexis smiled weakly. She needed a real meal, but cookies would have to do for now. Her deliveries were going to be late. "I hate to admit this, but I'm way behind schedule. I gotta go."

Sandy reached for the door handle, then paused, "Would you stop by my place tonight? I'd love to talk with you more." She picked up Alexis's clipboard and wrote her number on the bottom of the delivery list. "On Thursdays I'm off at eight. Give me a call."

Fortunately, the cookies were filling. Alexis stopped by a mini-mart and bought a little carton of milk and spent the rest of the afternoon nibbling on cookies and milk between the deliveries. Her delivery on 14th Street wasn't made until well after five. The place was a Chinese restaurant, and when she ordered a carton of the chef's veggie special and two egg rolls to go, the manager didn't seem to mind her lateness. He added a few extra fortune cookies to her takeout bag and made her promise to come back for a full dinner.

Alexis met up with Darcy on the bus ride home. She offered her a fork, and they munched on the Chinese food together. It seemed strange to feel so familiar with Darcy. All of the edginess of Alexis's crush had vanished, and now she was excited by the opportunity to really get to know her neighbor. Darcy shared a few stories about her day at work, including grading midterm exams, the thought of which made Alexis flinch. It seemed like a long time since she'd been in school, but exams still made her sweat. Darcy's car was in the shop for a tune-up. She was going to pick it up tomorrow morning and mentioned that she'd be taking a cab instead of the bus. Alexis was distracted from their conversation, thinking that she'd rather be talking about other things. Specifically, did Darcy really like Paula and what had happened last night. Unfortunately, these topics were still a little too personal. By the time the bus reached Westside Apartments, they'd finished the veggie special and were cracking open fortune cookies.

"Shit, I hate fortunes like this," Darcy complained.

"What's it say?"

"Patience makes sand out of mountains."

"That doesn't sound that bad. Mine says, 'Don't waste time counting egg rolls. Someone else might eat them.' How'd they know?"

"I don't believe you." Darcy took the slip of paper from Alexis. "Let's see what it really says. 'Don't waste time counting your money while someone else earns more.' Well, at least it's easy to understand. But I think I like the fortune you made up better. Maybe this means you should consider a career change."

"You think I could make rent if I took a job making up fortunes for a cookie company?" Alexis grinned. She thought of Sandy's peanut butter cookies and considered calling her. It was late and she'd had a long day, but she didn't want to wait another day to see Sandy. First thing on the list tonight was a long bath. She reached into her pocket for her keys and felt the corner of paper she'd ripped off the delivery sheet. Sandy's number. She'd call first and then take a quick bath.

Alexis and Darcy headed into the mailroom as soon as they entered the building. As usual, Alexis had an empty mailbox and Darcy had a pile of junk mail. They both complained about their mail woes and parted in good spirits. Alexis figured Darcy would be calling Paula soon. She'd made some reference to a date with Paula that night. Apparently, they weren't wasting any time getting to know each other.

Sandy answered the line after the first ring. "I was hoping it'd be you. Otherwise, I was ready to lie to some phone solicitor and tell them that there's no Sandra Webster living here."

"Wait a minute. Did you say that you were going to lie? 'Cause I need to know what I'm getting into before our second date," Alexis teased. "I don't date liars, you know. They're just as bad as players, really."

"Shut up, Lex. And we're not going on a second date. Friends don't go out on dates."

"Yeah, I know. We're just hanging out together. So I was thinking of inviting *my new friend Sandy* to Decker's to shoot some pool. Would I be completely out of line if I did that?"

"No. Not completely." Sandy paused. "Give me an hour and I'll meet you there. But as fair warning, I'm a pool shark."

Chapter 9

Alexis woke on Friday morning feeling rested for the first time all week. She was dressed and out the door well ahead of schedule, though she was dreading the weekly work meeting. Ace always announced the new Employee of the Month at the weekly meeting, and she wasn't looking forward to the coddling the other drivers would give her for winning the honor. She jogged to the cafe at the corner of her block and ordered a coffee, then waited at the bus stop with the steaming cup cradled in her hands. The weather was getting colder, and the feel of winter had already set in. The bus pulled up on time and Alexis found a seat toward the back, remembering that Darcy was taking a cab this morning, or more likely Paula would be giving her a ride.

It was surprisingly easy to let go of her crush on Darcy. Paula and Darcy seemed like such a good couple, and her own thoughts were filled with Sandy now. Their evening had gone surprisingly well. Sandy wasn't joking about her pool skills. She'd soundly defeated Alexis in four out of four games. They left Decker's just after ten, still on good terms. Despite Alexis's attraction to Sandy, confining their relationship to a friendship seemed more like a possibility after their "friendly" night together. They hadn't even held hands. In fact, the only time she could remember touching Sandy was an initial awkward hug in the doorway of Decker's and a couple exchanges of the cue ball during the game. Sandy had even suggested another "non date" for Friday. She'd invited Alexis over to her house for dinner and a movie. This sounded dangerously like a date, but Alexis didn't argue. Aside from another pottery project, she had nothing else planned anyway. Paula would be tied up with Darcy, and her next date with Elana wasn't until Saturday night.

What was more, it had felt very normal not to exchange a goodnight kiss with Sandy. They waved good-bye and headed home separately. Sandy offered to give Alexis a ride, but she declined. After their fight that afternoon, she wanted to keep some distance between them. She liked the independence she felt in turning Sandy's offer down, though it was only a small personal victory. She had convinced herself that she could block her emotions toward this woman and felt a small swell of pride saying, "Thanks for the offer, Sandy, but I'd rather walk tonight." Fortunately, the sky had cleared after an earlier rain, and the crisp air and nearly full moon made her decision a pleasant one.

Ace was in rare form for the morning meeting. He bustled in five minutes late, spent one minute thanking the loading staff for cleaning out their locker area and gave a special thanks to everyone for keeping an eye on the coffee machine. Then, without further ado, he launched into the "You all ought to be fired" part of the meeting. He started with a list of drivers who had an unusually high number of missed or late deliveries, then chastised everyone for yesterday's bungled schedule, and failed to mention that it might have been at least partly related to the four separate car accidents that had shut down the city. Ace also singled out drivers who had chronically late deliveries. If more than twenty percent of orders were delayed, the driver's name ended up on a printout on Ace's desk. This week, over half of the drivers were on the late list, and Alexis breathed a sigh of relief when Ace passed over her name. Finally, Ace went on to remind everyone that, "APO means Air Post *On-time*. I expect higher standards from everyone since we are just beginning the busiest quarter of the year. And to all of you who asked, no, there will be no holiday requests granted for the week of Thanksgiving."

Randy, one of the more ballsy drivers and a forty-something, king of the hill type, whispered too loudly, "Shit, I thought APO stood for Ass Pickin' Organization. Damn, I better leave right now."

His comment was followed by a low grumble of laughter from the guys around him. Alexis only shook her head, wondering when, or if, the men would grow out of their potty humor. Fuming, Ace continued in his ranting about missed deliveries, and then to catch everyone's attention, added that Christmas bonuses would only be distributed to those drivers who met APO's competence standards. He closed with a wave to Ron, who was giving out the morning delivery routes.

While Ron was doling out the delivery lists, Ace pulled Alexis aside. "I just wanted you to know that we're getting a new driver. She's a transfer from Seattle, but I don't know how long she's been a driver up there. Anyway, since she's female, I figured it'd be best if she does her ride along with another woman."

And being the only female driver, I get the new kid, Alexis concluded. "Sure, Ace, I don't mind."

"I didn't think you would. She starts Monday. You can show her the ropes during her training period, and then she'll take over Mossinni's old route. This transfer is a lucky one. We're going to be busy over the next couple months. Thanks, Lex."

Yeah, *the drivers* will be busy, Alexis thought. She nodded and repeated, "Sure, Ace."

Ace started to walk away and then called over his shoulder, "Oh, by the way, we need the delivery info for that last package of

Mossinni's that you delivered to Westside. Drop by my office later."

Ron called her name and Alexis went up to the dispatch desk to get her schedule, ignoring the jabs from the other guys about being the boss's pet. As she scanned her delivery list, Randy had the gall to say, "You can come by my office later and I'll give you a little info as well, sweetie."

"Info on what, Randy?" she shot back. "Ass picking?" Normally she rolled with the comments, doing her best to not stand out since she'd become the only female driver, but Randy was pushing her buttons this morning.

The other guys near them laughed, and someone slapped her shoulder, adding a comforting, "Give him hell, Lex."

Randy held up his hands in mock defense. "All right, I know how to back down when a little PMS comes between me and a girl."

Alexis fought the urge to slug Randy. She unclenched her jaws and calmly replied, "PMS? Is that your problem, Randy? Well, I've got something that will help when your cramps start." She walked away still pissed at Randy, but grinning. The other guys were nearly spilling their coffee with their chuckling, and Randy finally didn't have anything to add.

The morning route was busy, but she finished in time to have lunch. For the first Friday in the past few months, she didn't go to Blue's. Instead, she picked up a salad from the nearby supermarket's salad bar, adding extra croutons and extra mushrooms. She dropped in at Ace's office while he was at lunch, and gave his secretary the information for Darcy's package. Happy to have cleaned her hands of Moss's leftovers, she headed down to Ron's desk and picked up her afternoon schedule, which was surprisingly light.

The first afternoon stop was a radio station. Alexis had been there several times, though she'd never met anyone famous. Usually, she just dealt with the receptionist, a very handsome gay man with jet-black hair, light brown skin and stunningly long eye-lashes. His name was Amir and his hands were as soft as his voice, and both so seductive that Alexis questioned her own sexual tendencies after their first meeting. What did it mean if a card-carrying lesbian was attracted to a femme gay boy? She had decided not to try to psychoanalyze it and just looked forward to deliveries for the station.

Unfortunately, Amir wasn't at the front desk. His chair was empty, and someone had left a little sign stating that the station was closed for the next hour. Alexis didn't want to come back in an hour. She passed the front desk and walked down a hallway, calling out, "Anyone here? Hello?" She tried every closed door in the hopes of catching another employee who could sign for the delivery and was about to give up when she reached the last door on the floor. An On Air sign was posted on the door, with a handwritten message just below it that read, "Don't even think about knocking." So she tried the handle.

The place was smaller than Alexis had expected. A long desk lined the near wall with a pane of glass separating this space from what appeared to be a live performance studio. The desk was crowded with stereo equipment, phones, microphones and two computers. Wires lay everywhere like coupling snakes in a pattern that Alexis didn't even try to trace. On the opposite wall, CDs and promotional items were stacked, with a prominent poster of the Dixie Chicks and another of Jimi Hendrix. The station was serious about diversity, Alexis thought with a grin, remembering their well-advertised claims of "no repeats". There was room for four chairs, only one of which was occupied. The woman in the seat had her back to Alexis, and headphones hugged the side of her head. That's why she didn't look up when I pushed in the dolly, Alexis thought. She hasn't realized I'm here.

The woman pressed a few buttons on the soundboard and then started to speak into the microphone. Alexis listened to the station often while working, and as soon as the woman in the chair spoke into the microphone, she knew it was the afternoon disc jockey,

Mel Travis. Her voice was just as low and husky now as when she heard it crackling through the truck's speakers.

"And that was the last commercial you're going to hear for the next hour, so long as you keep your radio tuned to KREX. From here on out, we're playing listener's requests, and as always, you can call me with your pick. We're going back to the nineties for our first request with 10,000 Maniacs and 'These Are Days.' So, Andy, if you're still listening, here's the song you *just had to hear.*" After pressing a few keys on the soundboard, Mel took off her headphones and sat back in her chair. Her dark brown hair was cut similar to Paula's, but Mel's was a little longer on top and razor short in the back, revealing a beautiful slender neckline. Her ears were studded with both silver and gold in a way that gathered your attention to their perfect shape.

Alexis cleared her throat, announcing her presence. Mel spun her chair to face Alexis. She drew in a quick breath and Alexis immediately regretted startling her. Alexis thought to apologize but hesitated, bewildered by the look on Mel's face. To say the least, she was beautiful when stunned. She needed no makeup on her smooth skin, and the perfect curve of her lips was accentuated with a natural redness. Her petite size was exaggerated by the largeness of her chair, yet as soon as she stood, she seemed to fill the room. She locked her blue eyes on Alexis. "What the hell are *you* doing in here?"

"Sorry to barge in. The rest of the place is deserted, and I just needed to have someone sign for a delivery. It's marked urgent." Alexis pointed to the dolly that she'd wheeled into the room and the two boxes positioned on it. She could feel her cheeks warm with a blush and hoped that Mel wouldn't notice. Mel Travis was the reason that nearly all of the able-minded lesbians in Portland tuned in to KREX every afternoon. Her voice had seductive powers, and now Alexis had discovered Mel's good looks and sexy confidence really put her speaking talents in third place overall. She could feel a warmth between her legs and knew that as Mel continued to stare at her, she wouldn't be willing to walk out of this room without a phone number at least. Alexis forced herself to continue, "Again, I'm sorry about the interruption. I really shouldn't be here, I know. But since I am, do you mind?" She extended her clipboard toward Mel.

Mel smiled. "Shit, Lex, you really don't remember me, do you?"

Alexis shook her head, surprised by the question. She was sure she would have remembered sleeping with a disc jockey, especially someone as attractive as Mel Travis.

Mel laughed loudly. "Jeez. Well, forget about it. Sure, I can sign." She took the clipboard and pulled the pen off the clip on the side, then glanced up at Alexis, tapping the tip of the pen on the delivery list. "I just can't believe that you don't remember. Well, I sure as hell remember you, Lex Getty."

Alexis was at a loss. It was obvious by Mel's tone that she knew her more than just casually. Mel's hand swept over the form on the X-marked line. "Give me a hint?"

"Music."

Alexis stared at Mel's hand. Her fingers, long and slender with perfectly trimmed nails, tapped the clipboard. Music? Had they met at a concert? She couldn't recall ever meeting anyone like Mel Travis. Maybe they had taken a music class together in college. Alexis had taken a few seminars in music appreciation, and it was possible that Mel was in one of her classes. "Do you play an instrument?"

"Yes, the piano. Why?" She laughed. "You're racking your brain now, aren't you?"

She sighed, thinking that she was not going to remember Mel and might as well give up trying. "It's just that . . . you have musician hands. I'm not surprised you play the piano." Alexis felt a sudden rush of embarrassment, knowing that her comment sounded like she was flirting.

"Thank you for that." She eyed her own hands, stretching her fingers out. "I've been playing since I was a kid, but I'm not very good. And I always thought my hands should belong to someone with more talent." Mel seemed to take Alexis's compliment in stride, apparently ignoring any innuendo she might have noticed. She continued, "I was just thinking how nicely you've grown into your body. You're even more of a *hottie* than I remember. But unlike you, I can't politely ask about the features I appreciate."

So she hadn't ignored the innuendo, Alexis thought, pleased. "I don't mind if we skip politeness."

"And where are you suggesting that we should skip to?" Mel returned. She handed the clipboard back to Alexis. When Alexis reached out for it, Mel touched her arm. Her fingers traced the curves of Alexis's upper arm. "Christ, Lex, you must get whistles from your customers every time you lift a box. So who's the lucky girl that married you?"

"Still single." Alexis was growing more uncomfortable not remembering a prior meeting with Mel Travis. How did they know each other? And what had they done together?

"You're still trying to place me, aren't you?"

"I really could use another clue," Alexis admitted.

"I kind of like making you squirm." Mel leaned against the desk, carefully eyeing the On Air button. "Okay, how about this . . . You were a freshman at the time, and I was a senior with hair down to my waist and big glasses. We were listening to Bach."

"Oh, shit. Melinda Traverstein." Alexis felt like she'd just been blindsided. The image of a college dorm room and her music appreciation tutor suddenly flashed in her mind. Of course! Mel hadn't been in the music appreciation class, but that was definitely their bond. Alexis knew she would have never recognized her soft-spoken, and *self-identified straight*, tutor as the famous DJ. "God, you've changed!"

"A little. I'm a disc jockey instead of a concert pianist."

"You know, I listen to your sexy voice as often as I can." Alexis took her hand, loving the warmth and smoothness of it. Her mind was already jumping ahead, feeling Mel's long fingers between her legs. Or was it jumping back? She remembered her dorm room long ago and holding Mel's hand just like this.

"Radio voice." It was Mel's turn to blush. The rose color seemed to fill her cheeks. "You always were a little too forward."

"It's true. I haven't changed much, at least in that regard. Hell, I even still have one-night stands sometimes, if you can believe that."

"I've been guilty of that sin as well, whenever I have a good opportunity." Mel winked. Her dark blue eyes were beautiful without the thick glasses, and Alexis loved the fact that Mel's gaze was focused on her.

"Would now be a good opportunity?" Alexis whispered the question.

Mel didn't answer. She turned toward the computer screen and pressed a few buttons on the keyboard, keeping her other hand wrapped in Alexis's. The sexual energy that Alexis had felt with Mel eight years ago suddenly came flooding back. One night eight years ago, they had only spent one night together. At twenty-two, Mel had never been with a woman, and Alexis considered herself well experienced at eighteen. Alexis had initiated everything. They had started kissing after a heated argument about Bach, then somehow slowly undressed each other and managed to strip the blankets off Alexis's extra long twin bed as they wrestled on it.

Mel refused to talk about it the next day. She acted as if nothing had happened and seemed to regret that they would even be friends, using her position as a tutor as her excuse. Alexis also suspected at the time that Mel hadn't been ready for the sex. She'd seized up like a caught rabbit as soon as Alexis had bent her head to taste her clit. All in all, their one evening together had gone well, but Alexis knew that for Mel, it was a first time that left her shaking and scared. And after that night, Mel had receded into the closet and wouldn't even listen to music with Alexis later. Now it seemed she'd found her way out of the closet for good.

Alexis stepped toward the computer and glanced at the play list, ready for a distraction to break the tension in the room. "Barry Manilow? Someone requested that?"

Mel nodded. "Our listeners have a wide variety of tastes."

"And you? What are your tastes like now?"

"I still prefer Bach. And uniforms." She brushed her hand along Alexis's pants. "You still play softball?"

"No." Alexis had played on the college intramural softball team and had been wearing a softball jersey the last time she'd seen Mel. Mel had come to one of the team's last games, and though Alexis hadn't scored any runs, she had noticed that Mel cheered each time she'd been up at bat. "What about delivery uniforms?"

"Well, until now, I haven't really had an opportunity to appreciate them." Her hand had moved from Alexis's pant leg to the belt, and she ran a finger along the leather strap.

"How long do we have to catch up before you have to go on air again?"

Mel glanced at her watch and then at the computer. "The most I can get is thirty minutes. The computer has everything programmed in, with Mr. Manilow set to go last. Then I have to talk again."

"Thirty minutes? That's not long to chat."

"Maybe we shouldn't chat then."

"I like the way you're thinking." Alexis smiled. A half hour wasn't long enough to do everything she wanted to do to Mel, but they could abbreviate a few things. "What about the door? Can we lock it?"

"We don't have to. Everyone is out of the building until five o'clock. There's a business meeting . . ." Her voice trailed as she brushed her hands over Alexis's breasts.

Alexis couldn't relax and enjoy this knowing that anyone could come into the room. She backed away from Mel and locked the door. Mel took a step toward her just as the song changed. Janis Joplin's voice was pumping through the speakers now. Alexis still couldn't believe how much Mel had changed. The desires she'd felt all through the second semester of freshman year were filling her body again. She slipped off her shirt and reached out to catch Mel's hand. "You won't get in trouble over this?"

"No one will know. Besides, my boss loves me." She outlined

the curve of Alexis's breasts with her index finger. "My girlfriend would be pissed, but she's been out of town for six months and left telling me we should keep our relationship open. Long story." She freed her other hand and started working at loosening Alexis's belt buckle. "I haven't had many opportunities for one-night stands as of late."

"What a shame," Alexis said softly, feeling the seam of her pants ride against her clit as Mel pulled off her belt. The look of hungry desire was plain in Mel's eyes and Alexis was already wet.

"I wish we had more than a half hour. We'd have time for foreplay."

"Fuck foreplay," Alexis said, kissing Mel's neck. "I spent half of my freshman year waiting for you to give me another chance and suffering through endless bouts of foreplay."

"I was your tutor." She brushed her lips over Alexis's nipple. "And I couldn't let myself fall for a freshman anyway."

"You were scared of how you felt when you were with me," Alexis replied, matter-of-fact. She pressed her thigh between Mel's legs and got a satisfied moan in response. "But I'm glad you got over it."

Mel closed her eyes, hugging Alexis close as she rode the thigh pressed between her legs. In a voice more husky than the radio would ever allow, she responded, "Maybe I was scared. I've always wanted to meet up with you again and set things straight, I mean, right."

"Should we talk first?" Alexis asked, relaxing her leg for a moment.

Mel groaned as soon as Alexis pulled away. "Hell, no. We can talk later." She put her hand on Alexis's chest, pushing her against the wall.

Alexis felt the edge of the CD stack rub against her backside as Mel thrust her hips toward her. She unzipped Mel's pants and slipped her hand under the cotton fabric, feeling a warm wetness envelop her fingers. Mel's hands were busy exploring her breasts, tugging and massaging nipples until they tightened, erect and tingling with pleasure.

Pulsating under her fingertips, Alexis strummed Mel's swollen clit. She slipped her middle finger inside to press on the G-spot and then continued the finger flicking over and around the clit. Each movement of her hand enticed gasps of pleasure from Mel. Her hands were on Alexis's shoulders, gripping tightly. "Don't stop," she whispered, her breath warm on Alexis's ear.

Alexis felt her own body respond to Mel's wet skin, and she knew her boxers would be soaked soon. She rubbed her fingers on Mel's swollen clit, matching the rhythm of her pelvic thrusts and a moment later, pressed deep inside her. A wash of come bathed Mel's folds and her body trembled. Holding her fingers in place, Alexis brushed her lips along Mel's neck, enjoying her part in the climax. Mel squeezed her legs together, tightening on Alexis's wrist. Her fingernails dug into Alexis's skin, and she knew there'd be claw marks on her back as evidence of this encounter. Finally, Mel collapsed against Alexis.

"Damn, I needed that," she rasped. She relaxed her head on Alexis's chest, her breathing slowing a bit. "I wish I could have held out a little longer to enjoy your touch . . ."

"Maybe next time." Alexis slipped her hand out from Mel's pants. Instead of relaxing for long, Mel was already nuzzling Alexis's breasts. Their first time together, Mel hadn't even touched Alexis after she'd climaxed. Alexis had always wondered what Mel was like as a top. Her pants fell to the ground as Mel worked her hands down Alexis's legs. She was on her knees now and started to pull on Alexis's boxers. Alexis started to help, but Mel pushed her hands away. "I get to do this."

Alexis stepped out of the boxers once Mel had pulled them down to her ankles. Instead of standing back up again, Mel stayed on her knees in front of Alexis. "Spread your legs," she said.

Alexis knew better than to resist directions. She moved her feet apart and then braced herself with one hand on the boxes and the other on a CD stack. Mel's tongue was on her inner thigh, inching up to the part where Alexis needed to be touched. Her clit was throbbing for Mel's tongue. Instead of satisfying her, Mel skipped lightly over Alexis's middle and then started licking down the other thigh. With a senseless worry that this licking might be some type of torture, Alexis begged, "I need your tongue on my clit."

Mel gazed up at her, but continued working her inner thighs. Mel's hands moved from the back of Alexis's thighs to her butt. Finally, her tongue slipped between Alexis's warm center to stroke her clit. Alexis let go of the CD stack and heard a few cases fall as she reached for Mel. She ran her fingers through Mel's hair. "I want something inside."

Wordlessly, Mel slipped first one, then two fingers inside Alexis. She continued licking the clit and the pressure of her fingers sent Alexis nearly over the edge. She guarded herself, struggling to keep Mel on her for a moment longer. Her body was gripped in an orgasm a moment later. She felt every muscle tighten, from her clenched jaws down to her curled toes, and pulled at the boxes near her for support. Instead, the boxes tumbled to the ground. Still struggling to keep her balance, she reached for the CD rack. The CDs crashed to the ground. Finally a wave of nerves tingled through her, and relaxation followed. Her knees were weak and she shivered when Mel lifted her tongue off her clit a moment later.

The door handle clicked and a familiar male voice asked, "Mel? You okay in there? The door's locked . . ."

Mel caught her breath and quickly answered, "No, Amir, I'm fine. I was just changing out of my workout clothes and knocked over one of the promo boxes. I'm just a klutz, you know. No worries." Mel wiped her lips with the back of her hand and smiled up at Alexis. She whispered, "Guess the meeting's over early." Amir's footsteps could be heard as he padded down the hallway back to his desk. "You made a mess in here." Mel added, nodding at the boxes and the CDs that littered the studio.

"I'll pick everything up."

"No." Mel pulled up her underwear. "I'll take care of it. We just need to get you out of here."

"Is there a back way out of this place?" Alexis was already pulling her boxers on and searching for her belt. Her clit was still throbbing and she struggled to focus. She didn't want to think about what would have happened if she hadn't locked the door. Barry Manilow's voice filled the room.

"Behind the band equipment and the stage." Mel pointed to the room beyond the glass pane.

"Good." Alexis had her pants on and was placing the boxes back on the shelf. She gathered the CDs, but Mel took them from her.

"Relax, I'll organize them as soon as I figure out what to say when Barry's voice stops. That was the best half hour I've had in . . . I don't know how long." She brushed her lips against Alexis's cheek. "How often do you make deliveries here?"

"Every Friday." Alexis straightened her shirt collar and then bent to tie her shoes.

"Why haven't I noticed?" She shook her head. "Well, maybe you could drop by the next time you have a delivery?"

"As long as your girlfriend won't come after me." Alexis stood up and headed for the back exit.

"Like I said, she was the one who wanted an open relationship. It's good to see you again, Lex." Mel sat down at her desk and placed the headphones over her ears. She waved to Alexis, and spoke into the microphone just as the last note of the song melted in the air. "All right, folks, we've got a few more minutes for some requests, and I'm answering the phone lines now." Mel keyed another song list up on the computer and then continued, "And here's one that I need to throw on for an old friend from college who just paid me a visit."

Alexis paused in the doorway. Ani Difranco's voice filled the air, and she couldn't resist waiting for a moment longer. Alexis grinned at Mel as soon as she heard the chorus line. She remembered the last time she'd kissed Mel. They were listening to Ani then, too. Alexis had teased Mel about being too shy to have sex with her. Time had certainly changed things for Melinda Traverstein.

When she arrived at home, Alexis found a phone message from Sandy on her answering machine. Sandy left the address of her place and added, "I'll see you at eight. Been looking forward to this all week . . . By the way, I've got everything set to make this awesome veggie stir fry, and there's a fat chocolate cake already baked." Vegan too, of course, Alexis thought with a smile.

After scribbling down Sandy's address, she stripped out of her uniform and headed to the bath for a long soak. She hadn't seen Darcy on the bus ride home and there'd been no call from Paula all day. Things were obviously going well if Paula didn't send out a distress SOS. Alexis eased into the warm water, lying motionless as the faucet dripped on her toes. For the first time in a while, she hadn't checked her mailbox when she'd gotten home that night. It was always empty, but now the possibility of an undiscovered letter itched at her mind. Through the wall, she could hear the sound of Drew's radio. She could tell he was listening to Mel's station, but there was a different DJ on now. Alexis grabbed her shampoo and lathered her hair, thinking of Mel again. It had been very strange to have a freshman year fling surface again, and stranger still how much she'd enjoyed it. This thought bothered her the most. Could she ever settle in with just one person? Despite her best attempt at denying it, she had to admit she enjoyed being a player.

After dressing in a pair of jeans and a long sleeved T-shirt, Alexis combed her hair into place and studied her reflection in the small mirror. She was tired of the shaggy bed-head look and had been thinking of cutting her hair. On impulse, she found the phone book and called the salon on her block to see if they had any openings. They were one of the few places that kept long hours. The receptionist told her that she'd fit her in if she could be there in ten minutes. Alexis was out the door a moment later. She nearly careened into Drew and his puppy in the stairwell.

"Where the hell are you off to in such a rush? Slow down, sistah!" He slapped her butt as she dodged past him on the stairs.

"The salon. Last-minute appointment."

"Well, drop by after you get the new 'do so I can tease you," Drew hollered. Alexis was nearly to the last step, and she just waved her hand in response.

The stylist knew Alexis from Decker's and asked if she was going there later. Alexis admitted she had plans to go there tomorrow, not wanting to give any details about tonight. She still wasn't sure where she was with Sandy and doubted that things would work out for them as friends. With two inches clipped, her hair just reached the top of her ears and was even shorter in the back. It was nearly eight o'clock by the time she approved her reflection and paid.

As soon as Alexis stepped into Sandy's apartment, she felt a warm, comforting sensation. Sandy greeted her, strangely shy. She thanked her for bringing a bottle of wine and offered to take her coat. "Nice haircut," she said, just as she turned to hang the coat in the hall closet.

"Thanks. I was starting to feel a little shaggy." Alexis combed her fingers through the short hair, liking the new feeling.

"Can you give me a minute? I was just going to wash up. You can put the wine in the kitchen, just down the hall." Sandy headed to the bathroom, leaving Alexis to find the kitchen and then take a look around the front room. The walls, painted a rich amber, were dotted with several framed prints of pastoral countrysides, rivers and waterfalls. A dark green sofa with big velvet pillows took up the center of the space, flanked with a loveseat of matching fabric on one side and an end table covered in glowing candles on the other. Two tall bookcases, filled with hardbound classics, newer paperbacks and a few more candles, balanced the television and stereo that faced the sofa. Only the candles' soft glow lit the room, and the scent of burning wax mixed with an aroma of sweet curry drifting from the kitchen.

Sandy came out of the bathroom and glanced at Alexis, whose hand was brushing the velvet pillows on the sofa. "You like my garage sale furniture?"

"This room is so," Alexis paused, searching for the right word. "Serene. I bet you love to come home to this."

"It is nice, I guess." Sandy glanced around the place, as if trying to see it with fresh eyes. "But it gets too quiet. My neighbors are all seniors and I don't hear a thing after nine o'clock."

The expression on her face was either sadness or loneliness, and Alexis wondered what Sandy wasn't saying. She decided there would be time for inquisitions later. Changing the subject, she said, "Something smells delicious."

"I hope you like curry. I rarely make this recipe and when I do, well, I tend to make enough for a football team. Come on, I need a little help in the kitchen before we can eat."

Alexis followed her, noticing that the landscape art continued down the hallway and into the kitchen, with scenes from the rocky Pacific coast and hills covered in wildflowers. "I like the prints. Each one is so diverse, yet they have a similar feel, and all the mats are the same." One of the photos, the ocean scene, was signed, but Alexis could only read the first initial E. "Are they all from the same photographer?" As soon as she asked this, Alexis caught her breath. What were the chances?

"Yes, they are. You know, I came across this one," she pointed to the large print of the coastline with crashing waves and the shadow of seagulls on the sand, "at the farmer's market, of all places. The photographer, Elana Kingston, was there signing the prints."

"Small fucking world," Alexis said under her breath.

"What's that?" Sandy asked, handing her two bowls. Without

waiting for an answer, she continued, "Can you put a half cup of the basmati rice in each bowl?"

Alexis found the rice, still steaming in the pot, and measured out a portion for each bowl. Then Sandy took over, adding the vegetables to the rice. When they finally sat at the table, complete with candles and wine, Alexis couldn't help but ask, "So you're sure this isn't a date?"

"You mean the candlelit dinner? No, we're still just friends even if I light candles and cook." She laughed. "Though I'll admit, it feels dangerously like a date. Hell, don't give me that look. You brought the damn wine."

"I won't tell anyone if you don't." She took a bite and let the flavors coat her tongue. "God, this is delicious."

"Green curry is one of my favorite sauces." Sandy smiled with pride. She took a sip of the wine and patted her lips with the napkin.

"Better than amaretto chocolate sauce?"

"No." Sandy tasted the entrée and murmured her approval. "But almost."

"Can I ask you something?"

Sandy looked up from her plate but didn't answer.

"You told me before that you used to date a lot. I think you said *too much*. What did you mean by that?"

Sandy turned her fork in her hand. She stared at her wineglass, as if she was trying to avoid Alexis. "I meant that I used to go straight to bed with any girl I liked. Then I'd get a bad dose of reality when it turned out I wasn't interested the morning after."

"Sounds like you were a player."

"Eat your damn curry." She smiled. "Yeah, maybe. Enough to know one when I see one."

"Touché." Alexis couldn't help but wonder what had changed Sandy. She didn't seem like the type to fuck around.

They ate in silence for a few minutes and then Sandy asked, "Did you say you recognized the prints? The photographer was local, I think." She motioned to the prints. "I had a little trouble tracking down her prints at first. I only saw her once at the farmer's market, maybe three or four years ago. Then she just disappeared. Fortunately, I found her website and ordered the other prints online. But only the oceanscape is signed."

Alexis didn't want to lie outright, but she was reluctant to admit how well she knew Elana Kingston. "You know, I'm not sure. I bumped into an Elana Kingston at the last farmer's market. But she was selling apples, not prints, so it could be someone else entirely."

"Maybe . . . I miss going to the market. Last week was the end of the season, wasn't it?" She waited for Alexis's nod and then continued, "I didn't go enough this year. Stayed home or worked too much."

Alexis wondered why Sandy's face clouded as soon as she mentioned her home. She'd noticed that it was a two bedroom apartment, but only one of the bedrooms was furnished, while the other was nearly empty. "Have you always lived alone here?"

"No. My girlfriend lived here for a year. She moved out last month, which was, unfortunately, three months after we broke up. It was a hard summer."

"I'll bet. At least you had separate rooms."

Sandy nodded. "But it wasn't like either of us had separate lives. You can't exactly bring home a date when your ex is watching TV in her pajamas in the living room."

"A little awkward?"

"A pain in the ass, actually. I wanted to throw a party when she finally had her things all packed in the U-Haul." She sighed. "And the real irony was that as soon as she was gone, I missed her horribly. It took me two weeks before I stopped checking her room to see if she hadn't moved back in." Sandy's eyes shifted from her wineglass to Alexis's face. "Sounds crazy, doesn't it?"

"No. Not at all." And it didn't. It was obvious that Sandy had been in love with this woman and whatever had happened that separated their hearts must have been painful. Given Sandy's sensitivity to a monogamous relationship, she wondered if the ex-girl-friend had cheated on her.

Sandy smiled. "Eat up. There's plenty left for seconds if you like. Or thirds. But I'll warn you, there is a chocolate cake waiting for us as well."

When they had both finished eating, they took their wine-glasses into the living room and sank into the green couch. The overstuffed cushions seemed to envelop them, and Alexis leaned back against the pillows, feeling as though she could easily fall asleep there. "You know, that green curry was the best I've tasted. Honestly. I even liked the tofu."

"You mean you're not a tofu connoisseur?" Sandy asked with a hint of sarcasm. Of course she knew what Alexis ate at the café, and she rarely ordered anything with tofu.

"Actually, I thought I hated tofu," she admitted. "I guess it's all about the sauce, or maybe the chef. Anyway, you changed my mind. The thought of another helping was tempting."

"I've been known to convert people." Sandy winked. She took a sip of wine and got up to turn on the TV. "I'm not sure if we'll like this movie, but I figured we could always turn it off and talk if we get bored."

Alexis recognized the intro music on the movie almost immediately. "*Some Kind of Wonderful*. No way. I haven't watched this in years! This was my favorite movie when I was twelve."

"I think I was fifteen before I discovered it. Late bloomer, as you might have guessed," she said playfully. "I had a big crush on the drummer."

"Fucking hot," Alexis agreed. "It's too bad she didn't discover she was a lesbian," she added softly, as the movie started. Pointing to the teenager on the screen, Alexis continued, "This guy was all wrong for her."

"No kidding!" Sandy leaned back in the sofa, shifting closer to Alexis. Their knees bumped together but Sandy didn't move away.

Halfway through the opening scene, Sandy's hand was on

Alexis's thigh, further complicating things. Alexis had seen the movie enough times to not need to pay attention. She was distracted by the nearness of Sandy's body. Although they had made the *friend* boundaries clear last night, things were blurring now. She was confused as to what Sandy wanted, and what in fact she wanted. Her encounter with Mel that afternoon had left her with the realization that she was indeed happy to have her freedom. And since Elana Kingston had been brought up and her stunning photographs surrounded her now, she was forced to consider that relationship as well. She would easily give up dates with the likes of Tina and Bonnie, but she wasn't sure she was ready to stop flirting entirely to have a stable relationship with one person. And yet, of all the women she'd met, she felt the most comfortable when she was with Sandy. It was nearly impossible to ignore the erotic thoughts of pulling off Sandy's clothing and pinning her on the sofa to nibble on her breasts or press a hand between her legs. What was the value of a friendship when they could be lovers? Alexis tried to clear her mind and focus on the movie, but Sandy's hand still rested on her thigh.

After a while, Alexis shifted on the sofa and Sandy moved her hand away. Their wineglasses were empty, and Alexis used this as an excuse to step out of the room. "Can I pour you a little more?"

"Sure." She handed her the empty glass.

Alexis went to the kitchen, poured the wine and then turned off the lights as she headed back to the living room. Sandy met her in the hallway.

"Something's wrong, isn't it?" Sandy said softly.

Alexis shook her head, handing her one of the glasses. What was she supposed to say? "I'm just a little unclear about this friendship thing, I guess."

Sandy stepped forward and kissed Alexis. Her pressing, hungry need for contact was more than evident. Wordlessly, she took the wineglass out of Alexis's hand and set both glasses on a shelf in the hall. The next moment, Sandy's lips were pushing against hers again. Alexis gave in to the power of her desires easily, she wanted to feel Sandy's body, and her hands were already slipping under Sandy's blouse and loosening her bra. Sandy ran her fingers through Alexis's hair and then bit on her earlobes, whispering, "I want you naked in my bed."

Alexis murmured, "Is that a *friendly* request?"

"I think friendship's overrated." She kissed Alexis again, forcefully. Stepping away, she paused and eyed Alexis with a grin. "Unless that's what you want."

"I don't know." Alexis couldn't believe her own answer. Of course she wanted to sleep with Sandy, but what did that mean she was promising in return? "I don't know if I'm ready."

"For what?" Sandy was obviously upset. She crossed her arms and shifted back from Alexis. "I'm not asking for a commitment tonight."

"I know, but I can't even promise to just date you. I'm not very good at monogamy."

Sandy stared at the ground and then braved Alexis's eyes again. "I think we would be good together."

The comment stung Alexis. She felt like she was letting Sandy down, but she knew she had to leave before anything else happened. "So do I. But maybe we're not ready for each other."

"What do we need to be ready for? God, I look at you and . . . I want you so much. Maybe I don't need you to be monogamous." Sandy touched the pocket of Alexis's jeans. She placed her hands on Alexis's hips and stepped forward. "And I can feel how much you want me. You never pull away when we kiss. You only ask for another. I'm sorry about what I said before. That you were a player. I don't really believe that."

Alexis could feel her clit throbbing. "Damn, I want you so bad." Her body threatened mutiny if she walked away now, but she knew that was what she had to do. "But I think we should take it slow. I don't want to mess up with you."

"Okay. Maybe you should go." Sandy let go of her hips and turned away. She had whispered the words, and her pained expression made Alexis wish she could take back her last comment.

Sandy went to the living room and snapped off the television, watching uneasily as Alexis found her coat in the hall closet. Alexis paused by the door, unsure of what to say next. "The evening was going so well. I'm sorry I ruined things."

"Forget about it. It was my fault." Sandy sighed. She went to the door and placed one hand on Alexis's shoulder. "I was too honest with you about some things and left other things out. What I really should have told you, first off, was that I've wanted to fuck you since the first time you walked into my cafe. I don't want to just be friends."

"I only came back to Blue's for a second meal because of the hot chef. The first meal I had there was terrible. Juan made a grilled cheese that tasted like leather." She grinned. "After that, I always got the chef's special."

Sandy brushed her fingers through Alexis's hair and sighed. "Maybe you're right, Lex. Maybe we need to go slow. But don't make me wait too long." Sandy kissed Alexis on the cheek and started to open the door. "You have my number."

Alexis caught her hand and pulled her close for a last kiss. Their lips met and Sandy opened up, silently begging to have Alexis's tongue enter. Alexis pressed inside, loving the feel of Sandy's body surging against hers as they kissed.

Chapter 10

Alexis awoke on Saturday morning with the feeling that she'd forgotten to do something. She spent the first hour of her day sorting laundry and trying to think of what she could have forgotten about. Finally, she decided to get her mind off it with a run. Drew's apartment was strangely quiet all night, and she guessed he'd stayed at Ben's house. Thinking of the puppy, she took the spare key and went over to let the puppy out. She left a note for Drew, in case he came while she was gone, and headed for the park with the puppy in tow. She noticed that Drew had finally settled on the name Apollo, since the puppy now had a gold heart on a red collar inscribed with his name and Drew's phone number.

As usual, Apollo made it one lap around the park and then refused to run any further. Alexis picked him up and started for home, pausing just outside the park entrance when she heard someone call her name. She glanced back at the path and spotted Darcy jogging toward her.

"Alexis! How are you, hon?" Darcy reached the park entrance and paused to scratch Apollo's head. "Drew left you with his beast again?"

"I think he spent the night at a friend's place, and I didn't want to make the puppy wait to pee." Alexis set Apollo down when he started wiggling. He went to root around the bushes, sneezing as he caught a whiff of some smell in the ivy. "I hate to stop your run, but do you want to walk back with Apollo and me?"

Darcy nodded. "I had a long enough workout for the amount of sleep I got last night anyway. By the way, we're going to Decker's to go dancing tonight. Do you want to join us?"

"Sure, though I have to admit, I already had plans to be there with someone." Alexis remembered Elana's date, hoping that Elana wouldn't stand her up again. "Was Paula over last night?" Alexis asked, then instantly regretted the question. She didn't want Darcy to think she was nosy, or worse, jealous.

"Nope." Darcy answered with no hint of annoyance. She smiled coyly and added, "I was at her place."

"Wow, between you and Drew, I'm starting to feel like the nun on our floor."

Darcy held up her hand. "Don't even try to play the *innocence* card! I'm sure you weren't sleeping alone last night." She laughed.

"Actually, I was." Alexis sighed. "Had a date with a woman, but she's convinced I'm a player and wants a commitment for me to stop messing around before she'll even agree to dating. So we kissed and then I was sent home."

"Hmm, I don't blame her." Darcy shook her head as Alexis tried to argue. "Yeah, you can tell me whatever you like, but I've heard the stories. And despite how shy I used to think you were, I'd believe the wild stories more than your claims to being a prude."

"Wild stories?" Alexis shook her head. "You must have me confused with someone else." She winked at Darcy. "I'll admit, though, I'm not shy. The only reason I acted that way was because I had a little crush on you."

"Yeah, I noticed."

Alexis blushed and looked away. She wasn't surprised that Darcy suspected her feelings, but it made things awkward now. They had crossed the intersection in front of the park and turned down the next street. A bakery shop on the corner was bustling with Saturday morning customers, and the smell of cinnamon rolls was intoxicating. "Well, I got over it."

"Good. We wouldn't have worked together, judging from what I've heard." She touched Alexis's shoulder and then added, "But don't think that I wasn't hoping for a trial offer."

"What have you heard, anyway? I'm really not that crazy."

"No?" She grinned. "Well, Paula told me that you'd also slept with nearly every out lesbian at your college."

"It was a small school," Alexis defended. "And there were more than a few who would have turned me down." Not Paula, however, she added silently. "So did Paula also tell you I'm horrible at relationships? She usually points that out, first thing, to any of our friends."

"Is that why you two broke up?"

"No." Alexis had to stop herself from admitting the truth out loud. They'd broken up because Paula wasn't satisfying her. She wanted a chance on top and Paula wouldn't roll over. Simple as that. "It was . . . complicated. We're much better as friends."

"And do you think you're better at relationships now?"

Alexis shrugged. She thought of Sandy, wondering if it had been wrong to leave her last night. Her first impulse that morning had been to call and apologize. She didn't know what she wanted in return though. "I really hope things work out between you and Paula. As soon as I saw the two of you together, I realized how perfect your personalities would be together."

"It scares me a little." Darcy paused, reaching in her pocket for a set of keys. They had reached their apartment entrance, and she unlocked the front door, holding it open for Alexis. "We both just got out of relationships, and I don't want this to be a rebound thing, you know? But you never really know if something will work out until you try."

Alexis nodded. She was still distracted by thoughts of Sandy. A nagging voice suggested that maybe she should try being in a relationship with Sandy, instead of fighting it. She said good-bye to Darcy in the hall and went to check on her mailbox, idly hoping that she'd find something had been delivered on Friday. For once she wasn't disappointed. Inside her mailbox was a delivery receipt from the postal service and a key for the cabinet where oversized packages were placed. Unlocking the cabinet, she found a shoebox-sized package addressed to her with her mom's return address label. The box weighed at least ten pounds, and she knew instantly that it must be the clay her mother had promised. Apollo was impatient to go upstairs, probably hungry for his breakfast, and Alexis decided she could wait on opening the box.

With the puppy deposited back in Drew's bathroom with a bowl of kibble, she sat down to a breakfast of sugar flakes and banana slices before opening the shoebox. A fat hunk of red clay wrapped in plastic took up every inch of the box. On the underside of the lid she found the following note, "Dear Lex, Get muddy. Always makes everything else clear. With love, Mom." The note made her long to jump on a plane and go straight to her mom's studio. Visits to Arizona were few and far between, with APO's crazy schedule, and she doubted she'd have any time off to see her mom until after the holidays. Trying to ignore the pangs of homesickness, she devoted the rest of the morning to the pottery wheel and another attempt at making a coffee mug. Now that she had the right clay to mix with the Oregon water, the possibilities seemed endless, and she wished her skills matched her imagination.

Sometime after noon Drew dropped by to thank her for taking care of Apollo that morning. He was on his way to the deli for lunch and wanted company. She reluctantly agreed, hoping a break from the wheel would bring inspiration. She'd finished two mugs, but wasn't quite happy with either. They were well shaped and had good handles, yet neither looked very interesting. Drew offered that the right lacquer might improve them.

While listening to Drew expound on Ben's charms and his sudden domestic happiness, Alexis munched her sandwich and tried not to be jealous. Drew sounded just like Paula did when she talked about Darcy. Suddenly both of her close friends were acting as if they were ready to buy wedding bands.

Alexis headed back to her apartment, more depressed than before, and started to clean up the pottery equipment. The message light was blinking on her answering machine. Elana had called while she was out. "Hey, Lex, I hate to tell you this, but I got a call for a last minute photo gig tonight, which means I probably won't be able to go out later. If something changes, I'll call you. Sorry to flake like this. God, I hope you get this message and don't think I've stood you up . . . again."

Alexis deleted the message and started cleaning the pottery wheel. Strangely, she didn't really care that Elana couldn't go out now. Although she had been looking forward to a night of dancing and make out music at the club, she knew Elana wasn't emotionally invested in her, and for some reason that seemed important. Maybe she was just hanging around lovebirds too much as of late. For Elana, missing their date was nothing more important than a missed photo op. She could easily find another dyke if things with Alexis didn't work out. The reality was that Sandy was still on Alexis's mind. She picked up the phone and dialed Sandy's number, happy to get the answering machine. Alexis wasn't ready to say what she wanted to a live person. Instead, she left the following, "Hey, Sandy. I know you work on Saturday nights, and you mentioned you don't usually go to clubs, but I wanted to invite you out anyway. I'll be at Decker's around eleven, and I'd love to see you."

By seven o'clock, Alexis had taken a bath and changed into a tight black tank top and a pair of jeans. She added a white dress shirt over the tank, a thin black velvet choker, silver hoop earrings and her usual silver ring, right hand. She was debating what to make for dinner and staring at the open refrigerator, when someone knocked on her door.

Drew's voice called, "Hey, Lex?" Another knock. "Anyone home?"

"Yeah, Drew, the door's unlocked." She pulled out the orange juice and closed the door.

Drew walked in, followed by Ben and then Elana. Alexis smiled as soon as she saw Elana. She set the orange juice carton on the counter.

"Look, Lex, I found these kids out on the street. They wanted to know if I could buzz them in." Drew reached over and patted Ben's jean-clad butt. "I told them I would, but only if they played nicely."

"Wait, I never agreed to that," Ben returned quickly.

Elana blushed as soon as Alexis caught her eye. Alexis winked. "Well, well, we've got a party here now."

"And you're already pouring the drinks?" Drew asked, hopeful.

"If I had known, I would have picked up some vodka to add to this. As it is, I can only fill virgin orders."

"Virgin?" Ben asked. "I wouldn't mind a virgin." He glanced at Drew and smiled. Drew shook his head and then slipped his hand around Ben's waist possessively. Alexis had to stop herself from cooing out loud, "Oh, you look so cute together."

"No, let's skip the before dinner drinks," Drew suggested. "You ready, Lex? We're going to Blue's. Ben and I have convinced Elana that the food there is amazing. Not to be missed."

Elana finally spoke up. "I tried calling, but your line was busy. My gig ended early."

Alexis glanced over at the phone. Apparently she'd set the receiver down just out of place after her last call. Why did they have to go to Blue's for dinner? Shit, this was going to be sticky.

Elana continued, "I thought we could try a do over for last week. Ben and Drew already agreed."

"Sure . . ." Alexis glanced from Elana to Drew and Ben. A few hours ago she'd given up on her for what she thought was the last time. Going to Blue's was risky. If Sandy saw them together, she'd never agree to a date with Alexis again. Not that they'd been dating anyway, Alexis corrected herself.

"Come on, Lex, you look like you're already dressed to kill," Drew said. "Let's go. I'm starving."

"Okay. Give me a minute to grab my wallet and a jacket."

"By the way, it just started raining," Ben said, looking out the window. "Maybe we should grab umbrellas."

"It's always raining in this damn town," Drew said miserably. He liked the rain even less than Alexis. They'd had more than a few conversations complaining about the weather.

"Portland doesn't get that much rain. And where's the harm in getting a little wet, Drew? You can always strip and dry off." Apparently Ben liked Portland's weather. Just then a crack of lightning flashed outside and a low rumble of thunder followed. Ben had his nose pressed to the glass now. "Looks like we're in for a storm. It's really coming down now."

"It never rains, but it pours," Alexis mumbled. She had found her wallet and hung a black jacket over her shoulder. Elana eyed her. Alexis felt strange for not saying much. She held out her hand and waited for Elana to clasp it. "It's good to see you again. I was sad when I got your message."

Elana smiled. She pulled Alexis's hand close to her and then kissed her lips. "It's good to see you too."

They arrived at Blue's and found a full house. Gillian apologized for the lack of tables and added their name to the waiting list. Alexis hoped that Sandy would be too busy to notice them. She caught glimpses of her through the server's kitchen access. Again, she was dressed in the formal white chef's smock and black slacks. She was zipping around the kitchen as smoothly as a practiced orchestra leader.

When a table finally opened, Gillian seated them and doled out the menus. She came back later to take their orders and never acted any way but amenable to Alexis. Alexis wished that they could have had another waitress. She really didn't want to see Gillian, let alone think about tipping her. All four decided to order the chef's special.

"So, Lex, Elana told me that you delivered some film to her studio the other day. And you met her dad." Ben raised his eyebrows. "What'd ya think of Mr. Kingston?"

"Um." Alexis tried to think of something polite she could say about Elana's overbearing and rude father. "He's an interesting guy. Must admit, I envy his orchard. I've been eating his Pink Ladies all week. Unbelievably juicy and sweet."

Ben nearly spilled the wineglass he'd just lifted to his lips. "Pink what?"

"Relax, Ben, they're apples," Elana said, smiling at Alexis.

After a while, the dinner arrived and the conversation turned from fruit harvesting to a debate about the best nightclub in the city. Elana was eager to check out Decker's, admitting that she'd never been to a women's bar before. Alexis smiled when Ben offered the advice, "The first time I went to a gay nightclub I nearly peed my pants I was so scared. My advice would be to stick close to Lex your first time out there. If the women's bars are anything like the men's places, new faces are like fresh meat in a room full of hungry flies."

"Well, sure, when the meat is as tasty as yours!" Drew exclaimed, a little too loudly. Several other guests glanced at their table, and Drew forked up a bite of potato and popped it in his mouth, murmuring, "Mmm, god, I just love sinking my teeth in and feeling the rush of flavors spread over my tongue."

Alexis kicked Drew's leg under the table and whispered, "Cool it." Then teased, "This is a family place, after all."

Drew raised his eyebrows and rubbed elbows with Ben. "See? I knew we came to the right restaurant."

As they were finishing the meal of roasted new potatoes with dill and a vegetable risotto medley, Sandy appeared at their table. She glanced at Alexis and arched her eyebrows then set four forks on the table along with a fat slice of chocolate cake covered in raspberry sauce. Turning toward Ben and Drew's side of the table, she said, "Well, apparently you liked the meal last week well enough to come again, and with a friend." She smiled at Elana. Pointing to the cake, she continued, "I promised this slice to Alexis, but I figured she'd be willing to share with all of you."

"Damn, that looks good. I think you guys might have to fight me for a taste of this," Alexis joked. Ben and Drew immediately grabbed two of the forks and held them above the cake.

"Ready when you are, Lex," Drew said. "But keep in mind, I won second place in my fencing academy's children division when I was eleven."

"I knew you were as handsome as Lancelot, and as talented too, apparently," Ben teased, clanging his fork against Drew's. Everyone at the table was laughing, and the attention of many of the other diners had clearly shifted to their table.

Alexis realized she still hadn't introduced Sandy and Elana. She was battling the urge to simply not introduce them and hoping that Sandy might just walk away. But when the laughter ended, it was obvious that Sandy was waiting for something. "Sandy, this is Elana Kingston. Elana, our fabulous chef this evening, Sandy Webster."

Sandy stretched over Alexis to shake Elana's hand. "You know, we've met before." Drew kicked Alexis's foot under the table and gave her an "Oh, you're fucked" grin. Sandy didn't notice their exchange, clearly focused on Elana. "It's been several years now. You were selling prints at the farmer's market. I'm almost embarrassed to admit this, but I'm a huge fan of your work. It was a sad day when I realized I had run out of wall space and had to stop buying your prints."

Elana was beaming with the praise. "I'm so excited to hear you like my work."

Someone called Sandy's name from the kitchen, and she glanced toward the access space. Juan was trying to get her attention, obviously needing a hand with something. She nodded at him and held up one finger to let him know she was almost finished socializing. Turning back to the table, she apologized. "You know,

I'd love to hang out here, but we're slammed in the kitchen. I hope you all enjoy the cake." She smiled at Elana, "And it was nice meeting you again."

Elana asked quickly, "When are you off? We were going out for drinks after dinner and then over to Decker's. Maybe you could join us?"

Sandy glanced at Alexis and then at Elana. "Oh no, I don't want to be intruding on your evening together—"

"You wouldn't be," Alexis said, interrupting her. "We'd love it if you could join our little party." She wasn't lying. She wanted to spend the evening with Sandy, but hiding the fact that she'd been sleeping with Elana was going to be difficult. Hopefully Sandy would think that this was just a dinner among four friends, not a double date. "I have my cell phone. You can call us when you get off."

"Maybe." She was staring at Elana, not Alexis, as she said this. Just before she turned to head back to the kitchen, her leg brushed against Alexis's. No one seemed to notice the blush that crossed Alexis's face, as the rich chocolate and sweet raspberries created a stir when the other three dug in for a bite of the cake. Trying to ignore the feel of Sandy's leg against her, Alexis took a bite of chocolate and murmured her approval. It was unbelievably good and in moments it was devoured, among comments of, "I can't believe this is vegan!" from Ben and, "Chocolate has got to be good for you. And aren't raspberries supposed to make you brilliant?" from Elana and, "No, but I've heard chocolate and raspberries both improve your libido," from Ben again, and finally, "I think that last bite has my name on it. Not that I anticipate any libido problems tonight!" from Drew, of course.

After leaving Blue's, the group headed over to a bar, grateful for Drew's BMW, as the sky continued to pour down in relentless gusts of rain. They took over the pool table at the back of the bar, with Ben and Drew paired up against Alexis and Elana. Ben was obviously the pool shark of the crowd, and Alexis found herself wishing that Sandy was on their team so the women could have a shot at defeating the men. As it was, they lost all three games that they played, though the last one was close. Elana had finally relaxed, and Alexis watched her with growing affection as she joked about apple picking and wedding pictures. Elana teased Ben about his past marriage which apparently, she'd taken the pictures of, and then added that she really couldn't fault him since she'd come close to making a similar mistake.

The group got along so well that it was hard to part, but they had agreed to go to different dance clubs to round out the evening. As soon as Drew and Ben left, Alexis and Elana headed over to Decker's. It was a short walk, but the rain made the going slow. They dodged from one overhang to the next as they made their way down the four blocks. When they finally reached the club, they were drenched and welcomed the warm air that blasted out of Decker's along with the loud bass beats.

Elana took Alexis's hand and squeezed her palm while they stood in line at the entrance, huddled under the building's overhang. "I'm having a great time tonight. With you."

Alexis smiled. Her thoughts had been distracted by wondering if Sandy would actually call to join them. Hearing Elana say this focused her thoughts. Why should she worry about Sandy? Elana was awesome and right there in front of her. They got along so well, and Elana wasn't asking her to be anything but herself. She was only here for a good time. "I'm happy to hear that. I was just thinking the same thing." She leaned toward Elana and kissed her, tasting the moisture on her lips. Elana smiled as soon as their lips parted. Alexis continued, "You know, we're soaked. I've lived in Portland long enough that you'd think I'd remember to bring an umbrella."

Elana shrugged. "I brought one, but I didn't want to use it." She pulled a collapsible umbrella out of the large side pocket of her coat. "I wanted to feel the rain. And I like to see you all wet. By the way, I love your new haircut." She ran her fingers over the trimmed edge above Alexis's ears and then down the side of her neck. "Very sexy."

Alexis kissed Elana as soon as her hands reached the back of her neck. Elana let go of Alexis when someone in line whistled, apparently appreciating the display. They were nearly at the door now, and Alexis waved to the woman checking IDs. "We need to strip down when we get inside. Hopefully our coats will dry before we leave. Otherwise, we'll have a miserable cab ride home."

"We can take a warm bath at your place. I've spent quite a lot of time thinking about the last time I was in your tub." Elana arched her eyebrows.

The woman at the door overheard this last comment and said, "Oh, Lex, looks like you've got a reason to be smiling tonight. Are you sure you want to come in? You know this is a clean establishment. I don't want to call the bouncer to tell you to cool it down." She winked at Elana.

"We'll be on our best behavior," Elana promised.

Alexis smiled and crossed the threshold holding Elana's hand. The cashier waved her past the front counter when she pulled out her wallet. Elana laughed. "They know you well here, huh?"

"Yeah, maybe too well." She didn't want to hide anything now. "Let's just say, I know my way around."

Elana slipped her arm in Alexis's. "Then maybe you can show me where the dance floor is. I've been waiting all night to get my hands on you, and this music is perfect."

The music had a fast rhythm, and a woman's voice intermingled with the loud techno sounds. "It's not too fast?"

"Not tonight."

Alexis suspected Elana understood her question wasn't referring just to the music. Elana's earlier shyness had been replaced with a forwardness that set Alexis's body on fire. She couldn't wait to get her hands on Elana, and dancing seemed a cruel delay. As soon as they stepped on the crowded dance floor, Elana's swaying body, rubbing against Alexis made the temptation to strip Elana's clothing nearly impossible to ignore. Alexis directed Elana into a throng of dancers, already absorbed with their own partners. They were suddenly lost in a sea of swaying bodies, and Elana's eyes were wide as she scoped out the other women rubbing against each other. Alexis kept her own attention focused on Elana. She moved her hands from Elana's waist, up the swell of her small belly, along the skin-tight white cotton blouse, to where the swell of her breasts began. Elana backed away from her, shaking her head as though she were admonishing a child whose hands were in the cookie jar.

Alexis reached forward and caught the end of Elana's belt, tugging until she had pulled Elana back against her body. "I think I would like this music better if we were naked," she said in Elana's ear. Letting Elana's breasts fill her palms, she moaned with pleasure. Her knees felt weak as she tried to match Elana's dancing, tracing the edges of her bra through the soft fabric, and finally strumming the nipples to tense erectness.

"I don't think I'd be able to dance if you were naked." Elana was smiling as she moved Alexis's hands off her. "Lex, we've gotta take a break. At this rate, the bouncers will be kicking us out in about five minutes."

"They really don't do that," Alexis insisted. "Joan was just teasing."

"I could use a drink anyway."

They went over to the bar and waited to place their order. Alexis glanced around the bar, hoping she wouldn't recognize too many faces tonight. Paula and Darcy were on the couch facing the fireplace in the one quiet corner of the bar. Once they'd gotten their drinks, Alexis asked, "Do you mind if we say hi to some people? A couple of my friends are here."

"Why am I not surprised to hear that?" Elana smiled. "Sure, I need to meet more women anyway. And my mom has always said that the most likely way to meet your life partner is through friends." She paused and then added, "Or through your mother's friends, her hair stylist, the family dentist. Really the list goes on and on."

Alexis laughed. "Well, I usually try to avoid dating my friends' friends. Tends to cause jealousy. But I did notice a few cute women the last time I went to the dentist." She smiled as Elana jabbed her belly playfully.

"I bet you can't walk down the street without finding a date."

"What's the payoff on that bet? I just might take you up on it." Alexis enjoyed the lightness of their interaction. Elana seem to accept her and wasn't critical.

Elana shook her head. "Come on, introduce me to your friends."

Alexis led the way over to the fireplace. The music was more subdued on this side of the bar, and several couples were huddled around the fireplace, deep in private conversation. Paula and Darcy both stood when they saw Alexis approach. Once Elana had been introduced, they fell into a conversation about the weather, noting that Elana and Alexis were still damp from the rain.

Paula was repeating the weather forecast that she'd heard on the news and suddenly stopped mid-sentence. Alexis followed her gaze and realized why she'd stopped. Jen had just entered the club, arm in arm with, of all people, Moss. Alexis couldn't stop herself from laughing, Paula swore softly, while Darcy and Elana looked at each other with puzzled expressions.

"What were you saying about the rising temperatures?" Alexis asked, grinning.

Paula shook her head. She nodded toward the barstools where Jen and Moss had just sat down. "That's the chick I just broke up with, the skinny blonde, and the butch on her right . . . used to be my friend."

Darcy smiled. "I'm glad you're over her." She stepped in front of Paula, blocking her view of Moss and Jen, and kissed her.

Paula had no trouble returning the kiss. As soon as they parted, she said, "Mm-hmm, so am I."

"Hey, look, it's the chef from Blue's. I didn't think she'd come." Elana raised her hand and hollered, "Sandy, over here!"

Sandy had entered the club right after Moss and Jen, but Alexis had been too distracted by the first couple to notice her. She was now staring directly at Alexis and making her way toward the fireplace.

"Oh, shit," Paula murmured, only loud enough for Alexis to hear. Elana was a few feet away from her and smiling at Sandy. "Now you're in trouble."

"I've been in trouble all week," Alexis whispered back. She introduced Sandy to the group, noting that Elana was clearly happy to see that the chef had joined them. After introductions, Elana stood close enough to Sandy that the two looked like a couple. Alexis tried to ignore a feeling of impending doom.

"By the way, Sandy, that cake you made was amazing," Elana said. "I'd heard Blue's had good food, but I honestly wasn't expecting such a great meal."

"Yeah, we're kind of a hole in the wall place that's starting to get a reputation. I hope we can keep it up." Sandy smiled at Elana. "And I'm always happy to please people who have low expectations."

"You know, I haven't eaten at Blue's yet," Paula began, interrupting the unsubtle flirting between Elana and Sandy. "But Alexis has been raving about the chef for months now. Glad to finally meet you. I figured she just had a crush on you. Didn't realize that the food was the reason she goes there so often."

Darcy shook her head at Paula, obviously sensing the tension between the other three, and pointed to the bar. "Come keep me company at the bar, hon. I want to get a refill." Paula reluctantly followed with her own empty glass. Moss and Jen were standing at the bar waiting to order drinks as well.

As soon as they'd left, Elana asked, "So that's why you don't like to date friends' friends. Awkward moments at the local bar?"

"Among other reasons." Inclining her head toward Paula, Alexis explained to Sandy, "See, my friend Paula is also a good friend of Moss." She paused to point out Moss. "Or was. But now Moss is dating Jen. Um, yeah, the one she's kissing now. And Paula just broke up with Jen on Tuesday."

"Ah, how sadly typical. Lex, I'm surprised you're not the one having that awkward moment. I thought you were the one that had dated half the queer women in Portland." Sandy whistled softly.

Elana laughed. "Apparently you have a bit of a reputation, Lex."

Acutely aware of how awkward this moment was for her, as well as Paula, Alexis only shook her head. Just then she felt a hand on her back and turned to see Tina. Her stomach tightened.

"Hey, love, thought I'd find you here."

Before Alexis could fend her off, Tina stepped forward and kissed her. When Tina released her, Alexis rubbed her lips, stinging from the unexpected smack, and shook her head. She backed up, well aware that both Elana and Sandy had taken a sharp breath in as soon as Tina laid her lips on Alexis, and more aware that she had very little time to dig herself out of this mud bath.

"Uh, hey, Tina. How are you?" She glanced at Elana and Sandy. They both had expressions of disbelief plastered on their faces. "Tina, this is Elana and Sandy."

"Oh, you two are an adorable couple," Tina replied immediately. "I just think some lesbians were made for each other." She smiled graciously, then slid her hand up Alexis's leg.

Alexis stepped back. "No, I didn't mean that they were together." She shook her head, thinking suddenly that Tina was right. Elana and Sandy *did* look good together. "Tina, where's your husband tonight?"

"Out on the prowl, I suppose. Just like me." She laughed. "I need a drink. I'll find you later, love."

As soon as Tina left, Alexis dropped her head into her hand and sighed in relief. Whatever happened tonight, she was not going home with Tina. And now she knew Sandy and Elana were out as well. If either of them had thought she wasn't a player before, now they surely would know.

Sandy and Elana were both snickering, and when she looked over at them, it was Sandy who gave her the "I knew it" look. She rested a hand on Alexis's shoulder and said, "God, that was perfect. How the hell did you plan that? And how much did you pay her?"

Elana added, "Did you notice the rocks on her ears? I think that woman would be paying for Lex's time! So are you going to introduce us to any more of your friends tonight?" She slipped her arm in Sandy's and whispered something in her ear. Then in a louder voice said, "How about that motorcycle dyke in the corner?"

Sandy shook her head. "No, she's too tough for Lex."

"Right, okay then, the spray-on tan victim nursing the Budweiser over by the bar. She's got a pretty flower on the back pocket of those tight jeans."

Sandy nixed this one as well, but only after a half minute of consideration. "Possibly, but unlikely."

Alexis shook her head. Things had gone from bad to worse. Sandy and Elana were both attractive, and she knew few women would complain about taking either home tonight. Worse, rubbing up together they had made quite a few heads turn. The uncomfortable realization of being a third wheel had never felt so acutely painful. And now they were teamed up against her in an obvious game to find who else she'd *known* in the bar.

"Oh, how about the femme fatale that just walked off the dance floor? Check out those red curls!" Elana continued, "I wouldn't mind having that between my legs myself."

Alexis couldn't hide her dismay. How could Bonnie be here tonight? She wanted to slink out of the bar. Alone.

"Too much hair and lipstick for my taste." With a glance over at Alexis, Sandy continued, "But I think we may have a winner."

"No way! That girl. Really?" Elana eyed Alexis and then Sandy. "Well, well, well. Not bad for my first night at a girl bar. I'm already picking 'em."

Bonnie had spotted Alexis. She waved and made her way over to the fireplace. Alexis could feel her cheeks burn with a blush and wished she could escape, longing to be drenched from head to toe in the damned rain.

"Lex, I had no idea you'd be here tonight!" Bonnie began, giving her a peck on the cheek, and then leaving her hand on Alexis's neck for several moments too many.

Alexis didn't try to prevent her display of affection. She decided it was too late to save face, and pride was overrated. Finally, it was time to simply embrace the fateful evening. One day she'd look back and laugh at this, hopefully. "Bonnie. Good to see you." How horrible your timing is you may never know, Alexis added. "Meet my friends Sandy and Elana."

Bonnie slid her arm around Alexis's waist. "Damn, Lex, why didn't you ever tell me about these two! You gals look like you belong on some lesbian wall calendar. How long have you two been together?"

"Not long," Sandy answered, skillfully evasive.

"Why aren't you all out there dancing?" Bonnie interlocked her fingers with Alexis's and turned to the dance floor. "Come on, if you stand around here too long you'll get asked out by some freak!"

Lex heard the choked giggles of Sandy and Elana. She couldn't help smiling at her own fortune as they all stepped onto the dance floor. Sandy and Elana moved together, dancing as though they'd been waiting all night for the excuse, and keeping up their private conversation with only occasional glances at Alexis. Bonnie seemed unperturbed by her dance partner's lack of focus. She had her arms wrapped around Alexis and straddled her leg, rubbing like a cat in heat. Normally Alexis would have found Bonnie's movements erotic, though awkward on the dance floor. Now she was at a loss for words. Paula would say she'd earned this night. They danced the next few songs, and finally Alexis couldn't handle the sight of Sandy and Elana together, only inches from her, but untouchable. And she found Bonnie's possessive hold increasingly annoying.

"I've got to use the restroom," Alexis said, nearly shouting over the rising music volume.

Sandy admitted she had to as well and Bonnie piped up with, "Well, Elana, that leaves you and me to hold up the dance floor." To her credit, Elana showed no sign of fear as Sandy and Alexis left her in Bonnie's hands. Alexis couldn't help but wonder what had changed in Elana. She had lost her straight girl hesitations and was suddenly confident and in control in the middle of a dyke bar. Sandy and Alexis joined the line outside the bathroom door, placing bets on how long it might take for the chance to pee. Several of the women in line were more intent on making out with their partners than anything else.

"I just don't see why you even pretend you're not a player," Sandy asked, half-teasing but half-serious as well. "And since we're on the subject, why did you ask me to come here tonight if you already had a date with Elana? Did you forget about her? Or do you like to schedule two at a time?"

The last question had a definite sting to it. Alexis had been waiting for her to say something and expected she'd be upset. Even at Blue's she had guessed that Sandy could tell that Elana was more than a friend. "I'm not really dating her. We're—"

"Just friends?" Sandy's voice was sarcastic. She was silent for a moment and then asked, "Well, if you're not dating her, you wouldn't mind if I asked her out, would you?"

Alexis felt Sandy's words slam into her like a swift kick. Struggling to keep her voice even, she replied, "Well, I guess not." She eyed the women on the other side of Sandy. Their lips were locked, and it was apparent that they weren't conscious of anything other than each other. She knew the couple was friends of Mossinni's. They had been partners for several years. Alexis felt somehow betrayed by her mind as she realized she was longing for that. She was tired of dating. "Actually, I would mind."

"Yeah, I thought so," Sandy replied defiantly.

Alexis slipped her hand over Sandy's. "I'd be pissed, in fact."

Sandy blushed at Alexis's touch. She stared up at Alexis silently. "You're a player."

"Maybe I have been," Alexis acknowledged.

"And am I supposed to believe you when you tell me you want to change?"

"I never said that."

Sandy blushed again, stammering, "You . . . you're unbelievable. Do you know that, Lex? Un-fucking-believable."

"What is so unbelievable?" Elana asked, suddenly standing next to Sandy. Paula and Darcy were right behind her. Alexis hadn't noticed them come up, and judging from the start that Sandy made, neither had she.

Paula stepped forward. "Darcy and I wanted to ask you all if we could move this little party. I'm tired of the music tonight. This DJ sucks."

"What she really means is that her ex is making out on the dance floor with one of *your* old flings, Lex." Darcy interjected. "And she can't handle watching."

Elana piped up with, "Well statistically speaking that has to happen pretty often, right, Lex? How many women have you slept with in this place? Just an estimate."

Paula and Darcy both laughed, Sandy only shook her head. Alexis wanted to pull Sandy out of the bar. She wanted to be anywhere except here. "No comment."

"I think we all need a break from this place. Let's go to Westside," Darcy suggested. "We'll meet you all at Lex's apartment. Paula and I will pick up some drinks."

Somehow, Sandy and Elana agreed to Darcy's plan. Sandy even drove. Fifteen minutes later, Alexis stood in front of her apartment wondering if it was a mistake to leave the bar. Drew had left a bottle of merlot on her doormat with a note thanking her for taking Apollo out that morning. She picked up the bottle and stepped aside as Sandy and Elana filed in. They had spent the car ride bonding over the beauty of the Northwest and landscape photography before their conversation turned to women. Elana teased

Alexis again about Tina and Bonnie, but her tone was good-natured. Sandy replied that she didn't understand Alexis's taste in women at all, excepting Elana of course. Alexis couldn't get a word in edgewise, but she wasn't trying. She wanted to say as little as possible tonight, conscious that each word might dig her an even deeper hole.

"Who decided we should come to the bachelor pad?" Elana joked as they looked around for places to hang their wet coats.

Alexis pointed to the hall closet and went to the kitchen to open the wine. She hoped Paula and Darcy would show up soon to add in a distraction. The phone rang and Paula's voice came over the line. "We can't make it."

"What are you talking about? This was your idea."

"Lex, I know you're going to be in a tight spot with two girls and all . . . but I think you can figure it out."

"Fuck you."

"We're already in bed. We just can't make it."

"Yeah, okay. I understand. Have fun." Alexis hung up the phone. She didn't know how to handle the situation now. She couldn't kick Elana out without sending Sandy away too. She poured three glasses and went to the living room. As she stepped into the room, Sandy and Elana withdrew from each other. Elana brushed her finger across her lips, accentuating the fact that the two had just kissed. The tension was palpable.

Alexis shook her head and chuckled softly. Sandy stared at Elana and Elana had her gaze focused on the ground. Alexis wasn't sure if she ought to be jealous about the chemistry between Sandy and Elana or relieved. Breaking the awkward silence, she asked "Wine, anyone?"

Sandy took one glass and handed the other to Elana. "This is fucking weird."

"Do you think your other friends are really coming here?" Elana asked.

"I kind of hope they don't," Sandy replied.

"Paula just called to cancel. They're already in bed." Alexis noticed Sandy's blush. She was confused as to what Sandy wanted. Elana set her wineglass down and headed for the bathroom, leaving Sandy and Alexis alone. Alexis took a sip of her own wine and mumbled, "Leave it to my friends to set me up with a threesome."

"I have to admit I always wanted to try that. Unfortunately, I never had two attractive—and willing—women in the same room at the same time."

Alexis stepped closer to Sandy. "I don't want to mess things up between us. I don't think we should bring Elana into this."

"Into what? This isn't serious." Sandy glanced at the bathroom door. "We're just having fun."

Alexis winced at her words, but covered with a smile. She knew then that she wanted more than a one-night stand with Sandy. And why did Sandy suddenly just want to have a good time? Alexis finished her wine with a quick gulp. "As long as you're fine with everything."

"Do you have a CD player or anything? We could use some music."

Alexis left the room as soon as Elana opened the bathroom door. She turned on the stereo and slipped in a CD. The bedroom door creaked and she glanced over her shoulder. Sandy and Elana leaned against the doorframe, kissing. She moved toward them and felt Sandy's hands brush across her shirt.

"Nice make out music," Elana teased. "Now all we need are the candles."

Alexis pointed to the candles on the nightstand. "The matches are in the top drawer."

"Always prepared?" Sandy shot a knowing look at Elana.

No, not for this, Alexis thought. She flicked off the lights once four or five of the wicks were burning. Elana stepped behind Alexis and moved her hands on Alexis's hips.

"I think you're overdressed," Elana said, tugging at Alexis's belt.

Sandy nodded in agreement.

Alexis slipped off her shirt and then her shoes and socks. Elana whispered something to Sandy. Slow jazz music fought the sound of Elana's voice. Alexis felt a tightening in her stomach as she realized they were conspiring. Sandy rubbed her hand down Elana's leg and kissed her neck. She was still watching Alexis, eyelids half closed, "Mmm, I love a good show, don't you, Elana? Lex, can you take off that tank top next? Then the jeans."

Elana murmured her approval, while Alexis stripped in front of the women. Elana had her hands under Sandy's shirt now and Alexis fought back a swell of jealousy as Elana massaged Sandy's breasts. She stepped toward them, half naked and hot with desire to have her hands where Elana's were. Elana shook her head as she approached, "Uh-uh. You're not quite done with your show for us. The jeans come off next, and go slow with those buttons."

Alexis swallowed hard. She'd never felt such amazing temptation and had so little control. She unbuckled her belt and pulled it through the loops, then started unbuttoning her Levi's, only pausing when she heard Sandy moan. Sandy's hand was hidden from view, tucked behind her body and Alexis could tell by Elana's closed eyes that her fingers had just slipped between Elana's legs. She pulled her pants off quickly and went toward Sandy, intent on ignoring Elana if she tried to push her away again.

Elana was too distracted by Sandy's fingers. Alexis stood in front of Sandy, begging to touch her. Sandy stared at her, the corner of her lips upturned. "What do you want?" she asked.

Elana continued to murmur, "Oh yes, mmm, yes," over her shoulder.

Alexis leaned toward Sandy and kissed her lips. Feeling Sandy's mouth open to her, Alexis started unbuttoning her shirt, half expecting to be stopped, while her tongue played in Sandy's mouth. Elana was too intoxicated with Sandy's hand on her to notice anyone else now. Sandy was only encouraging. When she had the front of the blouse open, she unclasped the bra and tilted her head down to take a nipple into her mouth. She sucked the tip to a firm hardness, while kneading Sandy's breasts. Sandy's breathing quickened, and she gave a sharp cry when Alexis bit on her nipple. Slowly she moved down from Sandy's breasts, rubbing the tense stomach muscles. She kneeled and unzipped Sandy's pants then pulled them off her hips. Elana's cries were gaining in volume and her body was rocking against Sandy's back, helping to push Sandy's pelvis toward Alexis.

After pushing the panties to the side, Alexis dipped her fingers between Sandy's legs, finding the warm wetness she had been waiting for all night. Sandy pressed her hips forward again, and parting her skin, Alexis slid her tongue inside until she found the swollen clit. She encircled it with slow and steady pressure, loving the feel of Sandy's hand on her head, guiding her face deeper between her legs. She quickened the movements of her tongue as she felt Sandy starting to climax, her breathing shallow and fast. Sandy's muscles were shaking and just as Elana's cries sharpened, she tightened up around Alexis's hand. Alexis pushed her tongue inside once more and Sandy came in a sudden spasm, pulling Alexis against her just as she let go of Elana.

The two women stood above Alexis, holding each other and trembling still. Sandy opened her eyes and ran her fingers through Alexis's hair. "Stand up," she said. "I need to feel you."

After a moment, Elana pulled away and started undressing, complaining of wet panties. Sandy followed suit, and Alexis sat down on the bed, trying to watch both women at the same time. Naked, Elana and Sandy approached her.

"I think it's your turn," Elana said.

Alexis smiled nervously, more wet than she'd been all week. Sandy climbed on the bed, straddling Alexis's legs and then pushing her back on the covers. Elana lay down on the bed, rubbing against Alexis, and moving her hands over her chest. "Mmm, what do you think we should do first?" She had both breasts in her hands and started fondling them, winking up at Sandy.

"Pay back a few favors." Sandy moved lower on Alexis, shifting so her shoulders were between Alexis's thighs. She slipped her hands under Alexis's hips, tilting the pelvis up to her mouth, while she kissed along Alexis's inner thighs.

Elana moved from Alexis's side to sit on the pillows, placing

Alexis's head between her spread legs. Alexis could smell the scent of sex on her, just as she'd smelled it on Sandy. Elana's hands started massaging her head, then her neck. She leaned down and kissed her lips just as Sandy parted Alexis's warm folds and drove her tongue inside. Alexis couldn't concentrate on anything, lost in the overwhelming sensations of the women's hands on her. Sandy's fingers pushed in to fill her and then pulled out. Alexis reached for Sandy's hand and guided the fingers back inside. Sandy sucked her clit while Elana's kisses continued, down her neck, her ears and again on her lips. She lifted her hips up, rhythmically matching the timing of Sandy's hand, driving deeper inside her. Clutching at the sheets, she felt the muscles between her legs tighten suddenly. Sandy continued licking her clit, faster, then pushed her fingers in once more and held still as Alexis cried out, the pleasure of her orgasm rippling through her body.

Alexis lay on the bed completely relaxed, despite the tremors that raced through her body every few seconds. She let out a deep sigh, and then laughed out loud. Reaching to find Sandy, she said softly, "Damn, that felt good. Come here where I can feel you."

Sandy climbed up, settling her weight evenly over Alexis, and Elana moved to lay next to them, her hands massaging Sandy's neck and back. Alexis could barely hear whispers of their conversation. She was too spent to worry about what they were conspiring this time. After a while, Sandy moved off her and Elana disappeared as well. She heard the sound of water running and knew they were taking a bath together. For the moment, she'd leave them alone. Alexis rolled on her side, fitting the pillow under her head and staring out the window. The rain had started again. For the moment, she loved the rain.

Chapter 11

The next week passed, as weeks sometimes do, too slowly. Alexis eased herself out of bed early on Friday morning and went for a run. She was showered and ready to leave the house before her alarm sounded. "I'm getting in shape and sleeping eight hours every night," she announced, staring at her reflection in the little bathroom mirror. "Something must be wrong."

Ace's gruff voice that started the Friday meeting didn't bother her like it usually did. And she wasn't fazed by the guys who whistled under their breath when the new girl, Kimberly Hedd, was introduced. Kim was nearly six feet tall, with long blonde hair. A throwback to the times of Amazon women, really. Fortunately, that made her adept at carrying the heavy boxes without breaking a sweat. Unfortunately for her, there was no way she couldn't attract attention in a crowd.

"Just ignore them," Alexis said, knowing that Kim could easily take on half the men here and probably didn't care about their taunts.

"I always do. Having a last name like mine makes you used to that sort of thing."

Ace announced that Kim, who had been riding with Alexis that week to learn the area, would start on her own deliveries on Monday and that everyone should help her on the radios if she had questions on directions. Alexis heard Randy, one of the guys she least liked, whisper that he'd be more than happy to give Ms. Hedd directions. She hoped Kim hadn't heard the comment. Ace may have heard it, however, as he added that the reason Kim had transferred to Portland's APO was that her fiancé had changed jobs. This helped to quiet the group somewhat.

After the meeting, Alexis picked up the delivery schedule from Ron and then met Kim at the truck. "Sorry about the other drivers. They're harmless, but annoying as junior high school boys."

"Don't worry. I can take care of myself with the guys." She took a sip of her coffee and made a sour face. "This may be the worst coffee I've ever had."

"Yeah, I think someone burned the grounds. Toss it. We'll pick up some real coffee on our first stop. It's a cafe down the road." Alexis handed the delivery list to Kim and climbed in the truck.

"Two packages for Blue's Cafe?"

"Mm-hmm." Alexis's mind was already spinning. She doubted that Sandy would be at the cafe. Unfortunately, Juan always worked the grill on the breakfast shift. Alexis started the truck and pulled out of the warehouse. Kim was playing with the radio, trying to adjust the station, and humming country music. Why someone from Seattle would love country music was a mystery to Alexis, and yet, she hadn't minded the humming all week. For the most part, her thoughts had been distracted.

Since Saturday night, she'd heard nothing from Sandy. Elana had called Alexis on Sunday night to say that she was heading back to Santa Barbara. She had an offer to do a photo shoot for some actor and two weddings the following weekend. Elana said she'd probably be back in Portland for the holidays and that she'd look Alexis up then. She asked Alexis to say good-bye to Sandy and added that she'd had a great time with them. No regrets, Alexis thought.

195

Alexis tried calling Sandy several times and never got through. She left two messages and after that gave up. She didn't have the nerve to walk over to Sandy's apartment or track her down at Blue's. Obviously Sandy didn't want to talk to her.

With Kim along for the ride, Alexis had an excuse to not flirt with any customers. She'd also avoided Decker's and didn't return a call from Tina that was on her answering machine Monday night. Instead, she daydreamed about new things to make on the pottery wheel and spent her evenings hanging out with Paula and Darcy or Drew and Ben. Paula had teased her about losing her touch with the women, and Darcy quickly came to Alexis's defense arguing that sometimes you need time off dating. Alexis wasn't sure which side she believed.

Gillian greeted Alexis at the door to Blue's. "You're a little early for the lunch special, Lex."

"We've got a delivery for you." Alexis handed Gillian her clipboard and pointed to the first line. "Can you sign off on this?"

Kim had followed Alexis into the cafe, wheeling the dolly with the two boxes through the entryway. Gillian directed Kim to place the packages in the back hallway by the bathrooms. As soon as Kim disappeared down the hall, Gillian asked, "So who's the new gal? She's really tall."

"She's a new APO driver. Replacement for Mossinni."

"That's kind of like replacing a shrub with a redwood tree. No offense to the shrub." Gillian had known Mossinni as a loyal Blue's customer. "So should I warn Sandy that you're training a hottie?"

"Kim's engaged and not exactly my type," Alexis answered, trying to hide her irritation at Gillian's goading tone. "Besides, I don't think Sandy gives a fuck who I date."

Gillian stepped back at this and arched her eyebrows. "Oh really? So that's why she's been moping around here all week. You two broke it off?"

"According to Sandy, we didn't have anything going to break off." She stopped her explanation as soon as Kim returned with the dolly. Alexis wasn't sure what to make about Gillian's comments.

Was Sandy moping because of Saturday night? "Can we get two coffees to go?"

"Cream and sugar for you, Kim?"

"Yes, please."

"I already know what Lex likes." Gillian winked at Alexis. "The APO drivers come in here often enough for us to memorize their orders." She disappeared into the kitchen and returned with their drinks a moment later. Alexis tried to pay but Gillian insisted it was on the house since Kim was a new customer. She asked them to return for the lunch special and Kim quickly agreed. Alexis would rather have just paid, but as soon as Kim spoke up it was too late to say no. She didn't want to face Sandy after being ignored all week and would have rather skipped lunch entirely than come back for a chef's special. As they left, Alexis thought of last week when she'd stormed past Gillian after Sandy had pissed her off. As much as she wanted to see Sandy at the start of the week, now she was filled with doubt. Maybe Sandy would call in sick. And yet, Alexis hoped she wouldn't.

Alexis let Kim make the deliveries on Moss's old route by herself. She needed to get used to the customers anyway, and they weren't bonded to Alexis. While Kim was delivering a load to a dentist's office, Alexis called Paula.

"What's up, Lex?"

"Hey, I was wondering if you and Darcy were going out tonight. I think I need to go dancing."

"Dancing?" Paula paused. "Sure, we could go out dancing. You haven't made it one week as a stay-at-home single and you're already going stir crazy?"

"I want to get my mind off Sandy." Alexis didn't want to explain any more than this, but Paula pressed her. "She's been on my mind. To tell you the truth, I haven't been interested in anyone else since I started hanging out with her. I think I lost my chance with her after last weekend."

"Ah, the torrid little threesome." Paula chuckled. "But you wouldn't have given up that experience to just date Sandy, would you?"

Alexis didn't answer. She knew the answer was yes but hesitated to say it aloud. Kim came back to the truck whistling another country tune. She climbed in and tossed the clipboard with the delivery list on the dashboard. "Paula, I gotta get back to work. See you and Darcy tonight at Decker's?"

"Yeah, we'll be there."

Kim looked over at Alexis as she set down her cell phone. "Lunch break?"

"Yeah, I guess it's that time. You want to go to that deli we ate at yesterday? They're a little cheaper than Blue's, and I think the food is just as good."

Kim shook her head, looking a little confused that Alexis would be changing their plans. "We promised that waitress we'd go back there. We can't go somewhere else."

"Yeah, probably not," Alexis agreed. She glanced over at Kim and decided she ought to explain. "See, I kind of started dating the chef at Blue's, but then I took things a little too fast and she jumped ship. I'm worried about seeing her if we go there. Gillian, the waitress, doesn't know what happened."

"You called her?"

"She won't pick up the phone and won't return my messages."

Kim held up her left hand, displaying the gold band. "Something like that happened when I first started dating Greg. He showed up at my work and asked me to give him a second try."

They dropped the truck off at the warehouse at noon and walked over to Blue's. The lunch crowd had filled up nearly all the tables, but Gillian pointed them to two open seats at the counter. "Great. Now she won't be able to miss me," Alexis mumbled aloud, feeling miserable.

"We don't have to eat here," Kim offered. "We could just tell the waitress we need to get our food to go."

"No, it's fine. We'll have to eat too much fast food meals in the truck over the next month. The holiday delivery season is always crazy around here, and then we'll regret that we didn't enjoy more lunches with real silverware." They took the seats that Gillian had pointed to and Alexis shifted to face Kim, refusing to see if Sandy was working in the kitchen. "I'll just hope the chefs are too busy to look up at the front counter."

Kim's eyes darted to the breezeway between the counter and the kitchen. "Let's see, we have a dark handsome guy wearing a white apron and grilling burgers. He's got nice muscles . . . and a pretty brunette in jeans and a white tank top with a little red apron. That's all I can see from here."

At Kim's description of Sandy, Alexis couldn't help but look toward the kitchen. Sandy had just called for Gillian as she placed a dish piled high with mixed greens and a hunk of honey-colored bread on the shelf for pick up. Alexis met her gaze and felt the air rush out of her as the smile left Sandy's face. Sandy turned away quickly, going to the sink to rinse her hands, and then starting on the next order. "Damn, she hates that I'm here."

"How do you know?" Kim asked. "Maybe she just wasn't expecting you."

Gillian stepped up to the counter and asked for their orders. Alexis didn't have the heart to order the chef's special. She ordered the grilled cheese and handed her menu to Gillian.

Gillian's face scrunched up, and she scratched something on to her notepad, then paused. "You sure that's what you want, Lex? You know the special today is outta sight. She's made a mixed green salad with cranberries and vinaigrette dressing, butternut squash soup that really fills you up, and of course the homemade honey wheat bread comes on the side."

"Just a grilled cheese, please. I'm hoping Juan has perfected this dish since I last ordered it."

Gillian leaned over the counter to whisper, "He hasn't. Order the chef's special instead."

Alexis shook her head. She wanted to rip Gillian's notepad out of her hands and print grilled cheese all over it. Kim seemed to sense the tension and quickly piped up with, "Well, I'll have the special. If your grilled cheese is awful, we can share."

Gillian turned on her heels and disappeared through the door to the kitchen. Through the breezeway, Kim watched the scene in the kitchen providing a whispered play-by-play account of Gillian's interaction with the chefs. "Okay, so now our waitress is talking to the chef. Your girl. She's handing her the paper with our orders. The girl chef—what's her name, anyway?"

"Sandy."

"Sandy. Okay, so Sandy just clipped our order onto a rack in front of the guy chef. What's his name?"

"Juan. You know, Kim, you don't have to tell me what's going on in there. I really don't care."

Kim continued as if she hadn't heard, "Now Juan is shaking his head and laughing. He's cute. I'd ask him out. I mean, if I wasn't practically married. I'd probably ask Sandy out too, if I was gay. She's pretty hot." She chuckled softly. "Uh-oh. Your girl is looking over at us now. Sandy is, I mean. Don't look up, but I think she might be coming over here."

Alexis glanced at the kitchen door just as it swung open. Sandy stared at her for at least half a minute, and Alexis found herself wishing she'd come over to their counter. Instead, Sandy walked through the maze of tables, smiling at a few of the regulars and then headed down the back hall to the office.

Kim sighed as soon as the office door closed. "Well, I hate to say it, but I think you're in trouble. She looked really upset."

Alexis and Kim decided to get their orders to go after all. Gillian didn't even ask why. She just brought out two boxes and said she'd look forward to seeing Kim for lunch again soon. To Alexis, she gave a pat on the back that felt too familiar and added, "See ya next week, Lex. Don't give up too soon, okay, hon?"

They finished the afternoon deliveries and had the truck back at the warehouse just before five o'clock. "Thanks for showing me the ropes this week," Kim said as they headed for their lockers.

"No problem, I enjoyed having a partner. Kept me distracted. And if you need any help next week when you're on your own, call me."

Kim nodded and grabbed her purse from the locker.

Decker's was nearly empty when Alexis showed up at ten. It was early for the dancing crowd, but still painfully quiet. She found Darcy and Paula over at the pool table. "It's dead here tonight. Good thing I wasn't hoping to find a date."

"There's an Indigo Girls concert that started at eight. Apparently all the dykes in town went there instead," Paula said, chalking her cue stick. "We'll probably have a pretty good crowd here once the concert lets out. So even if you aren't *looking*, I'll bet you don't go home single."

"What're the odds on that bet, Paula? I'll put up ten bucks that says Lex doesn't take a girl home tonight. She looks too damn sad to flirt." Darcy rubbed Alexis's shoulder and asked, "Still upset about Sandy not returning your calls?"

"I saw her today at the cafe and she basically told me to get out of her life, without really saying anything at all. She stared at me for thirty seconds and then turned and walked away."

"Harsh." Paula aimed the cue at the solid green ball in the far corner, and her stick skipped off the ball without moving it more than an inch. Alexis picked up a cue and took Paula's shot. The green ball fell in the pocket, and Paula slapped her back. "Thanks, Lex." She glanced over at Darcy. "That counts, right?"

Darcy shrugged. "Lex, maybe she's just uncomfortable with what happened between you and her. Maybe she's not really mad."

"Well, a lot of people do stop talking when they're mad. But I thought you said she wanted the threesome. Why would she be mad now?" Paula draped her arm over Alexis's shoulders. "And as for you, Lex, why are you so caught up in this girl anyway? You had enough dates last week. Call one of the other girls up and get your mind off Sandy."

201

"That's the problem. I don't want to." Alexis crossed her arms. "I want . . ."

"You want the one that's playing hard to get?" Paula teased. Alexis pushed away from her and Paula continued, "Now don't tell me you finally want a serious relationship with someone. After how many years of fucking around?"

"I want a serious relationship."

"Well, I'll be damned. Darcy, do we have a recorder or something?"

Darcy shook her head. "I think it's perfectly understandable. You just needed time to find someone who you really wanted to get to know. As far as what happened with your little threesome, I'd bet Sandy just didn't think it all the way through. Probably you didn't either." Darcy aimed for her next shot and sank the cue ball instead of the striped yellow. "Hormones can get you involved in some sticky situations. Then after it happened, maybe she started to think that sex was all you wanted. Maybe she wanted more initially, but you both were having trouble defining boundaries."

"Thanks for the pop psychology," Alexis interrupted. She laughed half-heartedly. "I have to admit I don't like it, but you're probably right." When Paula missed her next shot, Alexis changed the subject. "You know, I don't think I've seen two worse pool players in a dyke bar in a long time. This game could go on all night."

"You're saying we're made for each other?" Darcy asked with a hint of a smile. "Hey, Lex, don't look now, but some cutie just walked in. Alone."

Alexis glanced at the door. Sandy was hanging her jacket on the coat rack. She headed for the bar, her eyes scanning the empty dance floor. Four women sat at the bar, chatting with the bartender, and as Sandy moved up to the counter all of the women turned their attention on her. Alexis watched as the bartender flirted with Sandy while filling a glass with rum and Coke. Sandy paid for the drink and then turned to face the far corner where the pool tables and fireplace were. She straightened up as soon as she spotted Alexis.

Alexis lifted her hand to wave and then paused. She thought of leaving. Somehow, she wanted to escape the tension Sandy's gaze made her feel. Alexis faked a laugh when Paula tried to joke about sticky chalk as her cue stick skipped over the cue ball. Had Sandy come here hoping to find her, or was she coming to meet someone else?

Darcy stepped next to Alexis to aim for her next shot. Her stick hit the cue ball, and Darcy turned toward Alexis. "How long are you going to keep her waiting? Go over and talk to her."

Alexis couldn't bring herself to move. "Shouldn't it be Sandy's turn? I've left messages, gone to her work . . ."

Sandy walked over to the fireplace and sat down on one of the couches. She took a sip of her drink and kept her gaze on the flames. Paula set down her pool stick and put her hands on Alexis's shoulders, angling her toward the fireplace. "Go. You look pathetically sad, and I'm not going to let you screw this up. Forget about the dyke dating rules. Go talk to her."

Alexis approached the fireplace slowly. She hadn't thought of getting a drink yet and shoved her empty hands in the pockets of her jeans, overly self-conscious now of every move.

Sandy turned her head and looked up at Alexis. "Want to sit down with me?"

Alexis sat down on the couch, careful to leave enough room between her and Sandy so that they wouldn't accidentally touch. "How are you?"

"I've had a bad week."

"I'm sorry. What happened?"

"I don't know exactly. See, there was this girl that I really liked and we did some things that, well, changed things between us. And I kind of freaked out afterward. So I didn't call her back. But I wanted to. Then I made an ass of myself when I saw her."

"Maybe she understands." Alexis felt the fire warming her skin and relaxed with the smell of the wood. She longed to reach out and hold Sandy's hand. "You could give it another try."

"Maybe." Sandy reached out to brush her fingers over Alexis's hand. She pressed her palm against Alexis's palm and squeezed tightly. "Lex, do you want to go out with me sometime? We could see a movie or do something stupid like bowling."

"Do you mean a real date, or is this one of those two friends hanging out dates?"

Sandy leaned over and kissed Alexis. Their lips pressed together and held, desperate for the time that had lapsed since the last kiss and longing for more. Sandy finally pulled away. "I think I'd go crazy if we tried to just be friends. Then again, I may go crazy trying to date someone like you."

"So how do you feel about monogamy?"

Sandy laughed. "I didn't think you knew that word."

"Well, I was thinking it'd be kind of interesting to try it out. You never know what might happen."

"I'll bet you're chasing after some new girl in a month."

"Wow, you think I'll last a month?" Alexis joked.

Sandy grabbed a pillow off the couch and swung it at Alexis. "You know what, I'll give you a week after that comment!"

"Give me a year instead."

Publications from
BELLA BOOKS, INC.
The best in contemporary lesbian fiction

P.O. Box 10543, Tallahassee, FL 32302
Phone: 800-729-4992
www.bellabooks.com

THE KILLING ROOM by Gerri Hill. 392 pp. How can two women forget and go their
separate ways?   1-59493-050-3 $12.95

PASSIONATE KISSES by Megan Carter. 240 pp. Will two old friends run from love?
                                                   1-59493-051-1 $12.95

ALWAYS AND FOREVER by Lyn Denison. 224 pp. The girl next door turns Shannon's
world upside down.   1-59493-049-X $12.95

BACK TALK by Saxon Bennett. 200 pp. Can a talk show host find love after heartbreak?
                                                   1-59493-028-7 $12.95

THE PERFECT VALENTINE: EROTIC LESBIAN VALENTINE STORIES edited by
Barbara Johnson and Therese Szymanski—from Bella After Dark. 328 pp. Stories from the
hottest writers around.   1-59493-061-9 $14.95

MURDER AT RANDOM by Claire McNab. 200 pp. The Sixth Denise Cleever Thriller.
Denise realizes the fate of thousands is in her hands.   1-59493-047-3 $12.95

THE TIDES OF PASSION by Diana Tremain Braund. 240 pp. Will Susan be able to hold
it all together and find the one woman who touches her soul?   1-59493-048-1 $12.95

JUST LIKE THAT by Karin Kallmaker. 240 pp. Disliking each other—and everything they
stand for—even before they meet, Toni and Syrah find feelings can change, just like that.
1-59493-025-2 $12.95

WHEN FIRST WE PRACTICE by Therese Szymanski. 200 pp. Brett and Allie are once
again caught in the middle of murder and intrigue.   1-59493-045-7 $12.95

REUNION by Jane Frances. 240 pp. Cathy Braithwaite seems to have it all: good looks,
money and a thriving accounting practice . . .   1-59493-046-5 $12.95

BELL, BOOK & DYKE: NEW EXPLOITS OF MAGICAL LESBIANS by Kallmaker,
Watts, Johnson and Szymanski. 360 pp. Reluctant witches, tempting spells and skyclad beau-
ties—delve into the mysteries of love, lust and power in this quartet of novellas.
                                                   1-59493-023-6 $14.95

ARTIST'S DREAM by Gerri Hill. 320 pp. When Cassie meets Luke Winston, she can no
longer deny her attraction to women . . .   1-59493-042-2 $12.95

NO EVIDENCE by Nancy Sanra. 240 pp. Private Investigator Tally McGinnis once again
returns to the horror-filled world of a serial killer.   1-59493-043-04 $12.95

PICTURE PERFECT by Jane Vollbrecht. 240 pp. Kate is reintroduced to Casey, the daughter of an old friend. Can they withstand Kate's career? ISBN 1-59493-015-5 $12.95

PAPERBACK ROMANCE by Karin Kallmaker. 240 pp. Carolyn falls for tall, dark and . . . female . . . in this classic lesbian romance. ISBN 1-59493-033-3 $12.95

DAWN OF CHANGE by Gerri Hill. 240 pp. Susan ran away to find peace in remote Kings Canyon—then she met Shawn . . . ISBN 1-59493-011-2 $12.95

DOWN THE RABBIT HOLE by Lynne Jamneck. 240 pp. Is a killer holding a grudge against FBI Agent Samantha Skellar? ISBN 1-59493-012-0 $12.95

SEASONS OF THE HEART by Jackie Calhoun. 240 pp. Overwhelmed, Sara saw only one way out—leaving . . . ISBN 1-59493-030-9 $12.95

TURNING THE TABLES by Jessica Thomas. 240 pp. The 2nd Alex Peres Mystery. *From ghosties and ghoulies and long leggity beasties* . . . ISBN 1-59493-009-0 $12.95

FOR EVERY SEASON by Frankie Jones. 240 pp. Andi, who is investigating a 65-year-old murder, meets Janice, a charming district attorney . . . ISBN 1-59493-010-4 $12.95

LOVE ON THE LINE by Laura DeHart Young. 240 pp. Kay leaves a younger woman behind to go on a mission to Alaska . . . will she regret it? ISBN 1-59493-008-2 $12.95

UNDER THE SOUTHERN CROSS by Claire McNab. 200 pp. Lee, an American travel agent, goes down under and meets Australian Alex, and the sparks fly under the Southern Cross. ISBN 1-59493-029-5 $12.95

SUGAR by Karin Kallmaker. 240 pp. Three women want sugar from Sugar, who can't make up her mind. ISBN 1-59493-001-5 $12.95

FALL GUY by Claire McNab. 200 pp. 16th Detective Inspector Carol Ashton Mystery. ISBN 1-59493-000-7 $12.95

ONE SUMMER NIGHT by Gerri Hill. 232 pp. Johanna swore to never fall in love again— but then she met the charming Kelly . . . ISBN 1-59493-007-4 $12.95

TALK OF THE TOWN TOO by Saxon Bennett. 181 pp. Second in the series about wild and fun loving friends. ISBN 1-931513-77-5 $12.95

LOVE SPEAKS HER NAME by Laura DeHart Young. 170 pp. Love and friendship, desire and intrigue, spark this exciting sequel to *Forever and the Night.* ISBN 1-59493-002-3 $12.95

TO HAVE AND TO HOLD by Peggy J. Herring. 184 pp. By finally letting down her defenses, will Dorian be opening herself to a devastating betrayal? ISBN 1-59493-005-8 $12.95

WILD THINGS by Karin Kallmaker. 228 pp. Dutiful daughter Faith has met the perfect man. There's just one problem: she's in love with his sister. ISBN 1-931513-64-3 $12.95

SHARED WINDS by Kenna White. 216 pp. Can Emma rebuild more than just Lanny's marina? ISBN 1-59493-006-6 $12.95

THE UNKNOWN MILE by Jaime Clevenger. 253 pp. Kelly's world is getting more and more complicated every moment. ISBN 1-931513-57-0 $12.95

TREASURED PAST by Linda Hill. 189 pp. A shared passion for antiques leads to love. ISBN 1-59493-003-1 $12.95

SIERRA CITY by Gerri Hill. 284 pp. Chris and Jesse cannot deny their growing attraction . . . ISBN 1-931513-98-8 $12.95

ALL THE WRONG PLACES by Karin Kallmaker. 174 pp. Sex and the single girl—Brandy is looking for love and usually she finds it. Karin Kallmaker's first *After Dark* erotic novel.
ISBN 1-931513-76-7 $12.95

WHEN THE CORPSE LIES A Motor City Thriller by Therese Szymanski. 328 pp. Butch bad-girl Brett Higgins is used to waking up next to beautiful women she hardly knows. Problem is, this one's dead.
ISBN 1-931513-74-0 $12.95

GUARDED HEARTS by Hannah Rickard. 240 pp. Someone's reminding Alyssa about her secret past, and then she becomes the suspect in a series of burglaries.
ISBN 1-931513-99-6 $12.95

ONCE MORE WITH FEELING by Peggy J. Herring. 184 pp. Lighthearted, loving, romantic adventure.
ISBN 1-931513-60-0 $12.95

TANGLED AND DARK A Brenda Strange Mystery by Patty G. Henderson. 240 pp. When investigating a local death, Brenda finds two possible killers—one diagnosed with Multiple Personality Disorder.
ISBN 1-931513-75-9 $12.95

WHITE LACE AND PROMISES by Peggy J. Herring. 240 pp. Maxine and Betina realize sex may not be the most important thing in their lives.
ISBN 1-931513-73-2 $12.95

UNFORGETTABLE by Karin Kallmaker. 288 pp. Can Rett find love with the cheerleader who broke her heart so many years ago?
ISBN 1-931513-63-5 $12.95

HIGHER GROUND by Saxon Bennett. 280 pp. A delightfully complex reflection of the successful, high society lives of a small group of women.
ISBN 1-931513-69-4 $12.95

LAST CALL A Detective Franco Mystery by Baxter Clare. 240 pp. Frank overlooks all else to try to solve a cold case of two murdered children . . .
ISBN 1-931513-70-8 $12.95

ONCE UPON A DYKE: NEW EXPLOITS OF FAIRY-TALE LESBIANS by Karin Kallmaker, Julia Watts, Barbara Johnson & Therese Szymanski. 320 pp. You've never read fairy tales like these before! From Bella After Dark.
ISBN 1-931513-71-6 $14.95

FINEST KIND OF LOVE by Diana Tremain Braund. 224 pp. Can Molly and Carolyn stop clashing long enough to see beyond their differences?
ISBN 1-931513-68-6 $12.95

DREAM LOVER by Lyn Denison. 188 pp. A soft, sensuous, romantic fantasy.
ISBN 1-931513-96-1 $12.95

NEVER SAY NEVER by Linda Hill. 224 pp. A classic love story . . . where rules aren't the only things broken.
ISBN 1-931513-67-8 $12.95

PAINTED MOON by Karin Kallmaker. 214 pp. Stranded together in a snowbound cabin, Jackie and Leah's lives will never be the same.
ISBN 1-931513-53-8 $12.95

WIZARD OF ISIS by Jean Stewart. 240 pp. Fifth in the exciting Isis series.
ISBN 1-931513-71-4 $12.95

WOMAN IN THE MIRROR by Jackie Calhoun. 216 pp. Josey learns to love again, while her niece is learning to love women for the first time.
ISBN 1-931513-78-3 $12.95

SUBSTITUTE FOR LOVE by Karin Kallmaker. 200 pp. When Holly and Reyna meet the combination adds up to pure passion. But what about tomorrow?
ISBN 1-931513-62-7 $12.95

GULF BREEZE by Gerri Hill. 288 pp. Could Carly really be the woman Pat has always been searching for?
ISBN 1-931513-97-X $12.95

THE TOMSTOWN INCIDENT by Penny Hayes. 184 pp. Caught between two worlds, Eloise must make a decision that will change her life forever.   ISBN 1-931513-56-2 $12.95

MAKING UP FOR LOST TIME by Karin Kallmaker. 240 pp. Discover delicious recipes for romance by the undisputed mistress.   ISBN 1-931513-61-9 $12.95

THE WAY LIFE SHOULD BE by Diana Tremain Braund. 173 pp. With which woman will Jennifer find the true meaning of love?   ISBN 1-931513-66-X $12.95

BACK TO BASICS: A BUTCH/FEMME ANTHOLOGY edited by Therese Szymanski—from Bella After Dark. 324 pp.   ISBN 1-931513-35-X $14.95

SURVIVAL OF LOVE by Frankie J. Jones. 236 pp. What will Jody do when she falls in love with her best friend's daughter?   ISBN 1-931513-55-4 $12.95

LESSONS IN MURDER by Claire McNab. 184 pp. 1st Detective Inspector Carol Ashton Mystery.   ISBN 1-931513-65-1 $12.95

DEATH BY DEATH by Claire McNab. 167 pp. 5th Denise Cleever Thriller.
                    ISBN 1-931513-34-1 $12.95

CAUGHT IN THE NET by Jessica Thomas. 188 pp. A wickedly observant story of mystery, danger, and love in Provincetown.   ISBN 1-931513-54-6 $12.95

DREAMS FOUND by Lyn Denison. Australian Riley embarks on a journey to meet her birth mother . . . and gains not just a family, but the love of her life.   ISBN 1-931513-58-9 $12.95

A MOMENT'S INDISCRETION by Peggy J. Herring. 154 pp. Jackie is torn between her better judgment and the overwhelming attraction she feels for Valerie.
                    ISBN 1-931513-59-7 $12.95

IN EVERY PORT by Karin Kallmaker. 224 pp. Jessica has a woman in every port. Will meeting Cat change all that?   ISBN 1-931513-36-8 $12.95

TOUCHWOOD by Karin Kallmaker. 240 pp. Rayann loves Louisa. Louisa loves Rayann. Can the decades between their ages keep them apart?   ISBN 1-931513-37-6 $12.95

WATERMARK by Karin Kallmaker. 248 pp. Teresa wants a future with a woman whose heart has been frozen by loss. Sequel to *Touchwood*.   ISBN 1-931513-38-4 $12.95

EMBRACE IN MOTION by Karin Kallmaker. 240 pp. Has Sarah found lust or love?
                    ISBN 1-931513-39-2 $12.95

ONE DEGREE OF SEPARATION by Karin Kallmaker. 232 pp. Sizzling small town romance between Marian, the town librarian, and the new girl from the big city.
                    ISBN 1-931513-30-9 $12.95

CRY HAVOC A Detective Franco Mystery by Baxter Clare. 240 pp. A dead hustler with a headless rooster in his lap sends Lt. L.A. Franco headfirst against Mother Love.
                    ISBN 1-931513931-7 $12.95

DISTANT THUNDER by Peggy J. Herring. 294 pp. Bankrobbing drifter Cordy awakens strange new feelings in Leo in this romantic tale set in the Old West.
                    ISBN 1-931513-28-7 $12.95

COP OUT by Claire McNab. 216 pp. 4th Detective Inspector Carol Ashton Mystery.
                    ISBN 1-931513-29-5 $12.95

BLOOD LINK by Claire McNab. 159 pp. 15th Detective Inspector Carol Ashton Mystery. Is Carol unwittingly playing into a deadly plan?   ISBN 1-931513-27-9 $12.95

TALK OF THE TOWN by Saxon Bennett. 239 pp. With enough beer, barbecue and B.S., anything is possible!   ISBN 1-931513-18-X $12.95

MAYBE NEXT TIME by Karin Kallmaker. 256 pp. Sabrina has everything she ever wanted—except Jorie.   ISBN 1-931513-26-0 $12.95